KILLER BLONDE

ALLAN EVANS

Bob,
I love my fellow authors!
Keep on writing!

Allan Evans

Immortal Works LLC
1505 Glenrose Drive
Salt Lake City, Utah 84104
Tel: (385) 202-0116

© 2021 Allan Evans
evanswriter.com

Cover Art by Ashley Literski
strangedevotion.wixsite.com/strangedesigns

ISBN 978-1-953491-11-4 (Paperback)
ASIN B08S6VV556 (Kindle Edition)

There once was a boy who famously called out from the backseat, his voice rich with exasperation, "Why do the thumbs have to be the fat ones?" This book is dedicated to that boy, Cade Evans, for without him there would be no Cade Dawkins.

CHAPTER
1

Death came on a two-lane highway.

Holly Janek saw the fast-approaching headlights in her rearview mirror. What could possibly be the hurry at a quarter to three in the morning? Drivers tended to be in one of two camps: too-slow idiots or too-fast maniacs. This one clearly belonged in the second category, as the car shot out into the oncoming lane looking to pass. Just as the car pulled alongside hers, it slowed and the driver flicked on his brights. Asshole. Blinded, Holly swore again and looked away from the mirror. Then the unthinkable happened.

In rapid succession, the blinding light turned towards her car, she felt a heavy bump, and the rear of the car slid to her right, threatening to take her off the highway.

Fighting the skid—one learned these things growing up in Minnesota—Holly steered into it. This is where the minuscule margin of error came back to bite Holly in the ass. Cranking the wheel to her left, Holly oversteered, sending her Camry into a clockwise spin. Holly could hear herself scream as the car spun out of control.

Abruptly, it was over. Dazed and banged up, Holly found herself in the ditch facing the wrong direction. Reaching for her cell phone—tantalizing inches from her grasping fingers in the center console—Holly didn't think to release her seat belt. The violent images of the last minute cycled through her head. What happened? Where's the other driver?

A tapping at the glass pulled Holly's attention away from the phone. The silhouetted figure rapped insistently on the passenger window, gesturing to the locked door. Fumbling, Holly managed to unlock the door. It opened, and a man slid into the passenger seat next to her. He studied her for a long moment, and asked, "Are you all right?"

Illuminated by the glow of the dome light, Holly looked into his eyes, not sure she liked what she saw there. "What happened?" she asked.

The man smiled but his eyes remained as cold as any governor denying a stay of execution. "Just a little accident," he said, his voice slow and monotone. "Just a little accident." He reached over, clicking Holly's seatbelt loose.

Holly's tears ran down her cheek as the man reached toward her. An impartial onlooker would think a moment of tenderness passed between the two as the man smeared the tracks of her tears and gently brushed back her long blonde hair. The onlooker would be wrong.

Viciously grabbing her by the hair, the killer—yes, he had killed before and he would kill again—slammed Holly's face into the steering wheel, feeling the impact all the way to the back of her head. Pulling his fingers from her hair, he pushed her limp head back against the seat. Blood flowed from her ruined nose.

The man paused, staring at her as if for the first time, though it wasn't. Long blonde hair, white silk blouse, dark skirt riding high on her taut thighs. Shiny black stiletto heels. "Mmmm," he murmured, running his hand up her thigh.

Forcing his eyes to look away, the killer slid his hand up her silk blouse. Almost tenderly, he undid her top button, enjoying the view of her cleavage. Her chest rose and fell as she breathed.

Not for long though, not for long.

CHAPTER
2

The dawn phone call. Almost a cliché for cops, it rarely brought anything but bad news. Of course, the bad news was never their bad news—it belonged to someone else. Most career cops learned to put up the wall and keep their feelings out of the equation. But, being human meant those the feelings were still there, buried someplace. One thing was for sure: the dawn phone call could be a life changer.

"Dawkins." His voice was still thick with sleep.

"There's an accident, a one-car fatality you should probably come look at."

His feet found the floor. When Bill "Crash" Simpson, veteran accident reconstruction specialist, told you to come have a look, you trusted his hunch and got out of bed. "Where?"

"Highway 5 in Lake Elmo, just past the roundabout. Look for the flashing lights, you can't miss us."

⚑

CADE DAWKINS, an investigator with the Minnesota State Patrol, was one of two full-time plain-clothes investigators working out of the east metro division in the Twin Cities. The thirty-one-year-old had already spent nine years in law enforcement and was a recent transplant, having previously been with the Minnesota Bureau of Criminal Apprehension—better known statewide as the BCA. He'd quickly made his reputation with a once-in-a-lifetime case. Taking down the highway shootout killers had made him the Patrol's golden boy in the eyes of the media.

Crash was right, you couldn't miss the lights. State Patrol, Washington County Sheriff, and Oakdale police were all on scene. As was standard procedure in fatalities, the road was closed, but a deputy waved Cade through. He parked behind Crash's SUV, not wanting to contaminate the scene. Standing just over six feet, Cade was solidly built from years of soccer and had blondish brown hair, which some of his peers in law enforcement gave him grief for always being messy. Zipping up his jacket against the cool morning air, Cade headed for the commotion.

Recognizing Mike Swanson, a veteran trooper, Cade asked, "What do we have?"

Swanson, a typical trooper with a buzz cut and no neck, was an adrenaline junkie who raced cars in the summer and snowmobiles in the other six months of Minnesota's year. He shook his head in the *I've seen it before and I'm going to see it again* way.

"A body was discovered in a one-car accident down in the ditch. An early morning commuter saw the glint of metal when the sun peeked out. The car had probably been down there for hours." Along the rural stretch of Highway 5 in Lake Elmo, where cornfields frame the road, and deer cross with reckless abandon, it wasn't uncommon for a crash to go unnoticed for long stretches of time. "Lucky for us, the sun was out this morning."

"Any day the sun makes an appearance in March is a lucky day. What do we have on the victim?"

"The victim, Holly Janek, was an event planner on the way home to Stillwater from a downtown Minneapolis event. Her live-in boyfriend said she left Minneapolis at approximately 2, so the fatality most likely happened around 2:30 a.m. To me, it looks to be an accident, like maybe she fell asleep at the wheel. But I'm just a simple road trooper. Crash is the man to tell you for certain."

Crash Simpson was a 50-something bear of a man, with a ruddy face and a ready smile—which, considering he spent his days looking into car crashes, seemed ironic to Cade. He slid down the muddy embankment toward the green Camry. The car faced the wrong direction in the ditch, but showed no major damage. "What do we know?" he asked when Crash, who knelt by the driver's side rear bumper, stood up.

"Let's look at the road evidence first," Crash said, leading Cade back up the embankment. "The marks tell the story. You can learn a lot from vehicle marks if you know what you're doing." He looked at Cade with a grin. "And lucky for you, I know what I'm doing."

Together, they walked along the road's shoulder. Crash stepped out onto the road and gestured. "The marks begin here, so this is where it started. And for the record, these aren't simple skid marks. Skid marks show forward movement without tire rotation—in other words, the brakes are locked up with the car's momentum carrying it forward."

Crash pointed up the road toward the crash site. "Instead, the road evidence shows yaw marks, followed by scuff marks. These marks are in an S pattern, which means the victim tried to correct, overcorrected and ultimately lost control and went off the road."

"Yaw?" Cade wasn't familiar with the term.

"Yaw is a sideways movement of a vehicle that's turning—basically movement of a vehicle in another direction than which it's headed. If you're driving too fast into a corner, you'll create a set of yaw marks. For some reason, our victim went from a typical forward motion into a yaw."

Cade held up a finger. "I've been told I'm a smart guy, so clearly what you're telling me is she didn't fall asleep and drive into the ditch." Crash nodded. "And clearly, she didn't have a reason to turn suddenly at full speed. This is a straight section of road." Crash nodded again.

"Let's continue," Crash suggested. He walked further along the marks. "Right about here is where she overcorrected and lost control. The vehicle was in a spin and exited the road, here." Crash moved to the edge of the pavement, roughly 35 yards from the Camry's final resting place. "She bottomed out with the far side of the ditch's upward slope halting her forward progress, leaving her facing in the wrong direction. The entire thing happened in less than three seconds."

They moved off the road, once again sliding down the embankment to the Camry. Mud caked Cade's boots.

"As I said, the road evidence suggests there's more going on here than another case of overtired driver meets the ditch. But all is not well here, either. Notice our victim's position and the state of her clothing."

Crash stepped back, allowing Cade to move into the open car entrance.

"Don't touch her, the Dragon Lady hasn't made her appearance yet." The Dragon Lady was the Ramsey County Coroner. A flamboyant spectacle of color, she was more often than not dressed in vivid purples or reds with an outrageous hat to top off her unique ensemble. Without having a coroner of their own, Washington County had to wait for one to come from St. Paul. As obvious as her death appeared to be, only the coroner had the authority to pronounce someone dead.

The door was open, with a woman still behind the wheel. The blonde woman's face was a bloody smear, with splatters on the Toyota's steering wheel. "As I said, the road evidence shows she spun out of control, which could explain these violent splatters," gesturing to the blood on the steering wheel. The airbags hadn't been deployed and her seatbelt wasn't fastened.

Cade took in the dead woman's disheveled appearance. Her shirt was open at the top, her bra showing, and her short skirt was pushed up and torn. "If I didn't know better, I'd say she looks like she's been out parking with her date." Cade looked up at Crash. "Could an accident have caused this?"

"It could." Crash's face suggested he didn't believe it, though.

"If the accident was violent enough to kill her, wouldn't her airbags have been deployed?"

"Not necessarily. There wasn't a major impact or collision." Crash looked almost child-like with his *I know something you don't know and I'm not going to tell you* smile.

"You're making me work for this, aren't you?" Cade asked. Crash simply shrugged in response.

"The biggest issue in my mind—besides her post-prom appearance—is her seat belt. It's not fastened," Cade said. "And if the spin was violent enough to kill her, it should have been violent enough to toss her from her seat. Which leads me to believe..."

Cade leaned in and slid a pen under the victim's shirt at her left shoulder. "Huh."

"What?" This time it was Crash being led down the path. "What is it?"

Cade stepped out of the doorway and faced Crash. "There's an abrasion on her neck consistent with seat belt restraints. Yet her seat belt wasn't buckled."

"It's possible she unbuckled after the accident just before her injuries took her life." Cade didn't think Crash believed it either.

A trooper slid down the embankment. "Crash, the Dragon Lady's here."

An explosion of purple stood at the top of the ravine. Dressed in easily a half-dozen shades of purple—from her oversized hat, to her long scarf, to her fluffy coat, down to her lavender boots—was the Dragon Lady. Minerva Adams had been the Ramsey County Coroner for longer than anyone could remember. As colorful in her quirkiness as she was with her clothing, she took total charge of her accident scenes. Truth be told, she intimidated many of the burly troopers.

"Young man." She addressed the trooper next to Cade and Crash.

"Yes, Miss Adams?"

"Are you going to make me get down there by myself?" The trooper actually looked down at his feet.

With the look of a boy being chastised by his kindergarten

teacher, the trooper scrambled back up the embankment. "No, ma'am. Sorry."

She held onto his arm as they made their way down the steep incline. "And if I ever hear you call me the Dragon Lady again, I will kick your ass all the way to the Wisconsin border. Am I clear?"

Cade turned away, not wanting to get busted by the Dragon Lady for his grin. Crash had done the same.

"Mr. Simpson. May I have a peek at your ICR?"

Crash handed a clipboard with the Incident Crime Report to the coroner. He stepped back while Adams glanced at the report, her face offering nothing. "Let's see what we have here," she said to no one in particular and knelt by the open driver's door.

Crash waved a finger at Cade and they stepped back to the Camry's rear. "Another thing for you to see."

A dent with deep horizontal scratches was evident in the dark green paint of the quarter panel behind the driver's door. Squatting next to the Camry, Cade examined the damage. "Recent?"

"Uh huh. Fresh damage will be clean. Like taking a cloth and wiping it. If it were older, there would be a layer of dirt and grime sitting on top."

"Like my car," Cade grinned. After a moment's hesitation, he frowned. "I'd expect there would be some paint transfer to the victim's car. But I don't see it. Am I wrong?"

Crash cleared his throat and nodded toward the coroner as she closed her medical bag and approached them. "I've made the pronouncement. Her body is released. Good luck with this one, gentlemen. Looks like you'll need it."

Grabbing onto the arm of the waiting trooper, the Dragon Lady headed back up the embankment and was gone.

Crash leaned in by Cade. "See? It didn't feel right to her either. And you're right about the paint transfer. Typically, the vehicle evidence shows paint from the other car—usually quite noticeable. The BCA can analyze the paint transfer, telling us the make, model and year range of the other car. But not when someone has wiped it off."

They walked around the back of the Camry and Cade faced Crash. "So, let's say you're correct about this being more than your typical late-night one-car fatality. The road and vehicle evidence suggest someone bumped our victim's car on this deserted stretch, and the bump sent her vehicle into an unrecoverable spin. She ends up dazed in the ditch, vehicle pointed in the wrong direction. So far, so good?" Cade looked to Crash for confirmation.

Crash nodded.

"I don't have a sense of how much trauma occurred from the spin, but I have to assume there was some. Our mysterious perpetrator then enters the vehicle, and in no particular order, kills her, molests her, and unbuckles her seat belt. He cleans off the dent, thereby removing any evidence of his vehicle's paint. He climbs back into his own vehicle, heads for home and the comfort of his own bed, leaving her to be found hours later—all without a single witness."

"Yeah, that about covers it." Crash stated. He held Cade's eyes.

"I'm guessing our perpetrator must have had some issue with our victim. Maybe her boyfriend or an ex-boyfriend. Wanted to make it look like an accident." Cade shook his head. "Odd way to go about it though."

Holding up a finger, Crash hesitated. "There's one more thing."

Cade's eyebrows went up, but he didn't say anything.

"Remember the early morning fatality last month on Highway 95? Black BMW, woman apparently fell asleep, a St. Paul attorney."

"I saw the report, but Rob handled the follow up. How do you remember all these cases?"

"It's all I do. I have no life."

"Sucks to be you. Anyway, what about it?"

Crash didn't say anything. That was until Cade prodded him. "Crash?"

Crash let out the breath he'd been holding. "It was the same victim."

Cade's confusion was apparent in both his voice and expression. "Same victim?"

"Appearance-wise anyways. The victim, Jennifer Allard, was an attorney from Bayport. She was tall and athletic, a knockout. Same long, white-blonde hair. Pretty similar style of dress as well." Crash pulled off his cap, running his fingers through his thinning hair.

"Maybe it's just a coincidence." Cade didn't believe it, though.

Crash replaced his cap and folded his arms, looking directly at Cade. "I hate coincidences."

"Me too." Head spinning with ramifications, Cade repeated, "Me too."

CHAPTER
3

The East Metro District Office of the Minnesota State Patrol was housed in a sprawling complex alongside Interstate 94 in Oakdale. Shared with the Department of Transportation, the building was serviceable, but by no means fancy. Cade parked the unmarked Chevy Impala next to a deer-damaged cruiser. In Minnesota, deer crashes were not uncommon. In fact, Cade had recently been called to an accident scene where a trooper—in his first shift in a brand-new Patrol cruiser—had hit a deer while traveling 120 miles an hour. As one might guess, the deer was obliterated and the cruiser totaled. Fortunately, the trooper was unhurt and back on the road the very next day—in an older Crown Vic.

"Hey Dawkins, the new captain's looking for you," was the greeting Cade received as he pushed through the entrance. Cade gave the trooper a thumbs up and wound his way through the clutter of admin desks. Receiving glances and a few smiles, he said his hellos to the staff who kept the place running.

Nick Javier, a trooper built lower to the ground than most law enforcement officers Cade had come across, chatted with another trooper. "Hey Cade, the captain's asking for you. Her first day here and she's already looking for trouble."

"That's what I heard." Cade paused and walked back to the pair. "Keep an eye on this boy," he said nodding down to Javier. "Did you know Nick's the only trooper who's short enough you can see his feet in his driver's license photo?"

They both laughed as Cade continued to the back where the captain's office was located. He'd heard Capt. Rejene had worked her way up through the ranks, after starting her law enforcement career out of state in Charlotte. Most recently, she'd been in charge of the Patrol's Rochester district. This was her first day in her new position.

The office's previous occupant's name was still stenciled on the smoked glass: Capt. Dickey. Cade was more than happy to see that officious prick transferred away in the aftermath of the multimillion-dollar theft from patrol headquarters. Which, coincidently, was the case that made Cade Dawkins a household name in the Twin Cities. The story had received national attention—at least for the several weeks the media had been interested before they moved onto greener pastures.

He could see a woman with her back to him as she reached up to place a photograph on a bookcase. He caught himself staring at her calves as she strained for the top shelf. Focus, he told himself. This was his new boss, and he'd better be careful.

Cade knocked lightly and pushed the door open. "I'm Cade Dawkins," he offered as he took her in. She wore the white dress-uniform shirt, a navy skirt and burgundy pumps. Brown curly hair, dark eyes, clearly too good looking to be his boss.

"Capt. Leah Rejene." She shook his hand with a firm grip. "I wanted to meet you. You come with a reputation." She seemed to size him up as the awkward silence filled the room.

"I hope it's a good one," Cade said. Plopping himself in the chair across her desk, he leaned back and hesitated. He was self-aware enough to know he'd always bristled under authority and needed to choose his words carefully when dealing with higher ranking members of the Patrol. "Can I run something by you?" he asked.

"Sure." Capt. Rejene sat back, but looked interested.

"You're aware of the Lake Elmo fatality this morning?" A nod. "May be nothing, but I'm seeing a red flag I can't ignore."

"Go on."

"Crash—Sgt. Simpson—called me out to the scene. The victim had gone off the road at approximately 2:30 a.m. Her vehicle ran aground in the ditch after spinning out on the highway. Initially, it appears she was killed by the facial trauma brought on by the violent spin. However, she was found with her seatbelt unfastened and yet there were seatbelt burns on her collarbone. And there was something about her clothes." Cade hesitated.

"Her clothes?"

"Well, it looked as if she was groped."

Capt. Rejene winced, but Cade continued.

"Her skirt was pushed way up, her blouse was unbuttoned too far —too far for her coming from a work event. Our victim was an event planner and was at a banquet in downtown Minneapolis."

"Tell me about the road evidence."

"Straight section of two-lane highway, yaw marks leading to S pattern scuffs. Crash said the victim tried to correct, then overcorrected and ultimately lost control and went off the road."

Capt. Rejene jotted a note on a desk pad and looked up. "The ditch stopped her forward progress?"

"That's what Crash said."

"Was there any other damage to the vehicle?"

"Yes, there was a crease in the driver's rear quarter panel that may have been a parking lot souvenir."

Rejene leaned forward. "It also may have been a bump designed to spin her off the highway. Sounds like a PIT maneuver." The Pursuit Intervention Technique was a maneuver taught at law enforcement academies all over the world to end dangerous high-speed pursuits. Cade had learned the technique years ago and had the opportunity to use it successfully. One well-placed bump and the suspect lost control with little damage to either vehicle, and no injuries.

"That's what we thought as well. It could have been a textbook case of the maneuver. The entire thing gets stranger though."

Capt. Rejene's forehead wrinkled. "You have my attention."

Cade stood up, handing her his iPhone. "Here's a picture of the deceased, Holly Janek. Several weeks back, another late-night one-car fatality happened out near Bayport. Check this out." He pulled a photo from the file on the deceased attorney. "This was the victim, Attorney Jennifer Allard. See any resemblance?"

Eyes shifting between both images, Capt. Rejene asked, "What was the conclusion on the Bayport fatality? Any damage to the vehicle?"

"A lot actually. The victim's BMW rolled after leaving the highway. It was Rob Zink's case. He thought maybe she swerved to avoid a deer or possibly another vehicle crossing the centerline. Something like that." Cade leaned back in the uncomfortable chair. "Sometimes you never know for certain. There are no traffic cams on these rural highways."

Standing up, Capt. Rejene moved around to the front and leaned against her desk. "I agree this is highly suspect as far as coincidences go. You'll need to look into both victims, see if there's a common bond, something beyond physical appearance. Go check on the lawyer's vehicle, see if there's any indication a PIT maneuver was used there as well. Work with Zink, we need to know what we're up against here. Maybe these are just coincidences, but I agree it doesn't feel like it."

Cade was halfway out the door when she stopped him. "Dawkins, one more thing. I'm a bit of a control freak, but a nice control freak. Keep me in the loop, and I'll give you plenty of rope. If there really is a nutjob out there killing blondes on our highways, we need to stop it. Until we know something for sure, this stays quiet."

"Jurisdiction issues?"

"Exactly. If this becomes a full-blown murder investigation, we'll be required to pass this off to the BCA. I would prefer to keep the investigation here with the patrol."

As a former BCA investigator himself, Cade felt no small amount of professional rivalry where the BCA was concerned and was more than happy to hang onto the investigation as long as possible. He smiled at his new boss. "I can see we're going to get along just fine."

CADE WAS one of two full-time investigators on the east metro division payroll. Although he'd been with the Patrol for just a year, he was considered the senior investigator. Rob Zink, the other investigator, was a recent transplant from St. Paul. He'd worked as a patrol officer for years in the capital city's west side. Switching between law enforcement agencies wasn't uncommon. Sometimes you simply needed a change of scenery to keep your career—as well as your sanity—alive.

Cade found Rob at their shared desk. It was a unique arrangement, both investigators sitting on opposite sides of the same desk much as they had opposite shifts. They overlapped on three of the days each week, which gave the two investigators a chance to get to know each other. Each had their own cases but assisted the other as needed. Clearly not overloaded by his caseload, Rob had his feet up and was playing with an iPad.

"Angry Birds?" Cade asked as he glanced at Rob's screen.

"No, Horny Penguins."

"Not going to ask. What you do with your screen time is your business."

"Funny," Rob said, looking up over the device. "So, you meet the new boss?"

"I did. Better than the old boss." Cade sized up his investigative partner. Rob was a large man—Cade's parents would have referred to Rob as husky—with a mop of blond hair sitting on top. "She said I should bring you in on something, that is, if you're not too busy."

Putting down the tablet, Rob smiled. "Lucky for you, court doesn't start until tomorrow. Have to testify in the Dearborn hijacking. Court never follows their own posted schedule though. Wouldn't surprise me if it gets pushed until next week."

Cade slid the paper file across the desk. "Remember the one-car fatality last month, the Bayport attorney?"

"Jennifer Allard." Rob opened the folder, scanning the paper. "This was my case. What about it?"

Cade handed him his phone. "Here's the victim of my one-car fatality this morning."

Rob's left eyebrow went up as he looked at the picture. "Really?"

"Really. Could be the same woman. And there are enough flags to suggest she was bumped off the road, then molested and killed. Capt. Rejene wants you to help me look into it. See if there's a connection between the two victims."

Rob stood up, tucking his shirt in below his ample middle. "I'm intrigued. Where do you want to start?"

"Let's go look at Allard's vehicle. It's in the Lakeland impound lot. Maybe we'll get lucky."

"It's been a while since I got lucky." Rob smiled, "Let's go find us a connection."

CHAPTER
4

L unchtime on Nicollet Mall could be busy. Make it the first sunny day of spring and the downtown Minneapolis avenue swarmed with worker bees. Men in conservative suits from the busy financial district and women in their trend-perfect outfits from the large retailer headquarters all shared the same crowded restaurants. As both worlds collided, love and sex were in the air. Nicollet Mall was the perfect hunting ground.

The killer walked the sidewalks with the herd of downtown office workers. Even though he knew he didn't belong with them, the killer knew he blended in with them. It was important not to stand out, you didn't want to spook the herd. Much like an anthropologist, the killer studied people. Through systematic observation much could be learned from the diverse human landscape. His fieldwork brought him here, wanting to learn her routines, as he always learned the ways of his chosen ones.

People were creatures of habit. If most of the human population were wild animals, the DNR ranger would have little use for the tracking collar. We go to work, go home, have a few favorite haunts and friends we see. Ninety-five percent of the time, this is the sandbox we lived in. Learn these patterns and we should be able to find someone when we need them.

This one was different. Her range was much greater. Her work took her around the metro area and into Wisconsin. Many nights away from home. He hadn't been able to discern a regular pattern so far. She was going to pose a much greater challenge than the others. But the killer was a firm believer in the end justifying the means. And there was no doubt he'd have her in the end. Now that he had chosen her, the killer would pursue her relentlessly.

Street musicians dotted the landscape of businesspeople hustling to grab lunch before their hour was up. The noontime crowds filling the sidewalks made it difficult to keep her in view. She was ahead, some twenty yards, walking on Nicollet Mall just past 8th. Now and again, the killer caught a glimpse of her white-blonde hair. The platinum hair was a magnet, drawing him in. He needed to get closer, be close to her. Picking up his pace, he closed the gap.

At the intersection waiting to cross, the killer stood directly behind her. It was a warm afternoon and she draped her suitcoat over her shoulder bag. Staring at her, he couldn't look away. Her impossibly long legs looking even longer sitting on top of her high heels. The need drove him forward. The rest of the world faded away as he found himself mesmerized at being so close. He could reach right out and touch her snug navy skirt.

After the bus and taxi traffic passed, the crowd began to cross, not waiting for the light to change. The killer elbowed an office drone out of his way to keep close to her. His vision has closed up, seeing only her. Outside of The Local, the woman met up with a friend at the Irish restaurant. Head down, the killer was caught unaware and ran right into her backside. Eyes averted, he mumbled an apology and kept moving. To be noticed would not be a good thing.

"That guy smelled my hair," she said, behind him. He didn't dare turn around as he listened.

"There's too many creeps these days," her friend offered. "They're everywhere."

"Ain't that the truth."

⚮

THE IMPOUND LOT was nothing more than patches of gravel and grass overlooking Highway 95. Rows of vehicles, some rusty and beyond recovery, some with shattered windshields and broken windows. Most showed the effects of collisions, inattentive drivers, and unsafe conditions. All were here because there was nowhere else for them to go.

The lot manager directed Cade and Rob over to the fence line where the black BMW sat. It was obvious this one had been in a crash: creased-in roof, passenger door hanging off, front quarter panel missing with exposed wiring, the driver's side window shattered, dents and scratches over much of the vehicle's top and sides. The decorative rear bumper assembly was gone and the front windshield, although intact, was a spiderweb of cracks. Cade plucked a weed sticking out from the front grill and turned to Rob.

"First off, who was she?"

"She was Jennifer Allard, an attorney from Bayport. On her way into work at 5:30 a.m. I guess those lawyers like to get to work early. Her coworkers said she usually was in the office between 6:30 and 7 a.m."

"Where was her office?"

"Downtown St. Paul."

Cade walked to the driver-side door. He peeked in, noting the debris strewn around. For many, cars carried their life. Shake up the vehicle and the contents spilled out into the open. "Find anything unusual in the vehicle?"

Rob shook his head. "Just the usual."

"What was the cause of death?"

"Blunt force trauma."

Moving back to the rear quarter panel, Cade examined the damage. "Looking for signs of a PIT maneuver," he said to Rob, who knelt beside the vehicle. Cade ran his hand along the depression and scratched metal. "This is a dent."

"Yeah, but it rolled down a rocky embankment, and there must be damage over 90 percent of the vehicle."

Cade stood and paced around the BMW. Scratches and dents were everywhere. The entire vehicle was covered in dust as well.

"We're not going to get much from this vehicle. The damage is too extensive."

At the rear of the BMW, Cade paused. Glancing at the trunk, something caught his eye. A quarter-sized decal sat beside the BMW emblem. The decal's honeycomb pattern was highly reflective, as it caught the afternoon sunlight, turning it into a miniature spotlight. "What is this? Seen one before?"

"No, but it seems unusual. You don't see many BMWs with bumper stickers or any sort of decals. BMW owners are particular people. They don't want to mar their pristine German luxury automobiles." Rob ran his hand through his hair. "Any idea why Ms. Allard would want this on her vehicle?"

Cade shook his head as he covered the decal from the sun. The glow diminished, leaving the decal looking white. "No, but it'd make it easy to follow the vehicle at night."

The two investigators looked at each other for a long moment. Neither said anything. Cade's internal wheels spun as he processed the ramifications. If this woman, Allard, was being followed—stalked, really—this wasn't a crime of opportunity. This was a killer who selected his victims, followed them, and then killed them. And this killer seemed to have a thing for blondes.

"How about your fatality this morning? Was there a reflective dot on her vehicle as well?" Rob squinted his eyes in the sunshine as he looked around for the source of a large engine. A flatbed tow truck, emblazoned with blue and red flames came into view. It carried a green Toyota Camry. "I guess we're going to find out."

Rob darted between rows of junkers, waving his arms. The driver nodded and brought the truck to a stop. A mountain of a man swung down and approached Rob. Cade considered Rob to be a large guy, but the driver made him look to be a great candidate for midget wrestling. Standing easily six-and-a-half feet, and weighing somewhere in the neighborhood of 300 pounds, the driver was clean shaven and wore thick black glasses. "What do ya need?" He leaned in close to Rob.

"We need to take a look at the Camry," he said hooking a thumb toward the transported Toyota. "Doing some comparison shopping." He looked up at the man who stared down at Rob in return.

Cade took a step toward the two men, unsure where this was headed.

"Bwah ha ha," the man let loose with a barking laugh sounding somewhere between a hyena and a donkey. The loud laughter echoed through the wrecked vehicles. He was still laughing as Cade, followed by Rob, headed for the rear of the vehicle.

"No reflective decal. Damn."

"Hang on." Cade scooped up a handful of the sand and fine dirt that made up the roadway. He swung up onto the back of the large tow rig. "I have an idea."

"Good," Rob said. "I'm fresh out. Go for it."

"Because the paint transfer was wiped, maybe he removed the decal as well. But even so, some of the adhesive might still be here." Cade approached the Camry's rear end and tossed his handful of road debris at the Toyota emblem. Cade looked up at Rob and the driver's open-mouthed faces. He followed their gaze.

A perfect circle of dust the size of a quarter appeared on the Camry.

CHAPTER 5

C ade winced and glanced over to Rob and shook his head at Capt. Rejene's voice on the speaker. "Tell me it was all just a coincidence," she requested. Never in the history of the universe did anyone like to disappoint their boss on her very first day.

Their hesitation clued her in. "You don't have good news, do you?" she asked.

No, not good news.

"I think there's some good news. Now we know." Rob said, in a brave effort to put a positive spin on it. He looked at Cade and shrugged. They were headed west on 94, moving past the sprawling 3M headquarters.

"There is a connection," Cade added, steering the unmarked Impala past a slow-moving SUV with Wisconsin plates. For some reason in Minnesota, the slow ones gravitated to the left lane. "Both vehicles appeared to have a reflective decal on them. The one on Allard's BMW was quarter-sized, with a honeycomb pattern designed to gather light and bounce it back. If you're following someone from a distance on a dark deserted road, the decal would make it considerably easier."

"Back up. You said both vehicles appeared to have a disk. What do you mean, appeared?"

"Allard's car had the disk, Janek's didn't. However, an identically sized circle of adhesive was in the same location. Clearly, the decal had been removed recently. The adhesive wouldn't have been sticky otherwise."

"What about signs of a PIT maneuver?"

"Her car rolled down a rocky embankment, so there was damage over the entire vehicle, but there was damage consistent with a PIT."

Rejene sighed. "All right. Look for a connection between the two victims. If we have someone stalking women, there has to be a connection. How did he find them?"

"We're on the way to talk to Allard's personal assistant. He should be able to give us an idea of who she met with and where she'd been."

"Send me pictures of the disk and the sticker residue. I'll put out a briefing, give the road troopers a heads-up and maybe we'll get lucky and spot one on another vehicle. I'll have Tessa search case files for similar incidents. And gentlemen, let me remind you: we'll need to keep this quiet. We don't need this to become a media shitstorm. This is looking like a murder case now, but until there's a smoking gun, I want the investigation to stay here with the patrol. Understood?"

"Copy that."

Cade hit the end button, disconnecting the call, however he was confident Capt. Rejene had beat him to it. "Looks like we're in for a ride," he said, swinging the vehicle onto the downtown St. Paul exit.

LINEKER & Marsh was headquartered in the trendy Lowertown neighborhood of downtown St. Paul. Overlooking Mears Park, the law offices were located on the top three floors of the newest tower in the capital city. Cade left the Impala parked behind the building superintendent's designated parking spot. "He shouldn't be going anywhere." But to be safe, he slipped a police business card onto the windshield. It never looked good to have your work vehicle towed.

"We're meeting with Allard's personal assistant, Richard Schusterman," Rob said as he opened the etched glass door on the 31st floor, waving Cade in first. "He knows her day-to-day life far better than anyone." The attractive redheaded receptionist gestured them to the luxurious waiting area, informing them that Richard would be available momentarily. Rob plopped down into a leather armchair and picked up a Fortune magazine while Cade stood at the floor-to-ceiling window and took in the view of the nearby river.

"Greetings, I'm Richard," a voice said. Cade turned to see a tall man with a clean-shaven head, and an expensive green suit. Richard looked to be in his mid-thirties and confidently led them down the hallway as they made their introductions. "Coffee?"

"I'm trying to limit my coffee to four cups a day," Rob replied shaking his head. Cade declined as well. Richard stopped outside an expansive office, pushing the door open.

"This was her office. We can meet here. No one has had the heart to move out her belongings." Cade took in the trappings of power. A wall of framed photographs dominated the room. Photos of Allard with sports stars, photos of Allard with judges, and photos of Allard with former sports stars who were now judges. On the opposite wall, a gorgeous mahogany and glass bookcase featured more photos of Allard. Cade recognized the governor, mayors of Minneapolis and St. Paul as well as both senators. Many local media celebrities as well. Allard was well connected. But more than that, the photographs made one thing obvious: Jennifer Allard was a knockout.

He picked up one of the frames. "She photographed well," Cade turned to Richard who hovered nearby. "Was she seeing anyone?"

Richard stepped next to Cade, hands in his pockets, his leather suspenders showing. "Several actually. As you might imagine, Jennifer turned a lot of heads. She had power and confidence. She scared away some men, but many others were drawn to her. I didn't get the feeling she was too involved with any of the men. Her focus was more on her career. It requires a fair amount of work to get to Jennifer's level. It also necessitates a fairly large time commitment to maintain that status. Not much time left for relationship building." He took the frame from Cade, returning it to the shelf.

Cade walked over to Allard's desk, a shining example of

minimalism. Bamboo and glass, the desk was more museum-quality than your typical office furniture. Richard followed close behind.

"Would you care for some sparkling water?" Richard asked.

"That would be nice." Cade waited until Richard left the room and looked at Rob. "I get the impression he's here to make sure we don't touch anything. He's never more than a couple of feet away."

Rob smiled. "Yeah, that must be it."

Richard reappeared with a silver platter. "I brought an assortment of cookies and pastries as well," he said glancing over at Rob. "Help yourself."

Cade walked behind Allard's desk, hiding his smile. "Do you have her calendar still?"

Richard nodded, lifting an electronic tablet from Allard's credenza. "Certainly. We maintain each of the partner's calendars electronically. It simplifies the support staff's job function." He looked up from the device. "What do you need?"

"In the last two weeks before her death, what had she been doing? Who had she met with?"

Richard scrolled down the tablet's page. "Dinners, personal trainer, fundraiser at the governors. A number of client meetings. I'll print her schedule for you."

"What about her cases?" Rob asked. "Had she received anything threatening recently related to her cases?"

"Recently? Try never. She's not that kind of attorney. She worked exclusively for 3M. Corporate law is procedural. It's positioning, covering the corporate ass, such as it is. The confrontations you'll encounter in other aspects of the law simply aren't there in corporate law."

"Was she on Facebook?" Cade asked.

"She was." Richard slid over the tablet. "Here's her page."

Rob stepped over with a large glazed pastry in his hand. They both studied the page as Cade scrolled down. Nothing threatening on her page, just talk about her comings and goings. And much like her office, there were photographs of Allard with all sorts of people. This was clearly someone who enjoyed being in front of the camera. And the camera definitely liked her as well.

"Check out her friend list," Rob suggested. "Maybe there's something there."

The list showed 342 friends. Cade moved down the list, not recognizing anyone.

Sliding the tablet back to Richard, he asked, "See anyone you don't know? Maybe she had an online stalker."

Richard folded his arms and made no effort to look at the list. Instead, he looked intently at both investigators. "So, it was more than a tragic accident. I wondered why you're following up on her accident almost a month after the fact." He held Cade's eyes. "Was Jennifer murdered?"

"I can't answer with complete certainty, however new evidence has raised some difficult questions. We're here looking for the answers. We've had another one-car fatality this morning that had some similarities. And I hate coincidences."

"We do," Rob added. "Because most of the time it's not a coincidence."

"Exactly." Cade leaned forward. "When we dug deeper into this coincidence, we found a pattern. And a pattern means human intervention. However, until we can establish the who and why, we need to keep this quiet. Are you okay with that?"

Richard nodded gravely.

"Good." Cade turned to Rob. "We should check her cell phone records, see who she was in contact with."

Richard cleared his throat. "I can save you the trouble. Partners are issued mobile devices and I'm able to access her call log. Would you like me to print it for you?"

In the elevator, phone logs in hand, Cade smiled. "I need a personal assistant like Richard. Sure would make life easier."

Rob glanced over as he pushed the lobby door open. "Yeah? Richard looked as if he was interested in you as well."

Cade held up his hand. "Stop. I'm not going to go there with you."

Rob's laughter echoed through the lobby as they stepped out into the afternoon sun.

CHAPTER
6

Holly Janek's boyfriend, Tom Soderholm, lived in a downtown Stillwater condo. A newer building, it was one of a series that had sprung up in recent years as the young and affluent crowd discovered Stillwater. The building took up most of a city block on Stillwater's main thoroughfare. Cade pushed the intercom button and was buzzed in.

Waiting for the elevator, Rob pushed the button in a vain attempt to speed the car's descent. "This guy may not be talkative at all. He just lost his girlfriend this morning. You never know how someone will react. Everyone handles their grieving differently."

Stepping into the car, Cade pushed the button for the third floor. "We'll have to take it at his speed. No one should have to have a day like this."

Soderholm opened the door with a smile and waved them inside. "Gentlemen, come in." He was a broad man, with a weightlifter's chest. The condo had a wide-open layout, and the floor-to-ceiling windows had a view of the St. Croix River. As they followed Soderholm past the kitchen, Cade slid his fingers along the countertops, noting the unusual pattern in the granite.

"You like that? Just had the countertops installed. It's Uba Tuba, from the mountainous region of China. Got it for an unbelievable $20 a square foot. Can you believe that?" Soderholm had a lot of energy.

Cade glanced over at Rob, who simply shrugged. Everyone handles grief differently. As Soderholm gave the highlights of the kitchen sink, Cade held up a hand. "Can you tell us a little about Ms. Janek?"

Soderholm nodded. "I suppose you didn't come to hear about my granite countertops." He sprawled onto a leather couch. "Holly was an event planner. She started her own company in the last year, Inspired Events. Before that, she'd been at the mall. And working at the Mall of America, it was trial by fire. They had more events than you'd ever believe. Holly loved the work but hated her boss. He was a lecherous old perv. Holly would catch him staring at her all the time. Eventually, he started hitting on her."

Rob glanced at Cade, giving him a raise of his eyebrows. "Could we get his name?"

"Sure. Not sure why you'd need it though." Soderholm grabbed a piece of paper off the kitchen nook desk. He handed it to Rob. The paper was a single sheet of gold-flaked heavy card stock. Across the top in fancy script, it read, "Mason Armitage Monroe, a life celebrated."

"Holly arranged for his funeral a month back. She said even though the guy disgusted her, work was work. And she wanted the chance to see her old coworkers again. So she made an event out of his funeral."

Monroe was a dead end if there ever was one.

Soderholm continued. "Holly usually planned corporate events. Mostly in Downtown Minneapolis, some in Uptown, others in St. Paul, Stillwater, Hudson even. She had a nice base of clients who kept her busy."

Cade paced during the conversation. He tended to think better while moving. Rob leaned back in a leather armchair, looking comfortable enough to nod off. "Do you have Holly's recent schedule?"

"Sure." Soderholm pulled down a page from the corkboard by the desk. "Here's a printout of the last month. It made it easier for me to keep up with her schedule. I'm in construction, so I have appointments all over the calendar. I try to work them around her events, so we'd have time together."

"Can I keep this?" Cade asked. Glancing at the page, roughly half the dates were filled.

"Sure. Can I ask why you're interested in what Holly had going this last month? Seems like an unusual approach to an accident investigation. Just saying."

Cade sat on the couch next to Soderholm. "To be honest, we're not convinced it was an accident. It's way too early in the investigation, but there's evidence suggesting Holly may have been run off the highway."

Soderholm leaned forward, his mouth hung open. And for the first time in their meeting, he didn't say anything. Soderholm's eyes had the watery quality one gets in emotional circumstances. Cade touched his arm. "Tom, we don't know anything for certain. Right now, we're trying to get a sense of Holly, where she's been, who she may have met with. Things like that. Looking for something not quite right. If someone hurt Holly, we will find them. Believe me, this is what we do—and we are quite good at it."

"I read about you last fall," Soderholm said, holding Cade's eye. "You were the one who took down those highway killers. Those maniacs got what they deserved." He nodded at Cade. "I believe you."

Cade looked over at Rob and nodded. Pulling out a notebook, Rob leaned forward.

"Can I get Holly's cell phone number? Sometimes phone records tell us a lot about a person. We'd be looking for anything unusual. Maybe she got a call on the way home last night. Or calls from someone she didn't know." Soderholm nodded and jotted down a number, passing it to Rob.

Glancing over Soderholm's shoulder, a half-dozen framed photographs of Holly were spread across the desk surface. Several more were on the wall above. Stepping past Soderholm, Cade picked up a silver-framed photo of Janek standing on a dock somewhere. She wore a summer dress of pastel flowers. Striking. Holly Janek was a head turner. And she looked a lot like Allard. They could be sisters, even.

Cade handed the photo back to Soderholm and sized him up for a long moment. Soderholm, his head down, stared at the image of his deceased girlfriend. He looked lost. Devastatingly lost. In many investigations, interviewing the victim's significant other meant you were interviewing the prime suspect. Not this time, Cade decided. Janek's boyfriend didn't have a threatening vibe or even a hint of subterfuge.

"How'd you guys get along?" Cade asked. He had to ask.

"Are you kidding me?" Soderholm marched right up to Cade. "I'd never have done a thing to harm her. I worshipped Holly. I mean, look at me, I'm just above average. I work out, have most of my hair." Holding up a picture of Holly, he continued. "But, Holly's amazing. By far the best-looking woman I've ever dated. I was doing really, really well."

Cade glanced toward Rob, who gave a subtle shake of his head. *Not this guy.* Someone else was responsible for the death of Holly Janek.

Soderholm walked them to the door. "Let me know if you find anything. I really loved her. She was one of a kind."

Stepping into the hallway, Cade thought that might not be true. There was another one like Holly—except she'd been murdered too.

CHAPTER
7

Reynolds DeVries was a rising star. A reporter, and weekend anchor for the 5, she was easily one of the most recognizable television news people in the Twin Cities. Reynolds' long blonde hair and even longer legs had garnered her no small amount of attention. Frequently the subject of the local paper's gossip column and favorite speculation of the morning radio boys, she knew her stock was rising. And with her audacious belief in herself, Reynolds knew she would go far.

A friendly face appeared over her office cubicle wall. Kenzie, the station's traffic manager, smiled. "Phone call, Reynolds. It's probably Good Morning America." Laughing at her own joke, Kenzie enjoyed teasing Reynolds about the network call they both knew would come someday. Reynolds picked up the phone, her finger hesitated over the blinking light. Well known in the medium-sized Twin Cities television market, everyone here knew it was simply a matter of time before the network called and she would move onto the national scene. But Reynolds knew she needed a catalyst, something that would catch New York's attention. It would take just the right story.

"Is this Reynolds? Reynolds DeVries? I'm a huge fan. I have a story for you." The man's voice was deep and somewhat muffled. Not a voice she recognized.

"Can I ask who this is?" Most stories came through the station's news desk and were assigned by the news director. However, as her profile rose, it wasn't exactly uncommon for her to receive tips directly.

"Just a cop who believes the story should be told. Before more women are killed."

"I'm interested," she replied coolly. On the inside, her mind raced. This could be something. Scanning her desk, there was never a pen when you needed one. Phone to her ear, Reynolds stood, waving her hand, looking for someone, anyone with a pen. "Tell me more."

"Women have been murdered." The man paused, letting his words sink in. "One just happened on Wednesday, the other three weeks ago. Both women virtually identical in appearance."

A production assistant, attracted by her gesturing, stopped and Reynolds' plucked the pen from behind his ear. "Wait, you're saying there's a serial killer here? In the Twin Cities?" The young assistant's eyes went wide. Reynolds held a finger to her lips. Shhh, this is *my* story.

"That's what it looks like." Frustratingly, the man's voice wasn't telling her anything. His short choppy sentences didn't betray anything about the man. In her line of work, reading people by voice often told her more than the words they spoke. Give her a minute with someone and she'd know what part of the country they were from, their socio-economic status, whether or not they had more of a passive or aggressive personality, how much of a factor their ego was and even which political party they were likely to vote for. And she'd artfully use all of this information to draw out the story behind the story. This man's voice wasn't giving her anything.

"Who's investigating this?"

"The State Patrol."

"Who should I follow up with there?" Reynolds scribbled down notes. She may be the only one who could read them, but the detail in her notes had saved her before. It was important to not only get down what was said but her questions and impressions as well.

"Remember the State Patrol guy who solved the highway shootings last fall?"

"Cade Dawkins?" Like almost everybody in the Twin Cities, she'd followed the story. When you have the owner of the state's newest sports franchise orchestrating mass killings during the evening rush hour in an effort to distract the State Patrol so he could steal back his confiscated cash from the Patrol's evidence vault, well that was big news in any market. And it was Cade Dawkins who had solved the case. As a card-carrying member of the news media, she'd been all over that story. Some of her reports had gone national even as the network picked up the story.

"Yeah, it looks like he has the lead on this one." And just like that, this just became a much bigger story.

"Hey, I really—" and the caller was gone. Reynolds took a calming breath and held it before gradually letting it out.

Time to move. Grabbing her notes and her jacket, she flipped the pen back to the production assistant, still rooted in place, and ran.

CHAPTER
8

Hands down, the least glamorous part of being an investigator had to be the desk time. In every case there's time spent being desk-bound following up on evidence, looking up criminal histories, and Googling persons of interest. It wasn't glamorous, but it was necessary.

Cade requested thirty days of phone tolls from Janek's cell phone service provider. After downloading all of her calls—both incoming and outgoing—he'd then obtain an administrative subpoena to get the subscribers for each of those calls. Cade hoped to find something unusual, some contact that felt out of place, and maybe determine how she was targeted. If he could figure that out, it just might point to who the killer may be.

"Cade," it was Hannah, the patrol's office manager, "There's a woman asking for you on three. Sounds a little breathless." She shrugged but didn't move away.

"Dawkins." He held Hannah's eye as he picked up the call.

"I think there's someone following me." The woman's voice was soft-spoken but agitated. "Every time I look back, I see the same guy. When I left Maplewood Mall, he's there again, so I took the Highway 5 exit because I remembered Patrol headquarters is there. I just pulled into the lot and...he's stopped. He's there, just waiting."

Holy hell. "Lock your doors. Stay down, I'm on my way." Cade sprinted toward the door. Amanda Curtis, a trooper recognized for her drug interdiction work along the 94 corridor into Wisconsin, was just tossing her gear onto a chair. "Curtis. Follow me. We may have a threat." They both sprinted for the door.

Outside, a white van with a massive 5 emblazoned on the side was parked in the second row of spaces across from the entrance. A tall blonde woman stood next to a cameraman. The camera followed Cade as he burst out of the Patrol's front door. Shit. This would explain why the woman knew enough to ask for me by name, Cade shook his head. Should have known better. He put his hand on Curtis' shoulder. "Mandy, never mind. I've got this."

Holding up his hand, Cade stomped across the lot, glaring at the cameraman. "Shut it down," he barked. "I am not going on camera." After a moment's hesitation, the man lowered the camera. Cade turned on the woman, jabbing his finger at her. "You've crossed the line. Give me one good reason why I shouldn't throw your ass into the county lockup." He stepped right into her space, locking eyes with the woman.

The reporter, a 5 news logo on the chest of her royal blue jacket, took a step back. "Look, I'm following up on a tip that several women," she said, as she glanced down at her notebook, "a Holly Janek and Jennifer Allard, both listed as one-car accidents, were actually murdered." She looked at Cade, searching his face for a reaction.

Cade held his emotions in check, not wanting to betray anything while his mind raced. How would this reporter have gotten her information—and so quickly at that? One obvious answer came to mind. A leak in the department. It wasn't as uncommon as most people thought. Police saw a lot, both good and bad. They witnessed a lot of injustice and didn't always agree with the way the legal system handled things. And like most people who knew a secret, they liked to talk. Of course, members of the media exploited this, cultivating their sources, stroking egos, giving out small perks, and playing on it's-for-the-greater-good sensibilities. When you got right down to it, having this information out was inconvenient, but not a disaster. The real disaster will come, however, when Capt. Rejene found out.

The reporter looked at him with eyes that would best be

described as determined. "If a killer is stalking women in the Twin Cities, we need to get the word out. If we can prevent another killing..." She was trying to play the greater-good card, but Cade was not going to let her off that easily.

"What's your name?" he asked.

"Reynolds DeVries, Five news." She looked surprised that he didn't know who she was.

"So, Reynolds, you're here to save the women of the Twin Cities. There are no headlines for you?"

Cade could see the wheels turning behind her pleasant smile. She was not going to roll over and give up—at least not without a shift of tactics. Shaking her head, DeVries stepped into his space. "Of course, the Twin Cities' women are important. With a brave officer like you," she said, touching his arm, "the innocent women will feel better knowing you're looking out for them."

Cade glanced down. Yep, she was definitely in his space. Her breast caressed his arm. She was using her presence—and a remarkably feminine presence at that—to draw him in. The thing was, he knew what she was doing, but he wasn't going to stop her. DeVries continued. "People know who you are, and they like you. If you're involved with a story this big, this could be national news."

Cade nodded, not willing to say something about himself that would show up on the evening news.

"Here's what I have," DeVries said. "Both women were athletic and roughly the same height and weight. Both had long blonde hair." She glanced at her notes. "And both were found dead on dark, deserted highways here in the east metro."

"Look, a couple of ground rules before we go further. I won't be on camera. I will confirm—as a law enforcement source only—that we are investigating a connection between Janek's and Allard's one-car fatalities. There are several similarities making us question the single car accident explanation. That's it. We don't have a smoking gun and we don't have any suspects."

"So, if you had to give me your worst-case suspicion..." DeVries left the sentence hang and held his gaze.

"I'd suspect we may have a killer who has something for knockout blondes."

It was the six o'clock news that ruined Capt. Rejene's day. Not that it made life any better for the people around her. Shit rolled downhill.

"Dammit." Rejene stood by her open office door, her fists clenched at her sides. "Who's talking to the media?" her loud question ringing throughout the expansive room. A sea of blank faces stared back at her, no one willing to risk their life stepping in front of this particular buzzsaw.

"Five News just broke the story that blonde women are being stalked on our highways." Rejene stepped out into the hallway and paced around the desks. She picked up steam as she moved through the room. "The weasels couldn't just come out and say it. No, they asked if the recent deaths of nearly identical women could be the work of a crazed stalker targeting Twin Cities' women. Bastards. Then, they asked if our highways are actually safe for our women to drive on." She stopped in front of the admin area, folding her arms, glaring at anyone who would dare look in her direction.

"Do you know whose job it is to keep people safe on our highways?" Rejene rolled on, not waiting for an answer. "Every man and woman of the Minnesota State Patrol. That's why we're here. That's why we get up in the morning and that's why we can sleep at night. Because we're out there 24 hours a day, helping accident victims, stopping unsafe drivers, looking for drugs and criminal activity before they can ruin people's lives. And I'm the one responsible for the Patrol's performance. If the roads aren't safe, it's my ass on the line."

Cade looked across the desk at Rob and shook his head. This was not a shitstorm to step into. Rejene stopped directly in front of their shared desk. "No one talks to the media without clearing it through me first. Understand? I like my ass just the way it is." She stormed back to her office, slamming the door. Rob caught Cade's eye, wriggled his eyebrows suggestively, while Cade slid his forehead down against his desk. Not a good day.

CHAPTER 9

Stillwater, the oldest city in the state, was recognized as the birthplace of Minnesota. A sleepy but picturesque town on the banks of the St. Croix River, Stillwater was known as much for its prison as the scores of antique shops, used bookstores and one-of-a-kind restaurants which drew in visitors from around the state and nearby Western Wisconsin. Cade had moved to Stillwater last fall after finding his dream home, a 100-year-old craftsman on the north hill in Stillwater. His first foray into buying real estate had been a good one, leading to a romantic relationship with his realtor. Unfortunately, as it often happens in life, the two drifted apart under the strains of their respective careers. It was a cold month since he'd last spoken with her.

Cade ate alone at a trendy eatery on the main drag in downtown Stillwater. The secret to having dinner out alone, Cade discovered, was to sit at the bar. No one thought you were a friendless loser when you were at the bar watching a game on one of the many flat panel televisions. You were simply an enthusiastic sports fan who valued the game over friends or family.

Cade dug into his pasta dish, enjoying the Italian food. A glass of wine and a basket of warm bread bookending his plate. An English soccer game, Liverpool versus Manchester City was on the big screen directly across from him. A longtime recreational soccer player, Cade enjoyed watching English Premier League soccer, especially his favorite team, Liverpool. Life didn't get any better, he thought as he watched another near miss by Liverpool's Brazilian star. However, a

glance at the empty stool beside him had Cade reassessing—
sometimes having one's options open was a lonely experience.

Being a cop meant you never sat with your back to the door. Call
it a control issue, but pretty much every cop Cade ever met needed to
face the front door. It's all about being able to assess the threat level of
everyone who enters. It's just how a cop's brain was wired. So, when
the door opened, he spotted her right away.

Cade hadn't expected to run into her so soon. Three women
pushed through the front entrance, the two brunettes in front,
laughing as they approached the hostess stand. The third was hard to
miss. It was Reynolds DeVries. Dressed in a bright spring coat, she
wore tight gray jeans and black heels. Her long blonde hair had more
curl to it than it had earlier in the day. Her friends were striking, but
all eyes were on DeVries as she walked across the room. Trying to be
subtle, Cade turned away, but still kept his eye on DeVries as she and
her friends got a table.

DeVries sat so she wasn't directly facing Cade, which was
probably a good thing. After the tension of their earlier adversarial
confrontation, Cade wasn't convinced he'd be able to rein in his anger
a second time. He shook his head thinking about her ploy to get him
out to talk. The woman had a lot of balls. He turned back to the
game, disheartened to see Liverpool had been scored on twice
already by City. It was funny how quickly one's day could go from
good to the toilet.

Fighting the urge and losing, Cade found himself drawn back to
DeVries as he swung the barstool around. Her smile was radiant as
she interacted with her friends. But it was her laugh that captivated
him. It was so bright and full of sunshine. Could anyone with a
sparkling laugh like that be a complete monster? Finding his earlier
anger fading, Cade turned back to his dinner with a newfound
appetite. Liverpool's Firmino received the ball with his back to goal
and flicked the ball up and over City's defender, who was doing his
best to smother him. Firmino spun around the much larger man and
received his own pass, flicking it with his left foot into the path of a

sprinting Salah who calmly tucked the ball into the corner of City's goal.

Cade's wine glass was nearly knocked right off the bar by his celebratory fist pump. *Yeah. Take that, you overpaid City prima donnas.* Now we've got a game.

Fork in hand, the urge to eat forgotten, Cade hung on every pass as the last ten minutes of the game played out. Manchester City's Argentine star had the ball and sent a blistering shot at Liverpool's goal. Playing the game of his life, Liverpool's goalkeeper dove at full stretch, plucking the ball from the air just before it crossed the goal line. The Brazilian keeper rolled to his feet and sprinted to the edge of his box, unleashing the ball with an overhand throw. It found the feet of Trent Alexander-Arnold who took off hell-bent for the opposite goal. The counter attack was on.

Alexander-Arnold sent the ball into midfield, finding the foot of Liverpool's captain, Jordan Henderson, while Alexander-Arnold continued his forward sprint. Calmly sidestepping a threatening player, Henderson launched a diagonal return ball right into Alexander-Arnold's path. Finding open space, Alexander-Arnold pushed the ball far out in front of him as the City defenders realized they were in trouble and sprinted back. Alexander-Arnold's next touch sent the ball across the mouth of the goal. With a diving header, winger Sadio Mané redirected the ball past City's sprawling goalkeeper. Goal. Tied up at 2-2 with only a few minutes left to play.

Cade set down his fork. No way he could eat at a time like this. The mass of blue in front of Manchester City's goal meant every last one of their players had come back to defend. The red of Liverpool's uniforms filled the screen, too, as they pushed their advantage, rolling with the change of momentum, every player pushed into their opponent's half of the field. Liverpool rapidly passed the ball from one side of the field to the other, looking much like a baseball team moving the ball around the diamond. When the ball got to the foot of Firmino, Cade stopped breathing and stood up.

Firmino cut to his left, switched the ball to his other foot, and cut back to his right. Two of City's players were left on the ground behind him, victims of his quick change of direction. Two more touches and Firmino was at the endline just feet from the goal. Rolling the ball with his right foot, he dipped his left shoulder, convincing the three City players around him he would be launching a ball across the goal. At the last second, he hung onto the ball and moved it across his body, putting a City defender between him and the goal. His unexpected shot wasn't seen by the blocked goalkeeper and the ball found the far corner of the net. The whistle blew, the game was over, and Cade stood with his arms in the air celebrating. *Take that Manchester City.*

Caught up in the moment, it took a few seconds before Cade realized someone was standing beside him. He lowered his arms as he took in her bemused smile. "Good game?" Reynolds DeVries asked.

"It was okay," Cade offered, trying to remain to cool.

She gave him that radiant smile of hers, not buying his coolness for a second. "Yeah, I could see you were having trouble staying awake. I would expect most people find soccer a bit boring. It's not like it's a real sport or anything." She held Cade's gaze.

Twice today this woman has gotten to him. Cade took a deep breath. Some people were simply born with the innate ability to push other people's buttons. Fighting to keep his anger down, Cade took another deep breath.

DeVries smiled, "Relax, I'm just messing with you. I was a former soccer player myself. Played D1 at UNC."

"Really? UNC?" DeVries nodded. Cade's estimation of DeVries had just taken a 180. In Division 1 women's soccer, North Carolina was *the* program. She just might be a better soccer player than he was.

Nodding toward the empty stool, DeVries asked, "Is this seat taken?"

She knew it wasn't but had asked anyway. Cade pulled the stool out for her.

"Look, I'm sorry about today." DeVries turned the stool to face

Cade. She put a hand on his knee. "It was a shitty thing for me to do. I'd received this tip and needed to get to the lead investigator—you— as soon as possible. No running around, no chasing through Patrol protocols."

"And your first thought was to lie? To falsify a crime report?"

"I know. I should have done—will do—things differently next time. I feel horrible about today." Looking into her eyes, Cade believed she was sincere. However, if she was just saying what he wanted to hear, she was a surprisingly good liar. Scarily good.

"About that tip you received," Cade said. "It obviously came from our department."

DeVries smiled, her hand still resting on Cade's knee. He was acutely aware of her hand, to the point of distraction. "A reporter's source is a privileged thing. You know that."

"You mean protected."

She shook her head. "No, I meant privileged. The idea behind the reporter's privilege is the protection of our confidential sources from disclosure."

"I wasn't asking for a name."

DeVries leaned back in her stool, moving her hand. "Good. He never gave his name, anyway."

"But it was a cop." Cade searched her face, not an unpleasant task.

Her lack of answer was confirmation enough.

THE GLOW of the decal was visible, even though her car was a good quarter mile ahead. The killer had followed her from a discreet distance for over a half hour now, ever since she'd left the restaurant in White Bear Lake. He was behind her as she dropped a friend off in nearby Mahtomedi, and then as she went all the way to North St. Paul to drop off another. Being patient was important when you were acquiring someone—when you were stalking someone, if he was being honest with himself. He was smart enough to know his need was building and it would consume him if he didn't act on it soon. He prided himself on his reason and superior intelligence, but the need threatened to overwhelm all that if he didn't act on it soon. And his killing cycle was a speeding freight train, gaining momentum as it went along, getting shorter. And shorter.

This wasn't his first rodeo; he'd been through the cycle before. Prior to his move, there were others. The first was a cocktail waitress at Excalibur, one of downtown Chicago's busier dance clubs. A redhead who drew no small amount of attention, she was popular with her customers. It hadn't been easy to find her alone. A true slut, she had a different male escort take her home most every night she worked. He'd watched her flirt shamelessly with several of her male customers before honing in on the one. It wasn't lost on the killer that her selection process didn't differ substantially from his own. Over the course of several weeks, he watched her as his need grew, but the opportunity never presented itself—she always left with a man.

Eventually, there came a time when his patience left him and he'd followed the woman's likely companion to the men's room just before closing time. Their encounter was swift and brutal, leaving the man with probable ruptured testicles, broken teeth and most certainly no desire for a night of sex with the redhead.

It had been a night to remember. And to savor.

The red Honda signaled, moving into the left turn lane. This wasn't the exit for her house. She must be making a pit stop at the 24-hour gas station on the corner. He had no choice but to close the distance between them and pulled in directly behind her as the light turned green. By circling around the back of the Fleet Farm gas station, he put himself in position where he could watch her and leave when she did.

The tall blonde looked unsteady on her heels as she exited the car to pump her gas. She was dressed in a short skirt and tall boots, a dark jacket covering up her top half. He'd seen the sales rep enough times to have a good idea what was underneath the coat. And his imagination was vivid enough to fill in what he didn't know.

She glanced in his direction, and he turned away, hoping she hadn't recognized him from the times he'd gotten close to her in recent weeks. He was careful but the need also brought out his riskier side—their Nicollet Mall encounter a perfect example. He had his cell phone up to his ear, obscuring his face, pretending to be on a call. It must have worked, as she turned back to the pump. In a minute, she was finished and back on the road, the killer right behind.

Highway 36 ran from Interstate 35W in the west to downtown Stillwater in the east. Some sections of the highway had more traffic than others, but fortunately, there were several deserted sections surrounded by corn or soybean fields—depending on the year's crop rotation. The killer knew the woman was headed for Somerset, which meant she was going to take the lift bridge across the St. Croix River. The bridge, located in downtown Stillwater, would still have too much activity around, even at 2 a.m. And it was imperative he took her before she crossed into Wisconsin. That left the dark stretch of highway when Highway 36 took a left turn and paralleled the river a mile south of downtown.

They were in a section with stoplights every few blocks. Too many stoplights, too many streetlights—which made it difficult to stay back far enough. The red Honda was a block ahead, his reflective decal leading the way. She approached the Greeley intersection as his own stoplight went from yellow to red. Tempted to blow right through, a pair of approaching headlights reawakened his cautious side. He slowed, and stopped, wanting to be discreet. Frustrated, he tapped a rhythm on the steering wheel, the beat existing in his mind alone.

A glance to his left brought home his brilliance. A State Patrol car was not five feet away. He could feel the trooper's eyes on him. This could be a disaster if... But the light turned green and the trooper raced off, leaving a welcome gap between them. The woman was blocks ahead now, going through the Osgood intersection, the last stoplight before the deserted section began. The killer goosed the gas pedal.

As meticulous as he was, all the planning in the world couldn't predict the effects of a chance encounter. Up ahead, the trooper activated his vehicle's emergency equipment, the lights painting a pattern across the killer's windshield. The good news was he wasn't the trooper's target. The bad news was, the trooper had pulled over the red Honda.

CHAPTER
10

W hen the flashers lit up the interior of her car, Stephanie Harding knew she was in trouble. It was always the "let's have one more drink" that got you into hot water.

Seeing Paige and Alex again was perfect. Traveling so frequently for her new job meant she didn't have many opportunities to hang with her old friends. Stephanie had been worried they'd drifted apart and would have little to talk about. Like most of her worries, reality was a lot different. They'd fallen into old patterns right away, laughing and getting along perfectly.

At the bar, they'd received no small amount of male attention and Stephanie soaked it up. Several of the guys had potential, but she wasn't looking to date right now. The demands of her career were just too much.

She signaled and pulled onto the shoulder. Stephanie turned on the dome light and placed her hands on the steering wheel as her father told her to do if she was ever pulled over. He said it would help make the officer more comfortable about his safety and convey a sense of personal control on her part. As a sales rep who traveled extensively, a DUI could be a disaster. A real frickin' disaster.

The State Patrol officer was at her window in a flash, rapping his knuckles on the glass. Stephanie lowered the window with a sense of dread. The trooper leaned down, studying her face. "Do you know why I pulled you over?" he asked. His expression hard, all business.

"I'm sorry, I guess I don't," she replied.

He studied her for another beat or so. "Have you been drinking?"

Damn. How are you supposed to answer a question like that? Do you tell a cop that yes, in fact, I had a few martinis and thought it was a perfectly good idea to climb in behind the wheel? Or do you lie and say no? That I was just driving home at 1:30 in the morning because our church bingo night ran a little long. In the end, knowing a lie would be discovered, Stephanie went with her sales training. If you'd prefer not to answer a difficult question, ask a question of your own.

"Why do you ask?"

The trooper looked at her, no expression to betray his thoughts. Stephanie needed to pee.

"You were weaving a bit around the Greeley Street intersection. I need your license and proof of insurance." Stephanie handed them over. "It'll be a few minutes," he said before leaving her to wait. A thousand thoughts ran through her head: *I've got a clean driving record. I cannot get a DUI. Tony will fire me if I lose my license. Should I cry when he gets back? I really have to pee.*

It was, in fact, three minutes before the trooper returned. He leaned down by her open window. "Please step out of your vehicle. I'd like to administer a field sobriety test."

Damn.

Stephanie walked back behind her car, bathed in the light of the trooper's spotlight. The officer followed her closely. At such a close range, she was confident the trooper couldn't miss the way her skirt fit. Stephanie wasn't above using all her assets to her advantage.

"I'm going to give you several tests which will allow me to gauge your impairment." The trooper said, pulling out a pen. "Just hold your head still and follow my pen with your eyes."

The trooper swung his pen from one side to the other and then back the other way. So far, so good. Stephanie gave him a quick smile.

The trooper led her to the shoulder and gestured to the white line. "Now, I'd like you to take nine steps, heel-to-toe, along this straight line. After taking the nine steps, turn on one foot and return in the same manner in the opposite direction."

Nodding, Stephanie stepped out with her right foot. Since she'd been walking for twenty-three years, this should be relatively easy.

After all, practice makes perfect. When she made her turn with her left foot, she almost lost it but recovered quickly. It was the high heels that messed up her turn, the very heels that attracted her to the boots in the first place. Sometimes, it's tough to be a slave to fashion.

When she was done, Stephanie stepped into the trooper's bubble of personal space. She had a knack for reading people, and when they accepted her presence—they didn't step back in other words—she knew she had them. "What's next?" she asked pleasantly.

"Last test. I'll need you to balance on one leg while you count by thousands. Lift your foot six inches off the ground. I'll tell you when you're done."

Stephanie smiled. "Really? You should try balancing on these heels."

"Just do your best," the trooper replied.

"I always do." Stephanie lifted her left foot. "One thousand one, one thousand two."

After roughly 30 seconds, the trooper held up his hand. "Okay, that's fine. I don't see obvious signs of impairment, so I'm letting you off with a warning." He looked into Stephanie's eyes. *Here comes the lecture.*

"It's not the fear of getting a DUI that should concern you next time you're out having a drink. Alcohol greatly impairs reaction time, and being behind the wheel puts you in the most unforgiving of situations. It could be the deer that jumps out in front of you or the minivan pulling into your lane. Or the stoplight you didn't notice. You do not want to diminish your reaction time. Plain and simple: it could kill you."

He handed Stephanie back her license and insurance card. "Thank you," she said, relief coursing through her.

The trooper nodded. "I've seen too many fatalities to take this kind of thing lightly. Please be careful." He turned and headed for his vehicle.

Back in her car, Stephanie glanced in her mirror and pulled out. The trooper right behind her. It made her nervous. What if he changed his mind and pulled her over again? She tightened her grip on the wheel, not wanting to give any indication of unsteadiness. Her speedometer read 54 miles per hour. He was still back there.

The Beach Road exit came up and the trooper took the turn. Relief again filled her. Stephanie followed the curve as Highway 36 turned north, the St. Croix River on her right. In a few minutes, she would cross the river into Wisconsin and be home in ten minutes. What a night.

꽃

THE KILLER WAS DEVASTATED when he saw the trooper's emergency equipment activated and the red Honda pulled over. He signaled a right turn at the Osgood light and pulled into the gas station parking lot at the corner. Shutting off his lights, he kept the engine running in case he needed to make a hasty retreat.

The trooper was out of the squad and at the woman's car in a moment. The Honda's interior was lit and he could see her blonde hair. She handed him something—her I.D. most likely—and the trooper returned to his squad. He could see the trooper's face from the glow of the dashboard laptop as he entered her information. Was this a traffic stop or a DUI stop? The killer hoped for the former, but when the trooper returned and had the woman exit her car, he knew it was the latter. The killer checked his mirror in the event the trooper requested a backup.

This wasn't the first time a meticulously planned killing had gone horribly wrong. The Hilton Towers on Michigan Avenue was a favorite place of his. Inside was an Irish pub, Kitty O'Shea's, where the waitresses wore frilly green dresses and had a playful attitude and everyone sang Irish tunes. He'd gravitated to a redhead named Annie. Her long curls and warm smile set her apart from the other waitresses working there. As was his custom, the killer followed her home and set out to learn her routine.

It turned out Annie had a part-time job at a gallery on Water

Street. While not exactly an art connoisseur, a little internet research prepared him for his gallery visit—or so he'd thought. Dressed in a conservative suit with an open collar, he ventured inside the Illumination Arts gallery a half hour before closing, knowing she'd be there. Annie wore a gray business suit with matching skirt and heels. She'd looked stunning.

At first, their interaction had been delightful as she'd shown him around, asking about his likes and dislikes, and what kind of art stirred his soul. The trouble began when he attempted to describe his feelings toward the gallery's art. He simply didn't have any. Sure, he could appreciate an artist's technique, but nothing "spoke to him." And it never would. He wasn't wired that way. The killer recognized the change in Annie's demeanor as she sensed the aberration in him. He'd seen it before.

Annie left him to peruse the gallery while she finished her closing paperwork. She was only gone for a minute or two, but it was enough to raise the killer's suspicions. He made an excuse and left just after Annie returned. She did not seem sorry to see him go.

He waited near her car, in the shadow of the dumpster. When he showed himself to her, there would be no going back. Normal people with normal motivations do not hide in the shadows. He would have to take her.

Moments later, he heard her heels on the pavement as she came around the corner and approached her vehicle. The killer stepped out of the shadows—only to be caught in the glare of headlights. Another vehicle entered the lot and came hurtling in his direction. The killer had no choice but to flee. He cut between a cluster of vehicles as he ran toward the other entrance on the south side. The pickup truck raced through the lot, clearly chasing him down. He had a handgun holstered in the small of his back but thought better of it. Despite decades of television cop shows to the contrary, a handgun wouldn't be terribly effective against a speeding half-ton pickup truck.

He'd slid across the hood of a taxi out on Water Street and

sprinted up the sidewalk, cutting down an alley and crossing to a side street. Forcing himself to slow to a walking pace, the killer needed to blend in. At this point, a man running in a suit would attract more attention than he desired. His car was around the corner from the gallery and he couldn't risk returning to it, so he simply kept walking.

Close to midnight, roughly three-and-a-half hours after he'd arrived at the gallery, the taxi dropped him off at his car, with no sign of the pickup truck or Annie. He'd never seen Annie again after that night. After all, there are always more women for the taking.

The killer watched as the trooper took Stephanie through the field sobriety tests. He was convinced this wasn't going to happen tonight. Sometimes circumstances just happened and there's nothing you can do. But he didn't leave, instead wanting to watch as long as he could. She looked unsteady as she did the walk-the-line routine, and so he was absolutely astounded when she was allowed to return to her vehicle, apparently free to leave.

The woman signaled and pulled onto Highway 36, the trooper several car lengths behind. After a moment's hesitation, the killer pulled out and followed.

A surge of power went through him when the trooper took the exit, leaving Stephanie on her own. The woman was headed for the deserted stretch of highway overlooking the river. This was going to be his night after all. He floored the gas pedal and the hunt was on.

*

STEPHANIE COULDN'T BELIEVE her luck when the State Patrol trooper let her go. Most of the stories she'd heard of people stopped for suspicion of DUI, the result was the polar opposite. It almost always started with a night in jail and ended with a year of expensive insurance and multiple court appearances. Of course, most people didn't look like Stephanie. She learned early on that boys—and men— were attracted to her and she learned to use that. Working in pharmaceutical sales had been the right choice. For Stephanie, she had little trouble getting in front of the busy doctors putting her way ahead of her competitors who were often left sitting in waiting rooms for hours. If you were given a gift, there was nothing wrong with using it.

The bright lights came up fast behind her. Was it the trooper again? The sudden impact caught Stephanie by surprise as she wrestled with the wheel as the Honda spun out of control. Stephanie fought the wheel realizing she was in serious trouble. Her scream echoed in the car as it left the highway.

And then the car was still.

Stunned, confused and scared, Stephanie couldn't believe she was alive. The highway was up above her. The Honda's front end was resting on something—a tree or a large rock, maybe. Even though the engine was still running, Stephanie wasn't going to be driving it anywhere. She was stuck.

A bobbing flashlight caught her attention as a solitary figure made its way down the embankment. The man shined the flashlight directly at her, blinding her with its harsh light. He tried her door and rapped the flashlight handle on the window to get her to unlock the door. Stephanie fumbled for the lock button, relieved to hear the door locks pop open.

When the man opened her door, he asked if she was okay. Stephanie heard herself say something about her shoulder but was too dazed to know for certain. She just knew it hurt. The man leaned into the car, reaching for her seatbelt buckle, awkwardly pressing against her. "Sorry about this," he said quietly.

Stephanie knew she was in trouble. When he leaned in, the man smelled her hair, triggering a flash of memory. This was not her shining knight coming to her rescue.

The last thing Stephanie Harding ever saw was the man's eyes as he grabbed her head, fingers entangled in her hair, forcing her to look at him. They were the deadest eyes she had ever seen.

THE KILLER WAS ON AUTOPILOT. Time was critical now. Get down to the Honda. Get down to the woman.

He was prepared to bust through the window glass if needed, but the woman let him in.

Opening her door, the killer asked, "Are you okay?" In his own way, he cared. Still playing the part of the hero coming to her rescue. Not for long.

She complained about her shoulder, talking disjointedly about the pain. "Let me get you out of here." He reached across the woman to release her seatbelt. "Sorry about this," he offered as he got close. The first sign of his slipping control was when he pushed his face into her hair and smelled. He knew it was a mistake when the woman went rigid. It enhanced the experience for him, seeing the utter shock as things clicked into place for the woman. This was not a rescue.

He clawed the fingers of his left hand into her hair and wrenched her head, forcing her to look at him. He could almost taste her fear, as he subconsciously licked his lips, looking into her eyes. Mmm.

With a quick jab to her face, the woman slumped unconscious. Breathing heavier now, he ran his hand up her thigh. With this one, the time for subtleness was gone. The killer grabbed her skirt, tearing the material.

Not much time left, he popped the top buttons on her blouse. Like the Janek woman, he felt her heart beating. One last time, he looked at Stephanie before he grabbed her by the back of her head. Even unconscious, she was beautiful. With a trace of sadness, the killer knew it was time to finish.

Stephanie Harding's face became one with the steering wheel as the killer killed.

CHAPTER
11

"There's been another one."

The adrenaline rush pushed Cade's brain to full alert. The clock on the bedside table read 4:20 a.m. There'd be no more sleep for him. "Where?" he asked. Standing up, looking for his jeans, pulling on his Duluth Pack sweatshirt.

"Stillwater, on Highway 36," Crash Simpson said, "Three quarters of a mile south of downtown."

Really close to home. "I can be there in five minutes. See you."

Cade grabbed a pair of socks and hustled out the door.

*

THE SCENE WAS LIT by the flashing of a dozen emergency service vehicles. A fatality brought in everyone: Stillwater police, Stillwater Fire and Rescue, Washington County sheriff's department and because it was on a state highway, the Minnesota State Patrol. The Patrol brought its own contingent of troopers and one larger-than-life accident investigator, Crash Simpson.

"This one's bad," Crash said in an emotionless voice. The haunted look in his eyes agreed with his words.

These things were never good. "How so?"

Crash leaned in closer. "He's not trying to hide it. Remember Janek's clothing? The way it resembled—as you so eloquently put it— a prom date's parking grope. This woman's body goes way beyond that. Her underwear was torn and her breasts exposed."

"Cause of death?"

"Head trauma. But it's worse than last time. You'll see."

They made their way down the rocky embankment. A red Honda sat nose up, lifted by an outcropping of rock, elevated roughly twenty degrees. The driver's door was open. Cade could make out a woman's body, dressed in expensive clothes, behind the wheel. Before heading for the woman, he veered for the rear of the Honda. Kneeling, he shone his flashlight across the trunk. The reflective dot was there.

The blonde woman was elegantly dressed, wearing a short skirt, silky blouse and over-the-calf boots. Blood was splattered across the windshield, the ceiling, dashboard and both side windows. The woman's face was a mess. Her blouse was open and her bra out of place. Her skirt was bunched up and torn. Cade felt his temper rising.

Backing out of the car, he looked at Crash, who simply nodded. "I'm going to start gathering road evidence. I'll call you before the chopper arrives." He headed back up the hill.

"Wait, chopper?" But Crash was already up the hill and hadn't heard Cade's question. Cade walked to the rear of the Honda, fishing out his cell. He got Rob after several rings and briefed him on the fatality. Rob said he'd be on scene in a half hour.

Next, Cade called Capt. Rejene, her voice thick with sleep. "It's not going to be good news, is it?"

"We've had another one-car fatality, this one outside of Stillwater. Another blonde woman who looked like she was assaulted before her face was hammered into the steering wheel. Much more violent than either Janek or Allard."

Cade could hear Rejene's sigh. "The media..."

"They'll be all over this one."

"Damn. What about her vehicle, any sign of a PIT maneuver?"

Cade walked to the side of the Honda, his flashlight dancing over the area behind the rear tire. "As a matter of fact, there's damage consistent with such an impact."

"And the reflective dot?"

"It's still there. No effort to hide it. Everything about this one is much more overt."

"Damn." Her expletive hanging there, neither one ready to add to it.

A long pause followed by a longer sigh. "I'm going to have to go to the BCA with this. I've got no choice."

"I know, but it sucks. I can do the same things their investigators can, plus I've got the background on this case."

"Out of my hands. Sorry." Rejene did sound sorry. Didn't help though.

Crash waved for Cade to join him up on the highway. "Trooper 7 will be here in a minute. Figured you'd want to join me in the chopper for the aerial view." They walked past the cluster of vehicles, and Crash said, "Don't want the chopper to contaminate the scene. Better to have it land a ways off. And all the same, I could use the exercise. If I don't watch my figure, no one will." Cade followed the portly man down the highway without comment.

Hearing it before he saw it, Cade scanned the skies for the State Patrol helicopter. Trooper 7 was used for emergency transport, manhunts and apparently for aerial views of larger accident scenes. So far, Cade hadn't had the pleasure of riding in Trooper 7—or any helicopter, actually. His stomach tightened as the chopper roared over the tree line and swung down to the highway.

Crash ducked and jogged to the chopper. He glanced back, seeing Cade still rooted in place and waved him to follow. Reluctantly, Cade joined him. "Take the front. I need to be in back to shoot pictures from both sides," Crash shouted over the roar.

Handed a headset, Cade shook hands with the pilot, a fifty-something trooper with a name badge reading "Hyde." Bushy hair, aviator sunglasses on his head, a toothpick hanging out of his mouth, with a face that's clearly avoided a razor for the better part of a week, Hyde looked the part of a veteran pilot. Didn't ease the growing turbulence in Cade's belly in the least. "Hang on," Hyde warned.

As the chopper bolted from the ground, the door next to Cade popped open. "Holy shit," Cade blurted. Under the mistaken impression that helicopter doors were meant to stay closed during takeoff, the sudden loss of said door dropped Cade's stomach. He leaned in, wanting to put as much distance as possible between him and the open door of death.

The air rushed in, the ground becoming trees as the pilot rolled the chopper up on Cade's side. The door slammed shut as gravity did its job. "Sorry about that. This old bird has her quirks." Crash busted a gut laughing at Cade's expense.

"You knew?" Cade jabbed his finger at Crash. "And you had me sit up here?"

Wiping away a tear, Crash said, "Yeah, it happens a lot during liftoff. Honestly, you looked so nervous already. If I had told you, would you have even climbed aboard?"

"I...well, probably not." He shook his head. "I almost wet myself back there."

Hyde laughed. "You should have seen your face. I've got to tell you; this job never gets old."

Crash got them back on track. "See my line there, the orange line? That's where the scene started. Same scenario as the Highway 5 crash. Yaw marks followed by scuff marks." On the road below the hovering chopper was a parallel pair of orange marks, looking much like an equal sign. Right after that was a series of red dots adjacent to black tire marks. Crash continued, "There is one difference, however. See how I've marked our victim's road marks in red? Now look down where her car left the highway. There are skid marks—just regular skid marks this time—that I've marked out in blue. When I'm plotting out the crash scene, I use orange spray paint to highlight where the scene begins and then again where it ends. I'll use red to mark the events as they happened to the victim's vehicle. If there's a second vehicle, I use another color of spray paint."

Cade nodded. "Hence the blue."

"That a boy," Crash said. "We have a second vehicle leaving behind road evidence this time. If I had to venture a guess, I would say your man was in a big-time hurry to stop and get down to the woman."

The marks were heavy and black. "Agreed. It feels like he's losing control. Everything about this is more overt. The subtlety is gone."

Crash looked back at Cade, serious. "If this continues, it's going to get real ugly."

Not knowing what else to add, Cade simply nodded. It was going to get bad.

CHAPTER
12

Somebody was in Rejene's office. Cade tapped lightly on her door, wanting to let her know he was back at headquarters and gave a wave as he headed back to his desk. He'd taken just a few steps when Capt. Rejene, standing at her open office door, called for him. "Dawkins, there's someone you should meet."

Rejene gestured to the man seated in her office. "Cade Dawkins, this is the BCA's Freddie Goodwin." Standing up, Goodwin stepped close to Cade and offered his hand. He towered over Cade's six-foot frame. Though Goodwin's proximity made him uncomfortable, he recognized the BCA man's intimidation ploy and stood his ground. Goodwin looked to be about forty and may have been in shape once, but his soft pudgy face showed a shift in priorities. His face had that dark leathery quality which suggested many hours spent in a tanning salon. Cade disliked him immediately.

"Nice to see you again," Cade offered. Goodwin had just joined up with BCA as Cade left. Prior to that, Goodwin had spent most of his career as a field agent with the FBI.

Goodwin stepped back studying Cade. "I hadn't realized we've met."

"I was just leaving the BCA as you were coming aboard. You were sort of busy decorating your office that first month." Cade caught a glimpse of Rejene's smile as she turned away.

Goodwin's eyes narrowed. Suspecting his status had gone from too small to notice to too large of a target for Goodwin to ignore, Cade tried to play nice. "I guess you're here to help with my case."

Goodwin had the pained smile of a waiter listening to the

restaurant's signature dish being mispronounced for the umpteenth time. He shook his head. "We were just discussing the case. My case actually. I'm going to need your case file and notes. After that, you're free to do whatever it is you do. I heard there was a fender bender on 94 this morning you could, um, investigate." He locked eyes with Cade.

Goodwin, a classic one-trick pony, stepped into Cade's space again. "I want to make sure you understand this. This is my case now. Here in Minnesota, it's the state patrol, not the state police. Our legislators—not usually the brightest bulbs in the shed—got this one right and saw fit to limit the scope of your responsibilities. You hand out traffic tickets and help little old ladies find their way home. I handle the murder investigations."

Each and every one of the muscles tightened in Cade's right hand. He held the fist at his side through sheer willpower.

Goodwin jabbed a finger at Cade. "If you mess with me or my investigation, I'll have my boss contact the chief of the State Patrol. And guess which one outranks the other." His smile returned.

Though he was aware of it, Cade's body was now on autopilot, the outcome predetermined by nature's fight-or-flight response. And flight was never an option. In a fraction of a second, Cade's weight shifted to his left foot and his right arm tightened.

Capt. Rejene put a calming hand on Cade's arm as she stepped forward. "Look, we're on the same side here. We want this maniac off our highways as much as you do. You'll have our cooperation. But don't forget where the investigation began. You wouldn't have this if it wasn't for the fine work of our lead investigator here. Okay?" She held Goodwin's gaze until he nodded.

"Fine. I'll throw you a bone at the press conference."

"Press conference?" Rejene looked to Cade who simply shrugged.

"At 4 today. BCA headquarters."

"Why? Don't we want to keep this quiet until we know more?" she asked.

"I'd heard you were from a small town, Captain. You're being naïve. The media can be a vindictive bunch and will punish us for not looping them into this from the get go. And quite frankly, the people need to know what's happened on the highways. They need to know they aren't safe." Goodwin seemed to be enjoying himself.

"And they need to know there's a new sheriff in town," he said hooking his thumbs in his belt.

"You know you're not actually a sheriff?" Cade asked and right away wondered if he'd gone too far.

If Goodwin noticed or cared, he didn't let it show. Instead, Goodwin paused at the door, looking Cade up and down. "And Dawkins, wear something suitable." He was still laughing at his joke as he rounded the corner.

Neither Cade nor Rejene said anything for a long moment. "Well, that sucked," Cade offered. He plopped down into a chair across from the Captain's desk.

Rejene's brown eyes burned. "That man is such a poser. I can't wait for him to get his. No way he should be treating us the way he did." She leaned on her desk, arms folded. "But you're going to have to be there at the press conference. There's no getting around that. We need a Patrol presence there or he's going to throw us under the bus."

Cade nodded. "He just might anyways. Goodwin is such the media whore." He shook his head, picturing the afternoon ahead. "It's going to be a helluva circus, isn't it?"

IT WAS A HELLUVA CIRCUS. When Cade arrived at the BCA headquarters, media trucks surrounded the place. Inside was worse. The cavernous lobby was packed with television crews, newspaper reporters and a multitude of others that Cade could only guess which outlet they represented. He skirted around the back and found

Freddie Goodwin in a conference room. A woman brushed Goodwin's hair into place, a bottle of hairspray in hand.

"No tie?" Goodwin asked without looking. Freddie wore his uniform from his FBI days: a dark navy suit, crisp white shirt with a burgundy tie. Cade suspected the suit sold for more than he made in a month. Cade had gone with a sport coat and slacks, leaving his only tie hanging in the closet. He preferred the comfort of the open-collared look.

"What's the plan?" He wasn't about to discuss fashion with Goodwin.

The woman patted Goodwin's hair into place, spritzing enough hairspray to make sure it wouldn't ever move again. "I'll make the introductions and give a timeline of the killings. Then I'll walk the media through our investigative process." He stood up. "And we'll end with a brief question-and-answer period."

"Remind me why I'm here," Cade asked. "It doesn't sound like I'll be needed."

Goodwin rolled his eyes. "Don't be such a media whore. I planned on mentioning you during the introductions." He gestured toward the door. "We better get started if we want to make the 6:00 news."

CADE FOUND a spot as far away from Goodwin as he could, standing at the end of a row of suits from the BCA. He suspected the only reason they were here was to make Goodwin look more important. Glancing around the room, he spotted Reynolds DeVries right in the front and center of the room. She was the first to break the story and now all the stations were here, no one wanted to miss the breaking story of the year. Cade caught her eye and she gave him a shy smile in return.

Freddie Goodwin confidently strode into the room, waving at members of the media. He leaned over a balding man, who Cade recognized as a StarTribune reporter. Following the aftermath of last fall's case, the reporter had interviewed Cade on several occasions. Goodwin clapped the man on the back as if they were old friends and moved to the front of the room. Much like a receiving line at a wedding, Goodwin shook hands with each of the BCA men in the row, starting with the man next to Cade. If the public snubbing was to teach Cade a lesson, the lesson was wasted. The less contact with Goodwin the better.

"My name is Freddie Goodwin, Special Investigator with the Minnesota Bureau of Criminal Apprehension. The purpose of this gathering is to notify the public of a serious threat on our highways." Cade could only shake his head in disbelief as Goodwin gave a dramatic pause, his eyes searching the room, before continuing. "Evidence has come to light of a serial murderer operating in the Twin Cities metro area."

The effect was immediate. Hands were raised, while other less-patient media people shouted questions. Goodwin held up a hand to silence the room, looking as if he were put out by the attention. The tightness at the corners of his mouth betrayed his actual pleasure.

"Three women have been connected to the killings so far. The first, Jennifer Allard, was an attorney from Bayport. Her one-car fatality was investigated as an accident approximately 45 days ago. The second victim, Holly Janek, was an event planner on her way home to Stillwater. She was killed approximately 12 days ago. Our third victim, Stephanie Harding was killed yesterday just south of downtown Stillwater in the early morning hours. All three women died of blunt force trauma to the head."

Goodwin shuffled through his papers. After a moment's hesitation, he continued. "State Patrol investigator Cade Dawkins, upon finding similarities between the three deaths, notified his superior, who in turn, notified the BCA. As we are better equipped to investigate murder cases, the BCA will own this case going forward."

Goodwin, with a slight smile, glanced in Cade's direction. "Since the BCA has just taken over the case, we do not have a suspect at this time. My educated guess is we'll have made substantial progress in the near future."

Looking around the room with the type of smile only other hyenas would recognize, Goodwin asked, "Questions?"

A dark-haired woman in the second row was the first to her feet. "Cynthia Margolis, Minnesota Public Radio news. What evidence tied the three women together? Can you be specific?"

"Well," Goodwin began, "all three were eerily similar in demographics, and the physical evidence found at the crime scenes pointed to identical methods to disable their vehicles. Also, a crude tracking beacon was used by the killer to follow each of the victims. Obviously, in an ongoing investigation, it wouldn't be prudent to elaborate further. Next question."

A reporter from the Fox affiliate spoke up. "I'd like to ask Cade Dawkins a question if you don't mind." Stunned, Goodwin simply shrugged.

"As a former BCA investigator yourself, and having solved the infamous highway shootings case last fall, aren't you equally qualified to work this case?"

With a grin in Goodwin's direction, Cade spoke. "Equally qualified? I don't know about that. Would I like to remain active in this investigation? Yes. However, it's not up to me."

Front and center, Reynolds stood as she commanded the room's attention. "Reynolds DeVries from the Five. Mr. Dawkins, in the interest of public safety, will you share with us the similar physical descriptions of the victims you discovered?" She had a twinkle in her eye.

Glancing at Goodwin, Cade spoke. "Each of the victims was female, ranging in age from 24 to 30, heights ranging from five foot seven to five foot nine. All three had long blonde hair and could be described as beautiful. Actually, as I think about it, all three looked remarkably similar to you, Miss DeVries."

That did it. The room went a little crazy after that.

CHAPTER
13

It was a cloudy morning in Woodbury as Mother Nature threatened one last snowstorm before spring made its presence felt. In Minnesota, the weather in March could be maddening. Just when you thought you'd seen the last of the snow and you finally felt the warmth of the sun on the back of your neck, the hammer dropped and the snow fell once again. Climbing out of his car, Cade glanced at the mass of gray hanging overhead and hoped the snowstorm would miss the Twin Cities.

Ever since the press conference ended in pandemonium, Cade was adrift. He hated having the case taken from him. What made it worse was he knew the killer was out there stalking the same highways he drove every day. The same highways his Patrol division was sworn to protect. But there was nothing he could do about the case now. However, the media didn't care and focused much of their reporting on him. In a deep, dark place inside, Cade didn't mind the spotlight turning away from Goodwin.

With his newfound free time, Cade shopped for a new truck. He'd found a Toyota FJ Cruiser on Craigslist that caught his eye. Hence his visit to the State Credit Union to meet with a loan officer.

For a Tuesday morning, the bank was busy. A half-dozen people stood at the teller windows, while several others waited with Cade to see a loan officer. A conservatively dressed blonde woman approached and glanced between Cade and the other man sitting across from him. "Cade Dawkins?"

"That's me," he said as he stood.

"Lindsay Miller," she replied as she shook his hand and led him back to her office, gesturing for him to take a seat. She rounded her desk and stopped, gawking at the lobby. "Oh dear."

Three heavily armed men had just entered the credit union and made a beeline for the teller windows. Cade was reaching for his Glock pistol when one of the men separated from the others and approached the office. He held a pump-style shotgun. Cade left the pistol in its holster.

"Come out here." He waved the others from the offices. "On the floor. Now." Miller and Cade got on the floor. He was careful to keep his holster away from the men. The man moved into a position near the entrance, his shotgun leveled at the group of hostages.

A woman cried out from the teller line as one of the men shoved her. "Over there. On the floor." The man corralled the remaining customers, brandishing his shotgun. Cade noted his jerky movements, recognizing that the man was amped on something far stronger than adrenaline. This one would be more unpredictable, making a tense situation even worse.

The third man was at the teller windows, swinging his weapon between the four bank tellers. The way the third man shifted his weight side to side, suggesting he might be on the same better living through chemistry routine the second man followed. Stepping close to a young woman in one of the middle windows, he yelled at her to hurry up. From the look on the teller's face, she was terrified. He knew the bank's protocol was to cooperate and hoped she would follow it to the letter. The combination of drugs and adrenaline in such an explosive situation could lead to a bad outcome.

Cade glanced at his loan officer. A track of tears went down her cheek, but she held it together otherwise. Cade found he could get out of view by leaning back under the counter that housed the deposit forms, loan applications, and suckers.

"Thirty seconds," the man by the entrance announced. Cade leaned forward, startled by the man's shout. At that moment, a woman entered the lobby and was immediately greeted by the gunman. He pushed her toward the others on the floor. Seizing the moment to take advantage of the gunman's distraction, Cade slipped out his cell and leaned back out of sight.

Cade hit the phone icon, glanced at the recent list and picked one to re-dial. He reached Capt. Rejene on the second ring. Before he could say anything, she was speaking. "Cade. Great, I'll put you on speaker," she said. "I've got Zink here, something's come up."

Unbelievable.

"I really can't talk," he hissed. Time was against him. "Listen carefully. I'm at the State Credit Union in Woodbury. There are three armed men, two with shotguns, and one..." he paused, sneaking a peek toward the third man at the teller windows, "And the third has an Uzi. Maybe a dozen hostages."

"Go notify dispatch," Rejene said, obviously directing Rob.

The second gunman moved into Cade's view. Keeping the phone out of sight, Cade leaned forward, praying the man hasn't seen what he was up to. The man took a step toward Cade and abruptly pivoted back toward the teller windows. Cade let out the breath he was holding. That was close.

Leaning back under the counter, he heard Rejene speaking. "I know you know procedures, so lay low and don't identify yourself. Leave the line open. Help is on the way."

"One minute," the man by the entrance calmly announced.

Cade lowered the cell phone and placed it on the floor against the counter. He leaned back out and glanced around at the hostage group. If anyone had seen him on his cell phone, no one gave any indication. The man who was waiting with Cade had his head buried in his arms and several of the women huddled together looking scared, while a mom and her young son sat on the floor as she bounced him on her leg. His giggle was surreal in the midst of the tense situation.

Scanning the windows, Cade caught a glimpse of white flashing by. Woodbury police had arrived.

"90 seconds. Time to go." The first man announced as he peered out the entrance. He was joined by the other gunmen, each carrying a sack. "And we have a cop car outside."

The third gunman, the one with the Uzi seemed to be in charge. "A complication, but not unexpected. Send out the hostages and I'll take the cop out in the confusion." This complication changed everything for Cade. He could no longer wait for someone else to take care of the situation. Not when a cop's life was in danger.

The second man held up his shotgun. "Everyone up on their feet. Now." He pushed the group toward the entrance where they were corralled at the door. "When I say go, you have five seconds to get out of here. You better run."

The man with the Uzi slipped into the group, the deadly weapon hidden inside his jacket. His plan obvious, he would blend in with the panicked group as they ran from the building. Most would run for the protection of the police car, and the officer would have little chance to defend himself when the Uzi made its sudden appearance.

Cade knew he had to act soon. The gunman by the door shouted, "Go, go." Everyone surged at the entrance, pushing out the door, a collective feeling of panic and hope driving them.

At the rear of the group, Cade found himself next to the nervous second gunman. Seizing the opportunity, Cade stomped down hard on the man's foot, pulling the shotgun from his hands. Reversing the shotgun, he drove the butt of the gun into the gunman's belly, doubling him over and dropping him.

Without hesitation, Cade moved to the man at the entrance, body slamming the robber into the wall. He ducked out the door, deperate to find the third man, the one with the Uzi.

Panic gripped everyone, and the pack surged, screaming and running toward the police car. The young Woodbury officer had his gun out but lowered it as the crowd of panicking hostages descended upon him. It was sheer pandemonium. No way the academy had trained him for situations like this. The mother scooped up her child and was the first to reach the squad. A group of four credit union staff followed them, three of the women holding hands as they ran. The fourth woman shouting for the officer to save her, her hysteria made her voice come out as a high-pitched screech. The gunman was directly behind the women, his Uzi coming up.

Cade sprinted forward, kicking the man's leg out. The gunman hit the pavement hard, his Uzi sliding across the pavement. Cade dove on top of him, his elbow connecting with the gunman's solar plexus, knocking the wind—and fight—out of the last of the would be bank robbers.

The Woodbury officer caught onto the threat and stepped around the women, his gun leveled at Cade. "Don't move," he barked. The officer's darting eyes betraying his nerves.

Cade, who was sitting on the back of the fallen gunman, held up his hands. "I'm a cop," he said. "State Patrol. There's two more inside. Incapacitated."

A flurry of activity broke out as three more squads arrived on scene. Officers dragged the gunmen from the credit union's interior. Rob and Capt. Rejene arrived shortly after, followed by the media.

Cade found himself surrounded by people with questions. Had he known or even suspected the bank heist was coming and that's why he was here? *No, I was here for a truck loan.* Why wouldn't you get a hybrid vehicle instead of a truck? *You can't be a badass in a hybrid.* Did the bad guys recognize him? *No.* Were you armed? *Yes, but I never had a chance to take out my gun.* Were you scared? *No, just wanted to keep a low profile so no one would be hurt—these guys looked to be amped up on something.* Was it dangerous to use your phone to call for backup? *Possibly, but given the perpetrator's agitation, I had to risk it.* What made you step up into an obviously deadly situation? *They were going to ambush the lone Woodbury officer and I couldn't let that happen.*

The last question of the day came from the Woodbury police chief. There had always been a friendly rivalry between law enforcement divisions with playful banter being the norm. The chief was no exception to this. "We'd heard you'd been with the BCA previously. Why would you want to be a trooper, anyway? I heard the lobotomy hurts like hell."

Cade paused and grinned as he looked directly at the police chief. "Doesn't hurt nearly as bad as the one you get when you're promoted."

CHAPTER
14

Cade, Rob and Rejene found themselves a coffee shop where they worked through the day's events. Leaning back in a leather armchair, Cade shook his head. "What a day. Never did get to talk to the loan officer about my truck loan."

Rejene leaned forward, speaking quietly. "Something's come up in Goodwin's investigation. And it's not good for the Patrol."

Cade moved toward his captain. "Really?"

Rob nodded. "Really."

Rejene folded her hands. "Minutes before Stephanie Harding was killed, she'd been stopped by a Patrol officer. A DUI stop."

"Who was it?"

"Sully. The thing is, Sully's dashboard cam shows he missed several clues of impairment when Harding performed the walk-and-turn test, including taking the wrong number of steps, pivoting on her right foot instead of her left, and using her arms for balance." Rejene winced in a my-migraine's-going-to-make-my-head-explode sort of way. "The video shows a very short skirted Harding getting uncomfortably close to Sully right after she failed the test. And then he let her drive away."

Cade shook his head. "And it had to be Goodwin who discovered this."

Rejene pinched the bridge of her nose. "I know."

"We're going to take one for not following procedure. Harding would be alive if Sully had followed procedure instead of his hormones. Damn him," Rejene spat out.

Cade held Rejene's brown eyes. "You're going to have to suspend him. Not that I'm telling you how to do your job, boss. But the public needs to see we're taking this seriously."

"I know. I know." Rejene rubbed her temples. "This hurts worse than my promotion lobotomy."

Cade looked up. "Oh, you heard that."

"I did." Cade noticed Rejene had a hint of a smile for the first time that day.

THE KILLER TURNED on the news, starting with the 5 broadcast. The lead story was the Patrol scandal, with Harding's picture plastered across the screen. The news anchor, John Mason, was reporting, "In a startling development, the BCA's investigation into the murders of the three Twin Cities women has discovered the State Patrol had stopped victim Stephanie Harding just moments before her untimely death. A routine DUI stop became anything but routine when Harding failed her field sobriety test—yet was allowed to leave the scene."

BCA Special Investigator Freddie Goodwin came on screen, his face tanned, his hair perfect. "Trooper John Sullivan stopped Miss Harding due to probable cause of intoxication. Autopsy reports bear this out with a blood alcohol concentration of 0.2 percent, more than twice the legal limit of 0.08 percent."

The screen switched to a grainy black-and-white video, with Goodwin's voice providing the narration. "The troopers own dashboard cam shows Harding taking—and failing—the walk-and-turn test. This is a divided attention test that is easily performed by most unimpaired people. It requires a subject to listen to and follow instructions while performing simple physical movements. Impaired persons have difficulty with tasks requiring their attention to be divided between simple mental and physical exercises."

On screen, Harding is seen walking and turning along a line, while a trooper stood nearby. "In the walk-and-turn test, the subject is directed to take nine steps, heel-to-toe, along a straight line. After taking the steps, the suspect must turn on one foot and return in the same manner in the opposite direction. The examiner looks for eight indicators of impairment: if the suspect cannot keep balance while listening to the instructions, begins before the instructions are finished, stops while walking to regain balance, does not touch heel-to-toe, steps off the line, uses arms to balance, makes an improper turn, or takes an incorrect number of steps."

The video pauses as the camera zooms in on Harding. "Notice how Harding uses her arms for balance. And right here she turns after only eight steps, using the wrong foot. These three indicators should have meant Harding failed the test and led to her arrest for suspicion of DUI."

Onscreen, the video resumed showing Harding standing right next to the trooper, clearly comfortable in his space. The video paused with Harding smiling up at the State Patrol officer. "Yet, this is the scene right after Harding should be arrested. Trooper Sullivan allowing an impaired Harding to get back behind the wheel. And moments later, Harding was killed."

Goodwin was back on screen staring intently at the camera. Shot from the rear, a reporter asked a final question. "So, what you're telling us, if the State Patrol had followed their own procedure, Stephanie Harding would still be alive today?"

Goodwin nodded gravely in a tight close-up. "That's exactly what I'm telling you. In a major embarrassment to the state of Minnesota, the State Patrol let us all down."

The anchor was back on screen. "The fallout from this incident is sure to reach high into state law enforcement circles. The 5 news team will have developments as they come out."

Co-anchor Leah McLean: "The day's other top story also involves the State Patrol, this time with a figure familiar to Twin Cities' viewers. Reporter Susanna Song has the story."

"Cade Dawkins, famous for his remarkable efforts solving last year's freeway shootings, including bringing down the criminal empire of Andrew Bishop, was central in breaking up a robbery this morning at the State Credit Union in Woodbury."

A woman reporter stood by a busy thoroughfare; vehicles of all sizes rolled in and out of view. The camera tightened focus on the reporter.

"It was a Tuesday, like most other Tuesdays. Some people go to work, some run errands, maybe picking up a coffee or stopping at the bank. However, this particular Tuesday, three heavily armed men came to rob this Woodbury credit union."

Onscreen, a dark-haired man in his early forties wore one of those fur collared jackets only a cop would believe was still in style. "Woodbury police chief Dana Thorson." The State Credit Union was shown across the parking lot behind Thorson. A reporter's microphone entered the shot.

"Chief Thorson, can you tell us what happened here today?"

The chief turned toward the building, and the killer could tell the photojournalist had trouble keeping Thorson's face in the shot. "At approximately 9:25 this morning, three males entered the State Credit Union. Two were armed with shotguns and the third was armed with an Uzi." He looked right into the camera. "We don't see many Uzis here in Woodbury."

Onscreen, Song thoughtfully replied, "I suppose not."

"Two of the perpetrators approached the tellers and obtained an unspecified amount of currency. The other perpetrator held the customers and the remainder of the bank staff at gunpoint."

Reporter Susanna Song: "Fortunately, one of those customers was State Patrol investigator Cade Dawkins."

Police Chief Thorson: "Dawkins contacted his supervisor to get emergency vehicles rolling. One of our Woodbury units was first on the scene. He was apparently spotted by the gunmen, who rounded up the hostages and sent them running out the door. The man with the Uzi ran with the group toward the officer, his weapon hidden from view." Thorson looked off into the distance, his pale blue eyes squinting.

"Dawkins apparently figured out their plan and incapacitated the two men remaining in the bank and went after the one with Uzi. He was able to disarm and subdue the gunman before my officer could discern the threat."

Reporter Susanna Song: "Sounds like it was a good thing Dawkins was there."

Chief Thorson nodded intently. "I'd say so. I would be notifying our officer's wife and daughter about now instead of talking to you."

The scene switched to a crowd of media people. The focus of attention was a man in his low thirties, with slightly unkempt blond hair with a bouquet of microphones pushed into his face. His handsome face wore the bemused smile of a man not entirely comfortable in the media spotlight.

"Investigator Dawkins, can you tell us how you ended up in the middle of this robbery?" It was the reporter from channel 9.

Cade shook his head, running his fingers through his hair. "I was just here to see about getting a loan for a new truck."

"So, you weren't expecting an armed confrontation when you arrived at the bank?"

Cade grinned. "No, not really. The loan officer sounded so nice on the phone."

The members of the media broke out into laughter. Reynolds DeVries from 5 News stepped forward. "What happened when the three men entered the credit union?"

"Two of the gunmen went for the tellers, while the third held the staff and customers on the floor at gunpoint. I was able to contact my boss, Capt. Rejene, and let her know the situation. And she got the cavalry headed to our rescue."

Another question from DeVries: "When did you realize you couldn't wait for help to arrive?"

Another shake of his head and Cade looked into the distance.

"The moment I overheard their escape strategy. A gunman planned to blend with the group of hostages sent running toward the Woodbury officer. In the commotion, the man was going to kill the officer. Because he would never see the threat coming, I had to intervene."

Channel 4 news reporter, Colin Souder: "Wait, so you decided to take on three armed men by yourself? And you were unarmed?"

Cade grinned. "No, I had my service weapon. I just never had the opportunity to take it out of its holster. Sometimes life moves pretty fast. And this was clearly one of those times."

The camera pulled back to Song in the parking lot. "The three men arrested for the holdup are currently in Washington County lockup after being treated for minor injuries. Their names haven't been released yet, however a law enforcement source has stated all three are well acquainted with the criminal justice system. Live from Woodbury, I'm Susanna Song."

The killer was ecstatic, pacing around the cluttered room, the old hardwood floors creaking underneath his feet. The news story confirmed what he'd known since he decided to come to Minnesota. Cade Dawkins would be a glorious challenge. A conquest to surpass all his conquests. And his planning, meticulous by every standard he was aware of, had put the case right in Dawkins' lap.

The killer abruptly stopped and his face contorted with growing anger. There was a problem, of course. A massive problem. The case had been taken from Dawkins.

Rage overcame him. The killer swept everything off his table, the glass shattering, papers scattering across the floor. The wall became his punching bag, holes appearing every foot or so. He kicked over chairs. Whatever he could find was hurled across the room and exploded on impact. The killer reached for a frame, ready to obliterate the metal-and-glass object when his eye caught his mother's face looking back at him. Her long blonde hair framed a pale oval face. For a long moment he held his breath, looking at the dead women's cheerful face, and began summoning his control again. He had the power, the intellect, and the sheer will to shape events to meet his objectives. He could push this case back to the Patrol, get it back to Dawkins. That was the game, after all.

And this Goodwin idiot needed to simply go away. Forever.

CHAPTER
15

Reynolds DeVries leaned back in her comfortable seat. A creature of habit, her butt was typically in this same chair most nights—at her favorite post-broadcast hangout—with her producer and several of the production assistants. She looked around the table at the three girls who kept her life simple. Jenna, Ronnie and Nata were her behind-the-scenes angels, working tirelessly to minimize all the little speed bumps that invariably came along. It was their nightly routine: A little late-night sushi and a glass of wine. And the time with her girls kept life in perspective, winding down each stressful day.

Ronnie was in the middle of her story about the fill-in weatherman pulling her aside to describe his ideal warm front when Reynolds' cell rang. Frowning, she didn't recognize the number. But, as a high-profile reporter, her network of sources could reach out to her on occasion.

"Reynolds."

Hesitation on the line. Then, "It's me, the cop who told you about the murders."

Reynolds held up a finger to her group and stepped away from the table looking for solitude. She found it in the hallway outside the restrooms. "I'm glad you called," she began. "Wait, how'd you get this number?"

The caller gave a gruff laugh. "Please, I'm a cop. And I know how to Google. Either way: easy."

"Fair enough," Reynolds offered. "What's up?" In other words, why are you bothering me at 11:15 on a Thursday night?

"Look, I'm following this case and it's not going well. The BCA's man, Goodwin is a major load and couldn't count his own balls and come up with the same number twice. All he cares about is the media —no offense."

Reynolds laughed. "None taken."

The voice continued, as the cadence of his speech accelerated. "Dawkins on the other hand is clearly the right man. I saw the channel 5 story about the Woodbury Credit Union robbery. Amazing. This man Dawkins is smart, brave and heroic. What better person to be on this hunt for the killer?"

The conversation took a different turn than she expected. As she'd become closer to Dawkins, she found herself drawn to him— against her professional judgment. "Well..." Reynolds offered noncommittally.

The caller was having none of it. "You talked to Dawkins after the robbery. Don't you agree?"

DeVries nodded to herself. "Yes, I agree. There's something special about him."

"With all three murders happening on state highways—which is the State Patrol's domain—the case belongs with the Patrol. Especially when the state's leading investigator was already on the case. When the same thing happened in Chicago, they didn't go switching the case to another department. I realize the scope of the Patrol's powers is different here, but why play politics with the lives of our women?"

Reynolds had trouble hearing the man, as other voices intruded into the call. It sounded like the caller was also in a bar or restaurant. Apparently, she wasn't the only one out on a weeknight. "I didn't catch all of what you just said."

⚓

"SORRY, IT'S NOISY HERE," The killer replied as he pushed through a crowd gathered outside a 1st Avenue bar. A busy night in the warehouse district of downtown Minneapolis, the sidewalks were full of Thursday night partiers. The first warm days of spring brought everyone out, it seemed. Intoxicated bar-hoppers wandered the sidewalks dressed to thrill, coming downtown to see and be seen. However, only one person here held the killer's attention. A tall, rather striking blonde was just ahead of him, turning onto Sixth Street.

He increased his pace to keep her in view. "Is it possible for you to give this some exposure? In light of Dawkins' bravery, people are urging law enforcement officials to get him back on this high-profile case. This killer is probably stalking someone right now. Another Twin Cities' woman could be this savage killer's next victim, and this Goodwin idiot is getting caught up in inter-departmental politics. Something needs to be done."

"No guarantees, but I'll see what I can do."

"It's all I can ask. Gotta run." The killer disconnected the call and slowed his pace. Now would not be the time to be obvious—though the time was fast approaching. He could feel it.

The blonde, wearing black tights under a short skirt, stopped in front of Gluek's. Talking on her cell phone, she looked up at the historic building. The killer approached carefully, keeping her back between them. When he was within five feet, he stopped to study her. Finding every inch of her fascinating, he was mesmerized. Her long blonde hair. Her impossibly long legs, her athletic body. Her impending death.

Morning radio personality Ellie Winters would be as high-profile a target as the Twin Cities offered. Admittedly, she would be more difficult and would require more planning. He would need to get her on the east side of the Twin Cities, as she appeared to spend all her time on the west side. But that's what made life interesting. Challenges.

CHAPTER
16

M orning. Not Cade's favorite time to be alive, but you have to start your day sometime. The one surefire way to pull a brain back into the land of the living was coffee. It certainly wasn't a trade secret of his by any means—if you were a cop, you drank coffee. It was that simple. Though most of his compatriots enjoyed the straight black variety, not especially caring if it came from a gas station, office pot, or even a vending machine, Cade's tastes were more refined. However, refined was not the word used when he was teased for his mochas or lattes. On the positive side, being on the receiving end of good-natured mocking was one sure sign of acceptance into the Patrol.

Walking up to the counter, Cade scanned the room. If there was ever a link between caffeine and electronics, this place had found it. Laptops, tablets and smartphones were in use at every single table. Most looked to be used by out-of-work middle managers, writers, or college students. One blonde, in particular, caught his eye. She was in a leather armchair by the fireplace, her feet up on the hearth as she pecked at her smartphone. Collecting his mocha, Cade headed her way.

"Hey," he said, dropping in the chair next to her. "Thanks for the invite." He flashed her his best grin. Reynolds DeVries smiled back at him, her radiant smile doing funny things to his concentration. Trying his best not to stare, Cade asked, "What's up?"

"I got a call last night from my source," Reynolds said. "This is the second time I've heard from him. Like our earlier conversation, he mentioned being a cop and was irate about the case being pulled from your hands. Said you were the right person, the only person, who could keep up with this killer."

"Nice to have support from the law enforcement community." It was true. Much of the time, the law enforcement community could be aggressively territorial about their cases.

Reynolds nodded and took a sip before continuing. "He mentioned the similar deaths down in Chicago. What's that about?" She paused, studying him.

Huh? "Chicago? I hadn't heard about any similar cases there."

"It was difficult to hear exactly what he was saying. It was loud and people were talking. Like they just came into a room or he had just walked by a group. Anyway, he mentioned similar killings in Chicago, saying when the same thing happened, they hadn't moved the case. I would have assumed you had looked into similar killings."

"We did. Nothing. Our killer exhibits a perverse interest in tall blondes and he's also gone out of his way to make each killing resemble an accident. Our killer clearly is a pattern killer and a nationwide law enforcement search didn't ping any similar patterns." Cade paused, taking a sip of the caffeine-laced beverage. "Though maybe Goodwin has done something after all. I'd be surprised if he found a link—but I'd be even more surprised that we haven't heard a single word about it. You know how Goodwin is about pandering to you media types." He gave her a grin.

Reynolds batted her eyes. "I wouldn't mind a little pandering from you, too, you know? A girl appreciates all the attention she can get."

REJENE PACED BACK and forth in her office, talking on her phone. She caught Cade's eye and held up a finger, motioning for him to take a seat. Watching her wear a path in the carpet behind her desk reminded him of the caged tigers at the zoo. Something about the way they paced back and forth for hours longing to be on the outside, made him wonder if she would last. Rejene had a wild streak that her management career had yet to tame.

After fingers were held up four more times, Rejene was off the phone. "Sorry about that. Playing politics with Washington County."

"No offense, but I'm glad you have your job and I have mine."

"Except you get the badass types shooting at you," Rejene said, her dark eyes twinkling.

"Rather have that than the politicians always looking to take a bite out of my behind." Cade flashed her a grin.

"Funny." Rejene straightened up, fun and game time apparently over. "I'm guessing you didn't stop by just to tease me."

"Reynolds DeVries got another call from her law enforcement source. Besides reiterating his very valid and justified belief that I would be the best investigator on the case," Cade paused, smiling. Captain Rejene's serious expression prompted him to continue. "Her source mentioned similar killings in Chicago."

"But we didn't come across any similar killing patterns, did we?"

Cade shook his head.

"So, Goodwin made a discovery we missed?" She held his eye.

"Rob and I both checked independently of each other. We didn't find anything. I have serious doubts Goodwin found anything we missed."

Getting to her feet, Rejene came around her desk. "I shouldn't be asking this, but do you still have a channel—an unofficial back door one—into the BCA? See if the Chicago reference is real."

Cade got to his feet, joining Rejene at her desk. "I do know someone."

"Talk to your contact, but keep it quiet, please. We don't need our interest getting noticed by Goodwin or the media."

"It feels like I keep getting sucked back into this case."

"If people are getting killed on our highways, it should be our case. Screw the legislature."

Cade laughed. "Are you sure you should be working around

politicians? Though you may be the best person to keep them in line."

"Exactly," Rejene said with a smirk. "If they don't listen to reason, I might just remind them I carry a loaded gun."

∿

GRACE FOX AGREED to meet after work at a Selby Dale neighborhood tavern. Grace was one of Cade's favorite people in his time with the BCA. An accomplished crime scene technician, they'd crossed paths on cases frequently. He found her to be intelligent, insightful and irreverent. And frankly, anyone who doesn't take authority—or themselves, for that matter—too seriously, was someone Cade could relate to.

He found Grace at the bar, a glass of water in front of her. "You know, most people here drink something a little stronger," he said, sliding onto the stool next to her.

Grace tucked her long brunette hair behind an ear and smiled. "I've never been like most people. You of all people should know that. And I'm running a half marathon in the morning. Just water for me."

"What's new at the BCA?" Cade asked.

"Hey, did you hear Sellwood wants to get out of forensics and go to med school?" Sellwood was one of the BCA's crime scene techs who tended to aggravate just about everyone who came into contact with him. Cade had disliked him almost immediately.

"The only way Sellwood will see a medical school is from the inside of a jar. The man is an idiot," Cade replied. Grace let out a belly laugh.

He ordered a beer and caught up with Grace for a few minutes before getting to the point of their meeting. "I appreciate you seeing me. I need someone I can trust."

"Don't we all," she said, her expression becoming serious. "I'm curious where this is headed."

Cade offered a wry smile. "I know this isn't our case now, but I'd heard rumblings about similar killings in Chicago. I'd looked for the same pattern, the blonde women, the unusual highway deaths, but never found anything matching this case. Has Goodwin found something I missed?"

Grace shook her head. "Similar cases? None that we've come across. But we haven't made any progress. Nothing is moving, nothing is breaking. Honestly, Goodwin doesn't know what to do next."

"Really?"

"Really. After making such a big deal of things, Goodwin hasn't been able to produce anything—other than discovering the Patrol's DUI shitshow. Sorry, no offense. But you know that's why he made such a stink of it. He had nothing else. I almost feel sorry for the guy."

"Almost?"

"Almost. The man is an asshole." Grace played with her straw as she talked, putting her thumb over the end and letting drops of water hit her crumpled paper straw wrapper. At times like this, Cade could see the young girl in Grace, not the tenacious crime scene technician infamously known for standing up to a state senator during a murder investigation. The man had viciously berated Grace as she steadfastly stood by the evidence she'd uncovered. Turned out the senator's mistress was the killer and planned on taking out the senator's wife next. Grace held her ground, and the senator was soon engulfed in the scandal and went through a high-profile divorce instigated by his wife. This happened during her first month on the job. Now several years later, Grace was the Bureau's lead crime scene technician while the former senator was a divorced alcoholic who sold double-wide trailers in rural Minnesota. And somewhere in Minnesota right now there's a former Mrs. Senator who's feeling pretty good about her life choices.

"So, Goodwin hadn't found killings with a similar pattern?"

"Absolutely not. Where did you get the idea we had?"

Cade took a sip of his beer, deciding how much he should share. "A friend of mine is a reporter," he began.

"Reynolds DeVries." Not a question. "I see something in her when she mentions your name."

Cade shook his head. Leave it to women to have this relational radar—bordering on ESP—which carriers of Y chromosomes missed out on. Would it be too much to ask for a level playing field?

"My friend, Reynolds," he paused and smiled, "has a law enforcement source who mentioned a similar case in Chicago."

Grace nodded, as she stared off into space. Cade waited for her to come back. It didn't take long. "And you say you never found the same pattern when you searched NCIC?" Known as NCIC, the National Crime Information Center was the computerized database for tracking crime-related information. As long as you knew what to search for, you could find criminal information nationwide, 24 hours a day, 365 days a year.

"No, didn't find anything at all similar."

Setting down her straw, Grace twisted her hair around her fingers, the picture of nervous energy. "You know we're essentially talking about a pattern killer. According to criminal profiling experts, they're called pattern killers because there's a pattern in their killing associated with the types of victims selected or the method or motives for the killing." She glanced at Cade. "With me so far?"

Cade simply nodded, not wanting to break her thought process.

"Good. Researchers have discovered that the seemingly erratic behavior of the Rostov Ripper, a Russian serial killer active in the 1980s, conformed to the same mathematical pattern obeyed by earthquakes, avalanches, stock market crashes and other sporadic events. The finding suggested an explanation for why serial killers kill. Though, the Russian sometimes went nearly three years between killings, on other occasions he went just three days. Even though the spacing of his murders seemed random, the researchers found they followed a mathematical distribution known as a power law.

"When the number of days between his murders is plotted against the number of times he waited that number of days, the relationship forms a near-straight line on a type of graph called a log-

log plot. It's the same result scientists get when they plot the magnitude of earthquakes against the number of times each magnitude has occurred—and the same goes for a variety of natural phenomena. The power law outcome suggests there's an underlying natural process driving the serial killer's behavior.

"The psychotic effects leading a serial killer to commit murder arise from simultaneous firing of a large number of neurons in the brain." Grace was on a roll, her cadence quickening. "In the brain, the firing of a single neuron can potentially trigger the firing of thousands of others, each of which can in turn trigger thousands more. In this way, neural activity cascades through the brain. Most of the time, the cascade is small and quickly dies down, but occasionally —after time intervals determined by the power law—the neural activity surpasses a threshold.

"In epileptics, a threshold-crossing cascade of neurons induces a seizure. And if the theory is right, a similar buildup of excited neurons is what flooded the Rostov Ripper with an overwhelming desire to commit murder. Sometimes he went years without his neurons crossing the threshold, other times, just days.

"The new findings are well-aligned with prior observations about serial killers, many of whom seem to behave like drug addicts. In both cases, withdrawal from their addiction causes longing to build until it hits a threshold trigger point. After which they must kill to release that longing. And as with drug addiction, withdrawal from killing may cause a buildup of hormones in a part of the brain called the amygdala, and this surprisingly unpleasant feeling can only be reversed by acting out whatever the addicting stimulus might be."

"Which in our case is murder."

"Exactly. So, our killer is caught in a loop, driven to kill when the need becomes too much. And I would presume our killer has done this before, otherwise the cycle wouldn't be so frequent." Grace paused, waiting for Cade.

"Makes sense," he offered.

"If our assumption is true that our pattern killer has killed before, there must be a reason why you didn't find anything similar." Grace took a sip from her water, which was mostly untouched.

Cade slammed his hand down on the bar. Several heads turned in their direction. "I got it! There's still a pattern. But the pattern was different."

Grace patted him on the knee. "Exactly. Look for a different type of victim, possibly killed in a different manner. But I wouldn't expect him to have strayed too far from the up-close methods used on your victims. A gun would not offer the same intimacy, the same satisfaction, that a knife would bring."

"Grace, you are frickin' brilliant."

Smiling, she patted his knee again, leaving her hand there. "I knew that. Just glad you figured it out too." Grace glanced down at her hand and looked up with a shy smile. "How come you never asked me out?"

"Grace…"

"Come on. You owe me an answer."

Looking into her blue eyes, only one answer came to mind. "I was worried you might say yes."

CHAPTER
17

Like most mornings, Reynolds DeVries woke up to the buzz of her cell phone. People didn't seem to realize her job entailed late hours, and getting a little sleep would be nice. She groaned, reaching, grasping and eventually finding the cell on her bedside table. The buzzing had stopped. The digital readout said 7:42 a.m., which elicited another groan. Too damn early.

The buzz started again. Reynolds flipped the phone over and recognized the caller. "Good morning, Ellie." Ellie Winters was a good friend with a lot in common. Also prominent in Twin Cities media, Winters was co-host of the morning show on the top-rated radio station in the Minneapolis St. Paul market. Ratings could be a fickle bitch, but at the moment, Winters and her cadre of male radio clowns sat on top of the ratings.

"Reynolds, someone is following me."

Glancing back at the clock, it still said 7:42. "Aren't you at the station?"

"Not right now. You haven't had your coffee, have you?"

"It's not even 8 a.m., Ellie."

"I've been up since 4:15, so you'll get no sympathy from me."

"So, you're being followed," Reynolds prompted. It would be nice to get another hour of sleep.

"Most days, I feel someone. I've caught a glimpse every now and then, but he's good. He stays just out of view. He blends with the people around him. I've had friends comment about a man staring at me. When I turn, he's moving away or has simply vanished. I know how this must sound, but there is someone following me. I'm sure of it. It has to be the same guy who's been stalking and killing those women."

Ellie Winters was a tall blonde with a gift for turning heads. She fit the killer's demographics to a T, Reynolds thought. She was a dead ringer to the three victims. "Ellie, you need to tell the BCA. They're on the case."

"I don't even know who the BCA is. Shouldn't I just call the police?"

Reynolds felt like slamming the phone against the table, however she reined in her frustration. "You've never heard of them? The Minnesota Bureau of Criminal Apprehension is the police, Ellie, the state police. Our BCA was the first in the nation to identify a suspect based solely on DNA."

A pause. "Okay, I have to get back on the air. Who do I talk to?"

"Freddie Goodwin is the lead investigator. Ask for him."

"Okay, I will. And Reynolds..."

"Yes?" Reynolds asked.

"Don't be so crabby. Mornings are supposed to be fun."

Winters hung up before Reynolds could formulate a proper response. She dropped the phone and rolled over. One more hour.

CADE WAS in his new truck enjoying the way the FJ Cruiser cornered as he turned onto Main Street in downtown Stillwater. In a moment, he'd be able to open it up and test out the truck's acceleration. The road overlooked the river which looked to be ice free. Some years the ice-out happened later, some years earlier. This year was earlier by at least three weeks. Spring was off to a good start.

A call came through on Cade's cell and he hit the speaker button, Rob's voice filling the cab. "Morning partner. You should be listening to Ellie Winters on KDWB. She's ranting about our case. Call me after." And Rob was gone.

Cade pulled up the radio station. Ellie Winters was talking: "We need to stop this killer. Now. I don't feel safe. In fact, I don't know many women who do. Why can't we be protected?"

Cade turned up the volume.

"There's a man out there who has killed at least three women we know of here in our community. Women, just like me and you, simply living our lives. We should be able to feel safe."

A male voice: "You said you don't feel safe. Tell us about that."

Ellie Winters: "Someone has followed me. I've been downtown, at restaurants, shopping, and I've seen the same man. He's stalked me all over the cities."

The male voice: "Has he followed you on the highway? That's where he likes to kill his victims."

Her voice went quiet. "I know. I'm checking my mirrors all the time. I've seen the same car behind me often."

The male voice: "Ellie, can you describe the man who's stalking you? Have you been able to get a license plate?"

Her voice trembling, Ellie spoke in a measured cadence. "No license plate. But I know he's big and has dark hair. He's almost a ghost. Every time I try to get a good look, he evaporates into the crowd. My friends, who have watched him as he's watched me, have mentioned his eyes. There's something about his eyes, their intensity as he watches me, that's so scary."

The male voice: "How can a killer stalk women on our highways, in our cities with complete impunity? What is law enforcement doing to stop this?"

Winters answered. "I'm told the investigation now belongs to the Minnesota Bureau of Criminal Apprehension—the BCA. But is the BCA the right organization to end this? The case was in the hands of the same investigator who stopped Andrew Bishop and his group of killers. But they took it away for political reasons. What about us? What about the three dead women? What about the man stalking me? Will the BCA stop him before he...before..."

The male voice again: "We need to take a break here. When we come back, we'll have group therapy for a woman in love with an older man. Is mature really better? What if he falls and breaks his hip? Back after these messages."

On cue, Rob called again. "Well, that should throw some gasoline on the fire. If Goodwin wasn't feeling pressure before, he sure will now."

Cade was nodding as he goosed the gas pedal, the truck making the first stoplight on Highway 36 as the light changed. "Do you think someone's actually following Winters? These murders are fueling a whole lot of paranoia."

"I'm at the computer now, looking her up. Ellie Winters is blonde, five foot seven inches," Rob said. "She looks more willowy, more like a fashion model than the others, but she looks like she'd draw a lot of attention. She has a look, if you know what I mean."

"So, she'd fit the killer's profile." Not a question.

"No doubt. At all."

"Let's see how Goodwin handles this," Cade said. "I'll be there in ten minutes," he said as he blew around a slow-moving Honda. He loved hearing the engine purr as the open road beckoned. Cade smiled and pressed harder on the gas pedal.

Rob Zink was at their shared desk, papers spread across the surface. Rob subscribed to the messy desk theory, that being surrounded by visual and mental clutter forced human beings to focus and think more clearly. Taking note of the overturned soda cans and the three coffee cups scattered among the files, he wondered if laziness might just be an equal factor at work here. "Morning," Rob said as he looked up.

Cade took his seat across the desk. "What do we have this morning?"

"A couple of accidents, a road rage incident..."

"What happened there?"

"The usual: men behaving badly. Someone gets cut off. Horns honk, fingers communicate, the offended driver escalates things by bumping bumpers."

"Idiots."

"Exactly," Rob said. "One driver follows another into the Walmart parking lot." Cade rolled his eyes.

"There's a confrontation. Pushing and yelling. Our trooper arrived to calm everyone down. Someone had seen the entire thing as it escalated and called it in. Both guys had small children in their vehicles." Rob shook his head. "Idiots."

"Anything else?"

"Vang had another drug interdiction. He looks to be hot after that stuff."

Cade laughed. "He's like a terrier on the roads. He sniffs it out and will not quit. I asked him about it the other week. He said he wanted to do more. There are troopers hammering out speeding tickets all day, well more power to them. Not him. He uses the traffic violations as a means to an end. Looking for dope, guns, etc. And working the 94 corridor from the Wisconsin border gives him ample opportunity to find the stuff as it enters the state."

"From Chicago?"

Cade nodded. "There's a pipeline from Chicago and points east finding its way into Minnesota. Having Vang on point seems to be making a difference."

Rob slid a file across the desk. "Why don't you take the interdiction? I'll follow up on the road rage incident."

Standing up, Cade said, "Sounds like a great way to start a morning."

"Rather be chasing down a serial killer," Rob said with a frown.

"Same here."

JA

THE KILLER WAS at work when he heard about Freddie Goodwin.

Winters must have stirred the pot and Goodwin had decided to personally watch her, perhaps bowing to the pressure. Musing, he thought the situation could work in his favor. It certainly opened up several possibilities.

CHAPTER
18

His prey was directly ahead.

The occasional long-haul trucker aside, the highway was deserted. Not quite yet 5 a.m., traffic would be sparse for another hour. A white Kia Soul—Winters' vehicle—was easy to track even without the reflective disk. One vehicle was between them, a nondescript Ford sedan. It was Goodwin.

Goodwin had been Ellie Winters' constant companion for the last week, while the killer was their shadow, lurking just out of sight. He learned their routes, their patterns and their vulnerabilities. Though there were many opportunities to take Goodwin out, he'd waited for the right moment, one with maximum impact. After all, he needed to make a point. The killer found his pulse quickening, his anger growing. Simply knowing the fraud Goodwin was right there—right within killing range—severely taxed his control. It was this tight control which allowed him to play out his game as he pulled all the pieces together, setting up each of the clueless participants, and then with a master strike, blindside everyone.

In Chicago, the police were onto his pattern after the third killing. He could feel them nipping at his ankles, hoping to box him in, vainly trying to outsmart him. Like that was going to happen. Like any good chess player, the killer was always several moves ahead. Planning for contingencies, he'd scouted and selected a series of potential victims, waiting for the need to grow—as it always did—and waited. Knowing time was in his favor while the police chased around frantically, he simply sat back and taunted the lead detective on the case. *You'll never catch me.*

They never did.

Interstate 394 served as a direct link for commuters traveling between downtown Minneapolis and parts of the western Twin Cities metropolitan area. Just short of ten miles long, the highway began at U.S. Highway 12 and changed into an interstate after passing Interstate 494. Each morning, Winters was on 394 for several miles before exiting at Park Place. The killer knew each mile of her route intimately. The stretch right after Highway 169, directly across from the sprawling General Mills headquarters, would be sufficiently visible to get his point across.

Speeding up, the killer closed the gap. Winters was a quarter mile ahead of Goodwin and wouldn't see what he did to the fraud. Just after crossing under the Highway 169 interchange, it was time.

Driving a half-ton Chevy pickup, the killer knew Goodwin's sedan would be no match. And given the Ford's drifting between the lines, Goodwin was either sleepy or distracted or both.

The killer punched the gas pedal to the floor and hit his brights, as he turned the pickup into the rear quarter panel of Goodwin's vehicle. The effect was instantaneous: The Ford's rear tires lost traction and started to skid. The killer jammed his brake pedal until he was clear of Goodwin's spinning vehicle. In a moment, Goodwin was stopped directly in front of the killer, while Winters continued completely oblivious of her protector's fate.

If that didn't wake up the fraud, I've got another surprise that will.

The killer was out of his vehicle in a heartbeat and at Goodwin's door as the BCA man stepped out, his gun hanging impotently at his side. It looked like Goodwin was in shock as his mouth hung open, and confusion colored his face. Before Goodwin could react, the killer's gun's barrel slammed down and Goodwin slid to the pavement, unconscious. A little more work to be done, the killer ripped open Goodwin's shirt, baring his chest. Reaching into his pocket for his knife, it was time to make a statement.

As he drove down Saint Paul's most prestigious thoroughfare, Summit Avenue, Cade pondered the cryptic call from Capt. Rejene. Apparently, he and his boss were both summoned to the governor's residence with no notice and no explanation. This governor was a career politician, a real political animal. And like most animals, Governor Ritter hated being cornered. In the last month, critics had publicly shredded him for his policies, saying they looked to be dictated by public opinion rather than his own convictions. After the patrol's public humiliation, Cade had to believe Ritter's summons would not be for the good of the Patrol.

He turned into the governor's drive and a State Patrol officer waved him in, pointing to a small lot. Cade knew many people didn't realize the State Patrol had a capitol security division handling the security for the governor and the Minnesota State Capitol grounds. He waved at the trooper, a man he didn't recognize. Cade pulled into a spot next to Rejene, who leaned against her vehicle. "Let's go," she said moving toward the mansion's entrance, not waiting for him. Cade hustled to catch up.

An aide directed them into Ritter's office where the Governor and a handful of staff huddled around a conference table. "We're going to need the room. We'll meet up after lunch," he told the others at the table. When the room had cleared, Ritter looked between Cade and Rejene. He sighed. "I have a big problem. Our serial killer struck again early this morning."

Cade glanced at his boss, but she kept her eyes on the governor. Ritter continued. "We've kept this one quiet, but the shitstorm is coming. When the media gets ahold of this, it's going to be bad, really bad."

"Was the victim Ellie Winters?" Cade asked. "This story will go national if it was."

Ritter put his head down. "Worse than Winters." He looked up, his eyes sunken and red. Clearly sleep deprived. "It was Freddie Goodwin," Ritter said, his voice soft and flat.

Captain Rejene looked shocked.

"Goodwin's dead?" Cade asked incredulously.

Ritter shook his head. "No, he's still alive. But I don't know if that's good or bad at this point. Goodwin had taken on Winters' security personally. Around five this morning, Goodwin was behind Winters on 394 as she headed to the radio station. He was forced off the road and the killer used a knife to carve a message—using Goodwin's chest as his canvas. It was the most gruesome thing I've ever seen."

"What was the message?"

"There was only one word." Ritter looked angry, his staccato speech betraying his emotions. "Goodwin's at Hennepin County, the docs trying to stitch him back together. But his head is messed up. He's paralyzed with terror and I'd be surprised if he ever comes back to law enforcement."

"What was the word?" Rejene asked again.

"Fraud."

Rejene and Cade traded glances.

"What about Winters?" Rejene leaned forward.

"She made it to work, completely oblivious. She's going to go ballistic when she finds out how close the killer had gotten to her. And I wouldn't blame her."

The room was silent, all three lost in thought. Cade was the first to speak. "So, now what?"

Ritter stood. He walked to the window and stared out for a long moment. He turned back, facing the two State Patrol representatives. "The media is going to crucify me. As it is, I'm going to take a lot of heat and the democrats are going to be coming after me, looking for my head. I can't let this get out without a plan. And that's why you're here."

Walking up to Cade, the governor held his eye. "I'm dumping this back in your lap."

"Governor..." Rejene started.

"There's no discussion Capt. Rejene." Ritter took a step towards her. His eyes grew dark. "I don't give even the smallest shit about jurisdiction. To me, Dawkins is our best chance to stop this killer. Executive orders hereby have been drawn up giving the Minnesota State Patrol responsibility for the apprehension of the serial killer preying on our highways. You'll have the full resources of the BCA backing you up. But make no mistake, Mr. Dawkins, you are the person in charge of the investigation. Succeed or fail, it's on your shoulders."

"I'm comfortable with that," Cade said and moved toward the door. "The case should never have left us, anyway."

"Make us proud and get the bastard," Ritter said, holding the door open for Cade. "Capt. Rejene, a word."

Ritter stood at the door, making no effort to close the door. Cade stopped to take in the exchange between the Governor and Capt. Rejene.

"I need to be clear about this: If Dawkins can't stop this maniac, I won't be able to save his job. There's simply too much media pressure to end this case."

"Seriously? You'd sacrifice Dawkins just to appease the media." Rejene shook her head. "Why am I even asking? Of course, you would."

Ritter took a step toward Rejene. "You had better tread carefully, Capt. Rejene. Insubordination does not sit well in my office. And be aware, the repercussions of failure will most certainly go further up the food chain than Dawkins." Ritter waved for her to leave, his message clear. "Just do your job and there won't be any issues."

Cade waited for his boss at the corner. If Rejene knew Cade overheard her discussion with Ritter, she didn't let on. "What was that all about?" he asked.

Rejene stopped. Hands on her hips, her eyes betrayed her fury. "If this case continues much longer, the bastard's throwing you under the bus to save his own ass. Ritter will crucify you, making you his public scapegoat. It's a brilliant strategy actually. Because if you catch this killer, he looks like the savior for putting you on the case."

"No worries then. I'm going to catch this guy."

"I hope so. I really hope so."

CHAPTER
19

With the governor's expectations starkly clear, Cade headed back to meet with Rob. As Cade brought him up to speed on his morning meeting, Rob listened without interruption. After a moment of contemplation, he asked, "Where do we begin?"

"First things first. We look for other cases. Grace over at the BCA said this killer has killed before. That's what killers do. The murders feel too precise to be the beginning of a killer's life cycle. And since Reynolds' source mentioned Chicago, it's a good place to start."

Rob shrugged. "But we've looked for similar cases, remember? And came up with nothing."

Nodding, Cade pulled out his notepad. "Grace thought the killer will have had a pattern, but a different one from what we've seen here. It might be a different type of victim, but there will always be a pattern. And she said the murder would still be an intimate encounter. Bare hands, maybe a rope or knife, but not guns or poisons. The killer is a hands-on kind of guy."

"So, we focus on finding a pattern, looking for similar cases."

Cade shook his head. "Not we, me. I have a Chicago connection I want to exploit, for lack of a better word. I'm taking a quick trip south, see what I can dig up."

"And me?"

"I'd like you to look into how he targets the victims. Each of the women was of a certain type, eerily similar in appearance. So, how does the killer find them? Look at what these women have in common, where they may have crossed paths with this guy."

Rob nodded. "One thing's for sure: he's not picking his victims at random."

Cade stood up. Pacing always seemed to improve his thought process. "If we can discern his method of targeting these women, we should be able to find the killer himself. Possibly set a trap. Catch him in the act."

Rob shook his head. "That's a dangerous game you're suggesting. A lot can go wrong."

"A lot has gone wrong. The stakes have become too high. We're going to have to take a risk or two."

Rob was on his feet. "It's not our ass you plan on risking, is it? What happens if it goes wrong? What happens when an innocent—an innocent you placed directly in front of the killer—gets brutally murdered? I want you to think this through before that happens." Rob's eyes narrowed at Cade.

Cade walked over to Rob. "Relax. I'm just thinking out loud. I'm trying to prevent anyone else from getting hurt, remember? Let's get his methods figured out before we do anything else." He patted Rob's shoulder. "Are you okay, big guy?"

"I'm a little caffeine-deprived." Rob had a hint of a smile.

"We can fix that. Grab the case files."

Rob hesitated. "I might be a little pastry-deprived as well."

"We can fix that as well. C'mon."

THEY STOPPED at a local coffee shop just off the freeway in Maplewood. Caribou Coffee was Minnesota's answer to Starbuck's, and like Starbuck's, they were everywhere. After ordering, Rob said, "We need to spread these files out and look for commonalities. If we're going to catch this guy, we need to find the connections."

Cade picked up his coffee and took a sip. "C'mon, caffeine, bring on your magic." They moved towards the seating area.

"Excuse me." It was the barista. "Are you cops?" she asked.

Rob looked at Cade and shrugged. Cade opened his jacket, exposing his Glock and the badge clipped next to it. "We are. Why do you ask?"

"I heard you talking. Are you looking for that killer? The one who murdered those women?" Her eyes searched theirs. "Holly Janek was my aunt."

"I am sorry. By all accounts, she was a great woman. Yes, we're working the case. And we're going to catch her killer or die trying. I'm Cade Dawkins, this is Rob Zink." Both men shook her hand.

"I'm Haily," she said, looking intently at Cade. "Dawkins. I've heard your name before." She gestured for the two to follow her. She pushed open a door to a glass-enclosed room with a large table. "This is our community room. Groups can use it for meetings or projects that benefit our community. I can't think of anything that'll benefit our community more than catching that bastard. Use it for as long as you want. And the coffee's on us."

Rob's eyebrow went up. "This could work."

⚊⚊

AFTER SEVERAL HOURS, the room had been transformed. Each of the victims' pictures was taped up, a large sheet of presentation paper mounted below it. Notes on the specifics of each killing were jotted down. Two more sheets were mounted on the adjacent wall labeled respectively, *Commonalities* and *Differences*. Rob stood in front of the blank sheets with marker in hand. Cade leaned back in his chair, taking the first sip of his third coffee. It was looking like it was going to be a long day. "Let's begin with the commonalities. Women."

"Brilliant." But Rob wrote "women" on the board.

Cade ignored him. "All were blondes. Each was of a similar type, similar build, similar look."

"They were all hot," Rob said as he shrugged. He jotted, "nearly identical victims."

"Agreed. Each of the killings took place at night. On quiet stretches of road."

Rob paused and turned toward Cade. "Is it at all odd each of the killings took place on state highways? In the east metro?"

Cade leaned forward. "Not if the killer lived in the area. Many killers work in small geographic areas. But what were you thinking?"

"I'm just thinking out loud, but the killings took place in the only area guaranteed the case would come to us. And when it was taken away from us, our replacement was attacked, putting it back in our hands." Rob ran his fingers through his hair. "I hate coincidences. I really do."

Cade nodded. "But I don't see the killer's gain. Why kill so the case goes to us?"

Rob shook his head. "No idea. And why is the killer targeting these attractive blondes? Unresolved mommy issues?"

Cade laughed. "I don't know about your mom, but mine didn't look like any of our victims."

"Not mine either."

"Stacy's mom had it going on, though," Cade said with a grin.

"I see what you did there. Nice reference."

Leaning forward, Cade considered his research into victim selection. "Serial killers tend to fixate on their targets by finding some quality that appeals to something dark within themselves. Experts agree these killers have a vision in mind of the type of victim they would prefer. This person would be thought of as their ideal victim based on race, gender, physical characteristics, or some other specific quality. But, it's rare for the killers to find people who meet these exact qualifications, so they seek out people with similar traits. This is why serial killings often seem to be completely random at first—each victim may have something in common that only the killer easily recognizes."

"But ours was never random," Rob said as he sipped his coffee. "It was obvious right from the start. Almost like we were supposed to notice. Having nearly identical victims killed within a tight timeline and a tight geographical area certainly caught our attention."

Cade paused, taking a sip of his coffee. "Yes. It did. But I'm not going down the conspiracy theory road, though. These killers have their own agenda, their own dark reasoning for doing what they do. When we figure out this guy's agenda, we will catch him."

Rob shook his head. "We'd better do it soon. I don't want any more victims on our watch."

"Amen brother, amen."

CHAPTER
20

C ade took the afternoon flight to Chicago. Sitting in the aisle seat next to a mother and daughter, he listened to their discussion on the reality show of the moment. Thinking it was probably the furthest thing from reality he'd heard in a long time, Cade had nothing to add to the discussion.

It would be good to meet up with his old friend, Alan Bowles. Formerly a detective with the Chicago police, Bowles was currently a private security expert. Originally from England, they were teammates years back when they played together on a summer soccer team.

Bowles had suggested they meet up at Smoke Daddy, the kind of barbecue-and-blues club that only Chicago could produce. Clearly not the sort of place to take a date, the club was loud and crowded. The customers look dangerous, like it would be no big thing to kill a man. The lighting was too dark to tell if the food could have the same effect, but it sure smelled good.

Bowles was at the crowded bar, staking out a place for Cade. A bottle of Carlsberg beer waited for him. They shook hands and appraised each other for a moment. Bowles had thickened since his playing days, no longer wiry in build. His eyes still held the spark and cunning which made him such a devastating goal scorer on the field. Cade once watched the opposing goalkeeper taunt Bowles mercilessly during a hot summer evening's game. Bowles never gave up, but sometimes you simply run into a keeper that's on top of his game. This keeper wanted to rub it their faces, though.

If the verbal sparring wasn't enough, the keeper took a shot at

Bowles during a scramble for a corner kick. Just as the ball was kicked and all eyes—including the ref—were on the kicker, the keeper sucker punched Bowles in the gut. Unfortunately in soccer, if the referee didn't see a foul, it never happened. Cade helped Bowles back to his feet, asking him what he wanted to do. He looked at Cade with that spark of his and said, "Just get me the ball."

As Cade played defense on the opposite corner of the field, it took some doing. But at the next opportunity, Cade picked off a pass and surged forward with the ball at his feet. Cutting to the inside, Cade looked up the field for Bowles, who was making a run to the right of the goal. Launching a ball over the middle third of the field, it was heading up and over Bowles' right shoulder. Somehow, Bowles had caught the ball with his right foot and flicked it over the defender. Cade watched in amazement as Bowles shifted his body to his left to receive his own pass, the defender hopelessly out of the play now as Bowles went right at the keeper. In situations where an attacker is closing in on goal, keepers are trained to come out with arms spread toward the shooter to cut down the angle to make less room to shoot. Bowles took another touch closer and pulled his left foot back to shoot. The keeper dove to grab and smother the ball before Bowles could get off his shot.

Cade had replayed Bowles' move many times in his head over the years, amazed each time at the result.

Bowles had faked the shot with his left foot and then pushed the ball to his right—just out of reach of the keepers' outstretched fingers. Bowles went around the sprawled keeper and his next touch rolled the ball into the back of the net. As he walked past the prone keeper, Bowles calmly held up his middle finger.

The ref saw his gesture and gave Bowles a yellow card for unsportsmanlike behavior. Since the rest of the team hadn't seen Bowles' gesture, they were incensed, believing the ref gave him a card for scoring a goal. That moment had become a legend in the team's history.

"How was your flight, mate?" Bowles asked and gestured to the waiting beer.

Cade, always one to give his friend a hard time, replied, "Have you been on a plane? Well, you know how it goes up in the air and then goes back down again? Well, it was just like that."

Bowles laughed and took a pull off his beer. "So, what brings you to Chicago? You mentioned it involved a case you're working on."

"I'm looking for a serial killer up in the Twin Cities, one who seems to have a thing for tall knockout blondes."

Bowles smiled. "He's not the only one, mate. All three of my ex-wives were tall blondes."

Cade smiled at the comment and picked at the label on his beer. "Before you got into your cushy corporate security gig, you ran the homicide division down here."

Bowles nodded.

"I've heard rumor the killer had been plying his trade down here before going north. But I never came across similar cases when I researched the killer's blonde M.O. Maybe I should be more general and ask if there were any pattern killers operating in Chicago recently."

The club was busy, and it was standing room only. A large man pushed his way to the bar, bumping Bowles as he was about to take a drink. Turning to face the man, Bowles was met with a stone-cold glare.

"Excuse me," Bowles said.

The man didn't say a word, instead leaning into Bowles' space. The large man put his hand in front of Bowles' face, squeezing his fingers into a fist. Both men could hear the thug's knuckles crack.

Bowles's eyes had that spark again. "Look, I've got no problem going back to prison," he said, his British accent more noticeble. "Just know who you're dealing with, mate." Bowles opened his coat, an extremely large pistol evident.

The man held out his hands, as he clearly reappraised his life choices. "Hey, I was just messing with you. No worries." He turned away and moved down to the end of the bar.

Cade laughed. "Go back to prison? You'd never willingly go anywhere you couldn't play golf."

Bowles shrugged. "You just have to learn to speak the native language and no one messes with you."

"Nice weapon, by the way. What is it?"

"Taurus. Raging Judge 28 Gauge. It's brilliant. Holds five shells, has a double-locking cylinder for added strength and uses a red fiber optic sight."

"28 gauge? It shoots buckshot?"

Bowles nodded. "It's a beast. I admit it. It'll put down whatever is coming your way. Whatever 'it' happens to be. How about you, what are you carrying?"

"Company issue. Glock."

Bowles made a face. "The Glock is basically what you'd get if Microsoft went into the pistol business. But I digress. You were asking about old cases."

"I was."

"We had a pattern killer at work down here. Stopped maybe a year ago."

"Tall blonde victims by any chance?"

Bowles shook his head. "The victims were all over the place. All female, but no matching characteristics. They were all waitresses though. The offender killed six women who worked at downtown Chicago clubs. Our lead investigator, God rest his soul, made the connection after the third killing. He'd flooded the clubs with undercovers, Martinson figuring he could outsmart the guy. He didn't."

"You never caught the killer?"

"No, after his seventh killing, he just stopped."

"How did he kill his victims?"

"The offender liked his knives. He'd cut them pretty good. Liked to hurt them, make them bleed before finishing the job. A real butcher."

"Hold on, you said he killed six women."

Bowles nodded.

"Six? But you'd just mentioned he'd stopped after killing his seventh. Who was his seventh victim?"

Bowles looked pained. "His seventh victim was our lead investigator, Shane Martinson."

"Shane Martinson," Cade said the name, feeling something familiar about the sound of it. "Shane Martinson."

Bowles nodded.

"Wasn't he the one who broke the Syrian terror ring case several years back? Tons of media attention. Made the national news. That the same guy?"

"That was him. Brilliant guy. Everyone knew he'd be the one who'd catch the waitress killer."

"But the killer got him first." Another nod from Bowles.

"No more killings after that?"

"No, not in Chicago anyway."

Bowles drained his beer and nodded towards Cade's. "Finish your beer. There's someone you need to meet."

Cade tipped his glass back, stood up and tossed a five on the bar. The man from the earlier altercation looked away as the pair passed by. Cade thought he saw a little extra swagger from Bowles as they went out into the early evening sunshine.

"Let's take mine," Bowles said, pointing to a bright red Hummer across the street. Parked at an angle, the wheels on the passenger side were up on the curb. Glancing at Cade, Bowles explained, "It's an H1 Alpha, the original Hummer."

"Alan, we need to talk," Cade remarked as he swung up into the beast's cab. "First it's the Raging Judge and now the H1. You are quite the cowboy."

Bowles laughed. "You nailed it. My love of American westerns is what first brought me across the pond. And the guns made me want to stay. I like guns, as you could probably tell."

"You mean your shotgun disguised as a pistol? How much did that run you, if you don't mind me asking?"

"Only $800."

"The corporate gig must be paying well. And these original Hummers must go for nearly $140,000."

"Something like that. What can I say? Business is going well."

"So, I see," Cade said, looking around the Hummer's spacious cab. "Where's the flight attendant on this thing? I'm getting thirsty."

THE SIGN READ ILLUMINATION ARTS. Broad etched glass doors opened into a spacious lobby, the sounds of a jazz quartet intermingling with the trickle of water running down a wall fountain behind the receptionist. Bowles headed for the woman, while Cade wandered off taking in the exhibit. He stopped at the first painting, a portrait of a dark-haired woman, her head tilted down, her dark complexion blending into the shadows of the background. Her light eyes were striking in the way they seemed to look right into you.

"What do you think?" a voice asked beside Cade. Cade turned to look at an auburn-haired woman standing beside him.

"It's mesmerizing. Her eyes bore into you like you're the only thing in her entire world."

"It must have been that way for the artist, Seth Olive, too. He painted her—Malena—37 times throughout his career. The ironic thing is, after painting her 37th portrait, Olive divorced his wife and married Malena. And then never painted her again."

Stepping to the next painting, another of Malena. This one from a high perspective, looking down as she knelt on a wooden floor, her skirt spread out around her. Again, her eyes were striking as she looked up. Cade glanced at the woman beside him. "Sometimes getting your heart's desire isn't always a good thing."

"You're saying that by getting the object of Olive's desire, it took away his reason for living? That's a cold way to look at life."

Cade shrugged. "I'm a cop. We don't always see the best in people."

"So you're exposed to the dark, seamy underbelly of society. Get over it," the woman said and smiled. "My dad always said, 'When life gives you lemons you paint that shit gold!' He was a former hippy."

"Former? He doesn't sound too reformed to me. I'm Cade Dawkins, by the way."

"Annie Feller. I'm the gallery manager."

"There you are," Bowles said as he joined them. "Annie has some relevant experience which might help your case. Is there someplace we can talk?"

Annie led them through a set of doors into a staging area. Works of art were scattered around, with a number of open shipping crates. She pointed them to a tall project table in the middle of the room and Cade climbed on a stool. "Relevant experience? I'm intrigued."

Bowles cleared his throat. "Several years ago, Annie had a part-time job at the Hilton Towers, working at Kitty O'Shea's as a cocktail waitress."

The light went on for Cade. "The killer went after you. And you survived."

Annie nodded. "It was him. The police were not so sure, though." Her eyes looked haunted by the memories.

Cade touched her arm. "Why don't you just walk me through the experience as you remember it? Tell me what happened."

Annie leaned forward. "I was here at the gallery. It was a quiet night and I'd let Francine leave early, so I was alone when a man came in, roughly an hour before closing. He was well dressed and had this perfect balance of charm and danger that I found rather appealing. At least at first. He said he was looking for a piece for his library."

"I take it he didn't buy anything?"

Annie shook her head. "No, things headed south before that

happened. It started fine enough, as we walked the gallery floor. He's spouting off his knowledge about art, but it's all surface stuff. Like he'd just crammed for an exam. You know, names and dates. I noticed he's not the usual, soft, Lakeshore Drive type who frequents galleries. He's rigid like he's military. And I began to pick up weird vibes from the guy."

"Weird? How so?"

"When I'm walking someone through the gallery, I'm looking for cues, subtle indications which tell me how a prospect feels about the art. As someone who makes their living in sales, it can make all the difference in the world if I can get a reading on a person's feelings. Only I wasn't getting any. I couldn't pick up anything. It was like his face was a mask—but there wasn't anything behind it either. This guy had nothing. I excused myself to call my boyfriend. He's a bouncer at Kitty's."

"So, what happened?"

"While I made the call, the guy let himself out. Because I park in the lot behind here, I told my boyfriend to meet me there just in case the man was still around. It was a good thing too—because the guy was hidden behind my car. My boyfriend saw him and ran him off."

Cade glanced at Bowles. "And you think this was the same guy, the killer?"

Bowles nodded. "I do. He fits the general description we have of the offender. But it's more than that, it's his intent to deceive Annie and the complete lack of feelings. It has to be our offender."

Cade looked to Annie. "You mentioned he was rigid, like someone in the military. Do you remember what he looked like?"

Annie tucked a strand of hair behind her ear. "Dark hair, dark complexion." She hesitated, clearly unsure where to go from there.

Cade took a step closer to Annie. "Was he taller than me?"

She sized him up for a moment. "No, he was several inches shorter than you."

"How about his build? Was he built similar to me? Or maybe more average like my friend Alan here?"

"Hey..." But Bowles was smiling.

Annie shook her head. "No, he was more muscular than you."

Bowles chortled.

"Long hair? Facial hair? Tats? Accent?" Cade asked.

Annie thought for a moment. "No to all of those. He wore his hair short, buzzed almost. But nothing else to set him apart."

Cade shrugged. She hadn't given him anything to separate the killer from thousands of other guys. "I need you to close your eyes for a moment. Now think back to when you walked the man through the gallery. As he talked, was there anything he said, maybe it wasn't the words, but the way he said it, that stood out? We all have our own way of speaking, a turn of phrase or expression worded in a distinctive way. Sometimes these can be particularly memorable."

Annie shifted her weight from side to side as she considered his question. Cade waited a moment and then spoke softly. "Take your time as you run the conversation through your head. If it helps, think about the pieces you showed him. Possibly they'll trigger something."

With her eyes closed, Annie spoke. "I remember walking through the Mia Bergeron section. Her work is incredibly vivid, capturing surface detail in dazzling color but revealing so much more of the inner person. I remember him saying her work reminded him of Alex Kanevsky's work. He went on about how both artists merged impressionism and hyper-realism. The thing is, Kanevsky's work couldn't be further from Bergeron's. It was like he prepared a little speech and was determined to give it whether or not it was at all apropos. I remember him saying he'd been to an opening of Kanevsky's and how he still couldn't scrape the amazing imagery off his mind's eye."

"An odd turn of phrase. Not sure what to make of it though. If anything else comes to mind, contact me," Cade said, handing Annie a business card.

ON THE WAY to the airport, Cade asked about Martinson's killing.

Bowles shook his head. "It was bad. We found him on the hood of his car, throat slit and blood everywhere. It was like he was displayed. heavy bruising on his face. The medical examiner said the heavy facial bruising was consistent with the killer holding Martinson's head in place so he could see the knife coming. The offender had to have been both unusually strong and highly motivated to kill someone as fit as Shane Martinson was."

"Where was he killed?"

"On the south side. Martinson received a tip someone was staking out a nightclub. Apparently, a man was parked across the street and watching the club three out of the last four nights. Martinson was waiting to see if the man would return."

"Where did the tip come from?"

"That's the thing. We never could confirm, but it sounded like it came from one of our squads. But no one ever came forward."

"Was Martinson lured into a trap?"

Bowles nodded, as he signaled his turn into the Midway airport complex. "The offender sure looked like he had a grudge with Martinson. Shane was in plain clothes, parked in his personal vehicle. No sign he was a cop."

"Yeah?" Cade didn't like where this was going.

Bowles pulled up to the Delta ticketing entrance. "Martinson was undercover, yet when we found him, his shield was shoved in his mouth. Our offender was trying to make a point, don't you agree?"

Cade opened the Hummer's door and shook hands with Bowles. "Looks like I might need to watch my back."

"You had better, mate. You had better."

CHAPTER
21

The killer was at work.

The nice thing about working security for the governor was the variety. You saw all walks of life and had the opportunity to travel as the governor met his political obligations. Even though his job was a means to an end, he still enjoyed his position. It gave him access. It gave him power. And best of all, it gave him victims.

The ironic thing about working security for the governor was it meant the killer worked for the Minnesota State Patrol—the same law enforcement agency tasked with catching him. The Executive Protection Unit was responsible for protecting the Governor and his staff. Comprised of State Troopers, it was a prestige posting anyone in the Patrol's nearly 900 employees would love to have. The killer was in the right position to succeed.

And Marlin Sweetwater was motivated for success. The opportunity to pit his intelligence against law enforcement's greatest minds was absolutely worth killing for. Of course, the downside of his deadly game would be his own death. He knew it was a very real possibility. But the game was everything to him, and there was no way he could stop now—he might as well try to stop breathing.

Back in high school, his IQ was off the charts when it was measured. His counselor told him he'd go on to do great things. Maybe study engineering and build immense structures. Become a scientist and discover life-saving cures. Become a leader in government and change the world. But Sweetwater knew different. He was acutely aware of how singular he was. He always thought other people pretended to be nice, but then at some point, he realized he was the one who was pretending. He was simply incapable of feeling what most people did—remorse, compassion, empathy.

Whatever brain rewiring soared his intelligence to such superior levels also stunted him emotionally. Of course, stunted might not be the most accurate term. Deadened, twisted, or deviant might be closer. Screwing him up beyond all human recognition would be an accurate assessment.

It had started with animals, as it always did. He'd killed his neighbor's cat to see what happens at the moment the lights go out. The animal howled and clawed as it tried to get away. He'd held it down as the knife did its work. Getting as close as he could, he wanted to commune with the feline as its essence drained away. Sweetwater had felt something, he was sure of it. From that moment on, he was hooked.

A variety of animals had followed. He'd trapped squirrels and rabbits after killing several of the neighborhood pets. People began to raise suspicions with all the missing animals. He'd learned from the negative attention the killings received. Recognized that he needed to put himself in a position of trust. And a position to give himself a steady supply of animals—he didn't want to get caught seeking out his next kill. His first job was at an animal shelter, and he'd taken the first shelter animal less than a month later. Sweetwater was 16 years old.

His first human killing happened the following year. Even though the need was building, in the end, necessity drove him to kill the woman. Carlotta Scott was a volunteer at the shelter. Sweetwater could see her suspicions grow as he took several animals. He hid his actions, always taking precautions against discovery. But the woman knew. Somehow, she sensed the wrongness in him.

He'd decided on a course of action before the situation got out of hand, and followed Carlotta home to a rundown rambler, the lawn neglected and overrun with weeds. The street was quiet, the neighbors at work on the cloudy Wednesday afternoon. Hunting knife in hand, he'd crept through the yard behind hers. Best to enter through the back door, as he knew Carlotta wouldn't open the door for him. His entry into her kitchen was simple as the door was unlocked. Sweetwater stood in her kitchen for several long minutes, wanting to feel her. He believed a person's essence permeated their surroundings and wanted to experience it before he took it away. Holding still, he took in several deep breaths as he willed himself to feel her. A calico cat stared at him with disdain and scurried around the corner. Sweetwater's inability to feel anything beyond his mounting frustration aggravated him.

He was startled by the phone's sudden ringing next to him. "Hold on," Carlotta called out as she stepped into the kitchen. Her eyes went wide when she saw him. Giving her no chance, the knife came up as he grabbed her. He slid the blade into her midsection as he pulled her close. Carlotta's mouth opened, but whatever words she had were forever gone as her life drained away. Her eyes dimmed right before him as he held her. It was a watershed moment as he trembled from the adrenaline coursing through him. It was so much better than another nameless rabbit.

The killings happened infrequently at first. Sweetwater knew he couldn't establish a pattern for the police to uncover. He'd read enough novels and saw enough media coverage to know the police would find the pattern and eventually tighten the noose on him. Sweetwater would hold out as long as he could as the need grew. Eventually, he would drive hours to another city as he sought out his next victim.

He'd never killed men; it was always women. Their vulnerability appealed to him. Sweetwater knew this said something about him, but he wasn't one to linger on self-diagnosis. He knew he was two fries short of a Happy Meal—as his first sergeant liked to describe the drug-addled street people living under the bridge. He might be crazy, but his brains kept him out of trouble.

His early recognition of the necessity for putting himself in a position of trust had cemented his decision to pursue a career in law enforcement. He'd attended Northwestern University in Chicago and his high marks in the Legal Studies undergraduate program guaranteed a position in the Chicago police department. Sweetwater knew the job would play to his strengths and gain him access to a variety of targets as well. The law enforcement job would allow him to be on the inside track of the serial killer manhunt that ultimately would follow.

Like many of life's defining moments, the realization came one sunny morning as Sweetwater lay in bed. Why should he have to hide his life's work? Sweetwater knew his intellect far surpassed those of his law enforcement contemporaries. How could they possibly catch him? He could kill and get away with it. With control and carefully planned steps for the killings, the detectives of the Chicago area law enforcement brain trust would be left scrambling. That was the fun part. In fact, he decided he could take it a step further and make it a game. A game played against the best minds the police department had to offer. A game Sweetwater knew he wouldn't lose.

To start the game, Sweetwater placed several murder kits around the city. These kits gave him access to the tools of his trade: a variety of knives, rope, and zip ties for when the right opportunity presented itself.

In any game, you need a worthy opponent. For Sweetwater—an avid media consumer—his opponent was an obvious choice. In Chicago, one detective had received the lion share of publicity. Shane Martinson was the Chicago Police Department's golden boy. The press had gone on forever about how brilliant Martinson had been in stopping the Syrian terrorists. And hearing members of his own squad talk about Martinson's brilliance was particularly aggravating. Sweetwater knew he was smarter than Martinson. He'd drawn in the detective, using the media and department back-channels to feed him information. He killed those women—all waitresses—wanting to create a pattern for the police detective to discover. The first woman was killed to create a statement. A statement the police couldn't bloody well ignore.

Martinson believed he was after a serial killer preying on the city's waitresses. However, Martinson missed one important fact: he was Sweetwater's target from the beginning. While enjoyable, the women were always a means to the end. Martinson's end.

☙

ADVANCE SECURITY RECONNAISSANCE was an important aspect of working on the governor's security detail. Much like the work the Secret Service performed in advance of the President's appearances, the State Patrol Executive Protection Unit scouted locations ahead of the governor's appearances. Detailing the Governor's routes as well as possible alternates, the advance team conducted thorough site surveys, assessing vulnerabilities and possible threats as well as needs for manpower, equipment, hospitals and evacuation routes for emergencies.

Today was a reconnaissance day. As part of the Governor's healthy lifestyle campaign, Governor Ritter was scheduled for an appearance in two days' time at the Minneapolis Athletic Club. Sweetwater was tasked with the advance and was meeting with the facility's manager. Sweetwater's assessment would be presented to the team lead who would accompany and drive Ritter to the event. Members of the Executive Protection Unit rotated through assignments with the most-senior members providing the actual executive protection. Sweetwater was scheduled for site security at the governor's mansion during the Minneapolis Athletic Club event. He much preferred the advance reconnaissance over the security guard-like function of his job.

Sweetwater left his squad in a no-parking zone in front of the historic brick and glass building. He took the marble steps two at a time as he checked his watch. He had a meeting with the facility's manager, Kouresh Abel, in less than a minute. A large black-and-white photograph of Rome's Coliseum hung inside the entrance, setting the tone for the opulent space. They met at the front counter of the facility, the hub of the Minneapolis Athletic Club. Abel, a tall man of Middle Eastern heritage, shook his hand warmly. "A pleasure to meet you," he said.

"I appreciate your time this morning. I'm looking to get the lay of the land here." Sweetwater glanced at his clipboard. "Specifically, I'll need to see each of the exits, elevators and stairwells—and the event location, of course. It would be helpful if you would walk me through the facility. I've never been here before."

Abel nodded. "You're in for a treat, my friend. The Minneapolis Athletic Club opened its doors back in 1912. Bustling with luminaries, diplomats and sports figures, it was the premier social club at the time and was as lively then as it is today. The original club was turned into the Grand Hotel back in 2000. Our 58,000 square feet of athletic facilities were carved out of the renovated hotel. Our third-floor gym is complete with expansive cardio, weight training, boxing, yoga, and Pilates rooms. Racquetball, handball, and squash courts are also nearby, along with a running track and stretch rooms. Of course, the former billiard and card rooms, bowling alleys, and the famed Stag Room included in the original Minneapolis Athletic Club are long gone."

As they walked through the spacious lobby, Abel did the mayor-walk, shaking hands with pretty much everyone he crossed paths with. After a tour of the exits and stairwells, they moved into the gym. "We recently held a Golden Gloves boxing match here. It was packed. This is where we'll hold the Governor's Healthy Lifestyles event. Take a look around."

Sweetwater walked the perimeter, getting comfortable with the room. It was unlikely Ritter would have any issues here. Just another routine appearance for the politician. After several minutes of wandering, he caught up with Abel. "Looks good to me," he said.

"Great, my friend. Let's walk through our weight training area. You look like you might know your way around a gym," Abel said with a smile.

Sweetwater nodded. "It goes with the job. It's hard to be

intimidating when you look like a strong gust of wind could knock you over."

The sprawling weight training part of the facility was busy as trainers and members worked together through the myriad of machines and free weights. Nice, but he'd seen it all before. He put his pen back into his jacket, ready to call it a day here. And then he froze.

One of the trainers moved towards them, an iPad in her hand and an overweight woman in tow. It was the trainer who riveted him. A tall blonde in her early thirties, the woman was stunning. Her long blonde hair pulled into a ponytail and her chiseled features captivated him. He watched her athletic body as she gracefully made her way through the maze of equipment. Though Sweetwater was aware Abel had said something, his focus was on the blonde goddess and everything else was simply a distraction.

Abel's hand was on his shoulder and the manager leaned in conspiratorially. "I see you appreciate our quality here. Miss Spring is one of our most popular trainers." Sweetwater found himself staring as the woman shook hands with her client, the training session over. "Allow me to introduce you. Miss Spring," he called to her.

Smiling, the blonde trainer walked over. "Officer Sweetwater, I'd like to introduce you to Candan Spring, one of our elite personal trainers."

The moment was awkward. Being tongue-tied in front of women was not exactly a gift from God, not that he believed in a divine higher power. It was only when he held a struggling woman's life in his hands, that he experienced a higher power. It was all Sweetwater could do to shake her hand.

The trainer had a firm grip. "Nice to meet you, officer." He didn't say anything—couldn't say anything. Sweetwater simply nodded as the moment stretched into awkwardness. But he was alive in the moment, feeling her hand in his, her skin touching his skin. And he knew.

CHAPTER
22

Reynolds DeVries was having one of those mornings. Her news director was being an asshole. Not that it was a rare occurrence. After all, this was television news. For some reason, the industry attracted assholes. And douche bags, fame-grabbing talentless hacks, as well as others who were so dumb they had to be watered twice a week. Reynolds heard the new weekend anchor, a young brunette from Philadelphia, described as both hugely ambitious and a man-chasing trollop—essentially the same thing in broadcasting.

Standing in front of the dressing room's mirror, Reynolds flipped her long hair back and smiled. It was a well-practiced smile from someone used to being the center of attention. She liked what she saw. Her complexion was perfect, as were her teeth. She was fit, not too skinny and not too heavy. Reynolds was proud of her breasts and legs. Both attracted admiring glances, and her wardrobe was tailored to show as much as someone of her status dared. She lifted the front of her blouse, flexing her abs. Her trainer had made a difference there, well worth the agony she endured twice each week.

Now if she could figure out a way to endure her news director's abuse. With the largest story of the year happening, he was constantly clamoring for more. More updates, more exclusives, and more appearances. How was she supposed to get more updates when the killer hadn't made any moves recently? Her connection to the lead investigator was promising, but she didn't want to jeopardize the relationship for her news director's benefit.

Reynolds gave an appraising look at her reflection. She was in her prime, with none of the lines time would eventually bring. She had the respect of her peers and viewers. Even the local newspaper gossip said nice things about Reynolds in her trashy column. This should be her year.

Her cell rang as she headed for the door. The caller ID said UNKNOWN. It had to be her source. "This is Reynolds DeVries."

Reynolds recently added an app to her phone for just this moment. She pressed 4 on her keypad, activating the record call feature. She doubted she'd be able to use the recording on the air, but it would be corroboration for her news director. The jerk.

Whoever was on the other end hesitated. She could hear him breathing. Since he called her—it was his agenda after all—so she waited. After a long pause, he finally spoke. "He's stalking a woman right now. This man, this killer, has picked out his next victim. It won't be long now."

"Do you have him under surveillance?"

A pause.

"Are you waiting for him to incriminate himself?"

This seemed to energize the caller. "He's smart, this one. I'd imagine his IQ is off the charts, so we need to watch and wait, hoping for a lucky break. It might be that plain old dumb luck could be the only way to catch him."

"It sounds like you respect him." Not a question.

"When you're involved in a game of cat and mouse—and you're the mouse—the only intelligent course is to respect your opponent. Otherwise, you end up dead. We can't underestimate his cunning." Starting off slightly above a whisper, the man's voice grew louder.

"What can you tell me about the killer's description? Is he actually deformed like they say?" Reynolds asked. She felt like provoking him for some reason—something about him raised her well-tuned red flag. Her intuitive warning system had kept her out of trouble many times before.

No pause this time. "What? I can't discuss specifics with you on an ongoing investigation—especially one of this magnitude. But I can tell you the killer is not deformed. In any way." He angrily punctuated the last three words. And he was gone.

Hmm, there had to be more to this story, an angle she hadn't considered. This couldn't be just a cop passing along news. That left only one option.

*

SWEETWATER PACED BACK AND FORTH. He kicked at an end table, upending it and launching the lamp. The metal-and-glass fixture shattered against the wall. He swore and kicked the table again.

He knew the woman was messing with him. But she couldn't have known who he really was, could she? It didn't matter, she'd gotten to him and he wanted—no needed—to keep his cool to have this play out properly. He was the one in control, the one dictating the game.

He kicked the table again until it was in pieces. It was time to ramp up the stakes. A calculated risk, but he needed to make sure Dawkins was fully on board.

Using his burner cell, he dialed the State Patrol's administration line, asking for Dawkins by name. Within a minute Sweetwater heard his opponent's voice. "Cade Dawkins." And he started the timer on his watch.

Sweetwater took a deep breath, savoring the moment. "I'm going to kill again soon." He imagined the shock on Dawkins' face as he heard his announcement.

"How do I know it's really you?" Fair question—and a nice delaying tactic as well. Six seconds.

"Goodwin was a fraud." Sweetwater could hear Dawkins' sharp intake of breath. *Yeah, it's me.*

Dawkins: "So...it's you." 12 seconds.

"I have someone special picked out. Someone nice, someone pretty. Someone just my type. And when I have her all to myself, I'm going to take my time with her. It will be glorious." 20 seconds.

"Why are you telling me this?" He could hear the frustration and anger growing in Dawkins' voice.

Sweetwater smiled. "To see if you're smart enough to stop me."

A pause and Dawkins began, his voice growing louder with each word. "Listen to me, you stupid sack of..."

29 seconds in, Sweetwater ended the call. He danced around the room, giving the remains of the end table another kick, this time from joy. Yes, Dawkins was definitely in. He just didn't have a clue what he was in for.

CADE WAITED for Reynolds in the lobby of KSTP, one of the oldest stations in the Twin Cities market. KSTP began as a radio station way back in 1925 and started broadcasting television several decades later. Renovated and expanded over the decades as the station grew in prominence, their headquarters on University Avenue was a historic icon. The lobby reflected their rich history with images and mementos from the years, including the very first television camera available from RCA, bought by the station in 1938.

It was a busy morning for Cade. Following the disturbing call from the killer, he'd met with Rob and Rejene. The meeting exploded with differing viewpoints and emotions. "Look, we know the killer is going to take another woman soon," Rejene said. Her face looked stressed and her eyes radiated her fatigue. "We need to be ready."

It was Rob's turn to show his frustration. "But how? Other than saying she was his type, we've nothing more to go on. How many tall blondes are there in the Twin Cities? There have to be thousands. And how would we find them all?"

"Clearly, we can't." Cade leaned back in his chair. "Perhaps we should focus on the one we do know."

"You mean your new girlfriend, Reynolds DeVries," Rob offered.

Rejene's head swung around from Rob to Cade. "Really? You picked this time to get involved with the most prominent newsperson in the entire city? The same one who has a source within our investigation?" Lt. Rejene did not look pleased. At all.

"Look, it just happened. I wasn't looking for anything from her, but sometimes things happen. And just so you know, she isn't getting anything from me."

"Information, you mean," Rob interjected.

Cade shook his head and held up a finger. "Reynolds isn't getting information from me. Her source is someone else."

Rejene leaned forward. "But you're saying she could be his next target?"

"It makes sense," Rob offered. "She fits his profile, and she's extremely visible with this story. DeVries has had more breaking stories about these killings than all the other stations put together."

Cade nodded. "Profilers have shown serial killers are drawn to their media attention. They need to see the impact their brutal crimes cause. So, if you're the killer, she has to be on the top of the watch list." Cade looked to Rob. "We should make sure her security is tight. Real tight."

Rob nodded. "It has to be tighter than a camel's backside in a sandstorm."

"And then," Cade paused, "Maybe we can use her to our advantage."

"Here we go," Rob said, standing up.

Rejene looked confused. "Wait. What am I missing here?"

Rob jabbed a finger in Cade's direction. "This one is suggesting we use Reynolds DeVries—his own girlfriend—as serial killer bait."

"That's cold," Rejene snapped. "But I'm listening."

Cade looked between the pair. "You both are jumping to conclusions. I'm simply offering a way to communicate with the killer and point him in the direction we want him to follow. Look, the killer has dramatically changed course with this call. Now, it's not just about this asshole killing another woman, he's challenging me. Saying I'm not smart enough to catch him."

"Don't you see you're playing his game now? He's sucked you into his twisted game."

"Exactly. That's his game. A game he's played before. Chicago had a series of killings several years back."

"Tall blonde victims?" Rejene asked.

"No, these were all different body types, with different hair colors. But a pattern was there. All were waitresses working in downtown Chicago. According to my BCA friend Grace, serial killers are wired to create patterns. Her point was, each series of killings may not follow the same pattern. Yes, there'll be similarities such as killing close up—you won't find these guys killing with a gun, for instance—but the need to always follow a pattern will be there." Cade was on his feet pacing as he talked.

"This killer in Chicago ended his run of six murders by breaking his pattern. His last victim was a man, a man who happened to be the lead detective on the case. Shane Martinson had received a ton of media attention for solving a famous case the year before the Chicago killing began."

Rejene nodded. "I remember the name. He found a terrorism ring operating out of Chicago. Took them down pretty much single-handedly."

"That was him. The case made national news. So, the interesting part is how this famous detective was killed. Martinson was found eviscerated on the hood of his car, his shield in his mouth. After his death, the killings stopped—at least in Chicago."

Rejene looked concerned. "I may not be the investigator that you two are, but I can recognize a pattern when I see one." She looked at Cade. "You believe our killer—the same one from Chicago—has an ulterior motive to establishing such an obvious pattern with these blonde women?"

Cade nodded.

Rejene continued. "And he purposely killed on the state highways so the case would end up in your hands?"

Cade nodded.

"And here's the thing: when the case was taken away from you," Rob said, "the killer made damn sure your replacement was decommissioned."

Rejene nodded. "And now that the case is back in your hands, he reaches out to you. He taunts you, says he's going to kill again and challenges you to stop him."

Cade smiled a grim smile. "That about covers it. Though I did learn a little something about our killer when I was in Chicago."

"What's that?" Rejene asked.

"After several killings, he'd made a play for a woman, but she got away. But, get this: the woman was able to give a rough physical description."

"What did you find out?" Rejene was all in, and moved closer.

"The witness said he looked rigid, like he was military. She said he had dark hair, dark complexion and was several inches shorter than me. And he had to be strong. He held down an extremely fit Martinson and forced him to watch the knife do its work, forced him to witness his own death."

"As I said, I'm no detective, but it's obvious we have a dangerous situation. He's strong and exceptionally intelligent—he outsmarted Chicago's top detective after all—and he's killing women so he can play cat and mouse with our top investigator. I don't like it. At all." Rejene shook her head.

"Neither do I. But as long as I know his goal, I'm miles ahead," Cade said. "And boss, don't be worried, you'd make a fine detective."

"That's not what I'm worried about. I just don't want to find out my lead investigator was forced to eat his shield while being butchered on the hood of a Patrol vehicle."

"I'm right there with you," Cade said. "Let's bury this guy. Enough is enough."

CADE WATCHED Reynolds walk toward him across the television station's busy lobby. She wore a light green silk blouse, black skirt and stilettos. Every eye in the place followed her as she gracefully strode toward Cade. Elegant and sexy, Reynolds quietly commanded attention wherever she went. There's a saying that suddenly made sense to Cade: The whisper of a pretty girl can be heard further than the roar of a lion.

She embraced him firmly, her perfume washing over him. "Let's go down to the cafeteria. I'll treat you to one of our warm cinnamon rolls. We can talk quietly there."

Cade followed her to the elevator, trying not to stare. Reynolds truly was an exceptional beauty. He gave her a grin as they stepped into the elevator. Several conservative-looking women in their forties were already in the elevator. They gave Cade and Reynolds a dismissive glance and turned back to watch the indicator lights. They all rode in silence as the car went down to the basement and the chime dinged signaling their arrival. Catching Reynolds' eye, Cade said, "If the door opens and it's all zombies out there, let's team up."

She was still laughing as they got to the cafeteria counter. Reynolds ordered Cade his cinnamon roll and a couple of hot chocolates and grabbed a secluded table. "So, what's up? You said it was important," Cade asked.

Reynolds nodded toward Cade's plate. "Try the cinnamon roll while it's still warm."

Cade shrugged. His mother told him to never argue with a woman. He picked up his fork.

"I received another call from my source this morning," Reynolds began.

"Amazing," Cade exclaimed.

"What?" Reynolds looked confused.

"This is the best cinnamon roll I've ever had."

Reynolds gave him a shake of her head. She was smiling though.

"As I was saying, my source called this morning." Reynolds

pulled out her cell and set it on the table. She navigated to an app, pushed a button and leaned back.

A voice said, "He's stalking a woman right now. This man, this killer, has picked out his next victim. It won't be long now."

"Do you have him under surveillance?" This was Reynolds now.

There was a pause. Cade held Reynolds' eyes.

"Are you waiting for him to incriminate himself?" Reynolds again.

There was another pause. Then the man spoke. "He's smart, this one. I'd imagine his IQ is off the charts, so we need to watch and wait, hoping for a lucky break. It may be that plain old dumb luck could be the only way to catch him."

"It sounds like you respect him." Reynolds' voice.

"When you're involved in a game of cat and mouse—and you're the mouse—the only intelligent course is to respect your opponent. Otherwise, you end up dead. We can't underestimate his cunning." Cade listened intently as the man's voice grew louder.

"What can you tell me about the killer's description? Is he actually deformed like they say?" Reynolds asked on the recording.

"What? I can't discuss specifics with you on an ongoing investigation—especially one of this magnitude. But I can tell you the killer is not deformed. In any way." There was a click and the recording stopped.

"So, what do you think?" Reynolds asked as she sipped her cocoa.

Cade leaned back and ran his fingers through his hair. "You might already know this, or at least suspect it: Your source is not a cop. He's the killer."

"Holy shit! I was right," Reynolds said. And not quietly, as she gained the attention of the entire room. Sheepishly holding up a hand, Reynolds glanced around and said, "Sorry, my bad."

She turned back to Cade and leaned in conspiratorially. "What makes you think so?"

"I received a call from the killer today and it was the same voice as your recording. Same guy. He wanted to let me know he would be killing again soon. And he dared me to stop him."

She set down her cup. "The more he talked, the more he didn't feel like a cop anymore. Cops take their cases personally when people are getting murdered. You don't refer to a butcher of women with such reverence. That's why I thought he might be the killer instead of a cop."

"So, what was that part about the killer being deformed?" Cade asked. "That never came from us." He sipped his hot chocolate.

"I told you, he was pissing me off."

Cade laughed. "You were messing with him there, weren't you? A dangerous game. Just don't do it again. I much prefer you in one piece."

Reynolds gave him a coy look. "You say the sweetest things." She looked thoughtful for a long moment. "He obviously has a high opinion of his intelligence," Reynolds said. "I once had a colleague who'd gone to Harvard. Every chance he got, he'd mention it. It was the same with this guy, he kept referring to his IQ and cunning. It reminded me of the Harvard guy, and it annoyed me."

Cade smiled. "I can see that."

"Why do you think the killer contacted me in the first place? It made sense when it was a cop wanting to get the story out there to warn the public. But a killer usually tries to hide their crimes to limit exposure and the chances they'll be caught."

Cade nodded. "I've been thinking about that. This killer has established a remarkably obvious pattern. Even though patterns are one of the defining characteristics of a serial killer, our killer has established a pattern more obvious than most. He wants this pattern to be recognized."

"But, why?"

"This killer has a game he plays. He sets up an obvious pattern to draw in a specific investigator—one who's had high-profile success—and plays cat and mouse with him. He wins this game by outwitting the investigator and making a public execution of him. He contacted you because he wanted you to publicize the killings to draw me into his game." Cade studied Reynolds for a long moment. "But there's another likely reason you were contacted."

Reynolds looked impatient. "What's that?"

"As I said in Goodwin's press conference, you match his victim profile perfectly." Cade pointed to an outstretched finger. "One, you're tall."

"I'm five foot seven."

"In heels, you're tall. And two, you are blonde. Three, you are attractive. Remarkably attractive, in fact."

"Thank you."

"Serial killer profilers believe victims are selected based on certain physical or personal characteristics that reflect their ideal victim. Perhaps this ideal victim represents someone who wronged them, someone who traumatically affected them or maybe they represent the killer's mother—you know how many people have mother issues."

Reynolds rolled her eyes.

"Either consciously or subconsciously, the killer is drawn to you because you're a match with his ideal victim this time around."

Reynolds leaned back and tucked a strand of hair behind an ear. "Am I in danger?"

"Yes, you are. You haven't endeared yourself to the killer with your deformity question. And the killer told us he's watching his next victim. For sure he's watching you on his television."

Reynolds smiled. "I've always said the more viewers the better. Just so he keeps his distance."

Cade put his hand on hers. "We will watch over you. There will be a team keeping you under observation. Of course, I'd feel better if I were the one watching you."

Holding his eyes, Reynolds nodded. "Stay with me tonight."

"There's nowhere else I'd rather be. I'll pick you up after your broadcast. And no mentioning the killer's deformity. Please."

Cade saw the fear in her eyes as she nodded in agreement.

CHAPTER
23

"You're not going to believe what that asshole did," Cade announced as entered the community room at Caribou. Rob turned around at the sound of Cade's voice, allowing Cade to see Haily the barista seated across from him. "Oh shit," he said reflexively, "I didn't realize you have company. Sorry about the language."

"You kiss your television anchor girlfriend with that mouth?" Haily asked. The teen had a large grin on her face, clearly enjoying herself.

Cade turned on Rob, who simply held up his hands. "Haily has decided our case is more important than working, so she's here helping. A lot. And your name may have come up in conversation. Anyway, she's working on how the victims were targeted, looking for correlations. She's got a pet theory it might be through Facebook. She said our victims were too old for other social media like Twitter and Tumbling."

"Tumblr," she corrected.

"Tumblr. Got it. And she's getting me free coffee. I'm on my fourth cup. But I'm sure you can't tell." Rob's eyes were wide and he looked like an ADHD kid on sugar cereal. Cade had to laugh.

"Can't tell at all."

"Didn't think so," he said. "Haily has found Facebook accounts for each and every one of the victims, including Ellie Winters. Do you know if Reynolds has one?"

Cade shook his head. "She doesn't. I'm not sure if that puts her behind or ahead of the curve, technology-wise."

Haily nodded. "Ahead, definitely ahead. Facebook is mainly for old people now."

Rob waved his hand. "Hang on, I have a Facebook page. And I'm only thirty-three years old."

Haily nodded again. "My point has been made. Thank you."

Rob covered his eyes with his hands. "Oh Haily, where is the love? Thirty-three is not old."

"It is if you're seventeen," Cade said. "Now sit down before you fall and break a hip, old man." He laughed as Rob held up a finger.

"Have you found the victims have common friends or associations? Maybe they're in the same group."

"Working on that now," Haily said.

Cade pulled up a chair and turned it around to face Haily. "I'm not convinced you could target these women just by stalking them through Facebook. It's not like you can search Facebook using tall, knockout blondes as a search term. Wouldn't you already have to know someone's name to find them?"

Haily shook her head. She leaned in. "The killer could be trolling through his friends, looking at their friends, and then reaching further out to their friends."

"I don't know," Cade said. "You're telling me our killer spends most of his waking time trolling on Facebook? Our profile puts the killer as extremely strong, extremely dangerous, and possibly ex-military. A man of action. Most people I come across who spend hours upon hours on Facebook look like they spend hours sitting in front of the computer. They're overweight, soft, and squishy. No way they are capable of holding a strong police officer down so he could witness his own murder."

"I see what you mean," Rob said. "But maybe the killer is using it to research his potential victims. See their interests, where they spend their time."

"Back to square one then," Cade said. "He still has to find his victims somehow before researching them. Where does he find them?"

Cade stood up, clearly frustrated. He put a hand on Haily's shoulder. "Don't stop what you're doing, though. We may find commonalities between our victims through social media yet." He turned to Rob. "I know you're working on creating timelines for each victim. You may discover they all ate at the same place or frequented the same coffee shop," Cade said. "Maybe each of the victims had their car serviced by the same mechanic, went to the same hairstylist, worked out at the same gym, or had their waxing done at the same salon."

Cade's last comment had the desired effect: Rob raised an eyebrow, while Haily rolled her eyes at him. What was it about teenage girls that made them want to pass judgment on others with their eye rolls? What did it say about Cade that he received such immense satisfaction in provoking that very same reaction? Growing up with an older sister had honed his button-pushing skills to near-perfection. But no one should feel sympathy for his sister, as Abbey could always dish it out with clinical precision, offering up a well-timed comment designed to chop him off at the knees. Cade's family had a way of putting fun into dysfunctional.

"So far, there's surprisingly little overlap between victims," Rob said as he moved over to where the victim's pictures hung on the wall. "You'd think with all our victims being from the east side they would go to the same places, but no. Jennifer Allard, the first victim, and Stephanie Harding, the third victim, both had treatments at Vitality Med-Spa in Woodbury during the last year. However, there's no record of Holly Janek or Ellie Winters ever going there. Otherwise, there are no commonalities other than driving and dying on the state highways. Our victims led contrasting lives. Jennifer Allard was an attorney and hobnobbed with an elite crowd. She was part of a roundtable discussion with the Governor a month before her death.

"Holly Janek, Haily's aunt, was an event planner. She was all over the metro area and western Wisconsin planning weddings, funerals and corporate events. Conservatively speaking, Holly must have interacted with thousands of people in her last two months."

Haily nodded as she listened. "Holly was always busy. She loved her work, though."

Rob continued. "Stephanie Harding was a sales rep for a medical device company. She'd been with them for a little over six months and visited clinics and hospitals all over Minnesota and Wisconsin. None of the other victims went to a hospital or clinic in their last several months.

"Ellie Winters was the most high-profile of our victims. I'm guessing 75 percent of her listening audience knew exactly what she looked like. Her pictures are all over the radio station's website. She was immensely popular. And our killer most likely focused on her based on her outspokenness about the killings. Winters' comings and goings probably won't lead us anywhere."

"We have to keep digging. There is a connection there between these women, and when we find it, we'll find the killer." Cade stood up. "But it better be soon. This bastard says he's going to take another woman."

Rob shook his head. "I still can't believe he called you. He's treating this like a game."

"Oh, it gets worse," Cade said. "Reynolds took a call from her cop source today. After listening to the recorded call, I know who her source is."

"Wait, what? Who is it?"

"The thing is, it's not a cop. It's actually the killer. It was the same exact voice as my call from this morning."

"That makes sense. What did he tell her?"

"He said the killer had picked his next victim and was stalking her right now. He went on to say how the killer's IQ was off the charts and the only way the police would catch him would be through dumb luck."

"What an egotistical douchebag." Rob folded his arms, clearly taking the remarks personally.

"He said we're the mice in the killer's game of cat and mouse—and we needed to respect the killer and not underestimate his cunning. Otherwise, we'll end up as dead as the Chicago detective."

"What an arrogant prick," Haily said. "I didn't think I could possibly hate him more."

"No way am I letting him get the best of us. I don't care what it takes," Cade said through clenched teeth.

"That's what I'm worried about." Rob stared intently at Cade. "Let me ask you a question. Is there a line you won't cross to stop this guy?" Rob held his eye.

Cade locked eyes with Rob for a long moment before finally shaking his head.

REYNOLDS ABSOLUTELY SHINED in front of the camera. Cade stood alongside the officer charged with providing Reynold's security. When he'd arrived, Cade told the Saint Paul cop he was free to leave, as Cade was there to watch her. "No way am I missing out on this," were the officer's exact words. The pair of law enforcement officers sat side by side enjoying the spectacle of television news. Every time a pretty reporter made her way onto the set, the St. Paul officer nudged Cade. "Check her out," he whispered. Cops were the same no matter where you went.

It was crazy pandemonium leading up to the moment they went live. Somehow, some way, everything came together at the last possible second as the news team slid into place and Reynolds calmly introduced the evening's 10 p.m. news.

Reynolds was clearly the star. In front of the lights and cameras, her smile, laugh, and eyes captivated as her presence radiated. Dressed in a muted violet blouse with a snug black skirt and purple high heels, she looked amazing. And the parts hidden below the set were equally enthralling. Her legs were without question the best he'd ever enjoyed looking at.

"You have a bit of drool there at the corner of your mouth," the cop whispered. Cade felt like he was back in high school as he tried not to laugh. A production assistant shot them a nasty look, causing Cade to pretend he was sneezing into the crook of his arm.

"How'd you like it?" Reynolds asked after the broadcast was over. "Most people would never imagine the chaos happening behind the scenes."

"It was amazing to see all the commotion with you so calm in the middle of it all." Cade paused and smiled. "I have to say, I was completely entranced watching you. No wonder your ratings are so high. You light up the entire studio."

Smiling shyly, Reynolds said, "It's nice to hear you liked it. Your cop friend seemed to be enjoying himself."

Shaking his head, Cade grinned. "Men can be such pigs."

Reynolds laughed. "Pot. Calling the kettle black." She playfully poked him in the chest. "You were enjoying it too."

"Well, aesthetically speaking, there was a lot to enjoy. The set was decorated quite tastefully." Cade gave her his best grin. She gave him her elbow.

She leaned in close enough for Cade to catch her scent. It was fresh with a hint of lavender. "Take me home."

"You don't have to ask me twice," Cade whispered.

"I hadn't planned to," she said huskily as she nuzzled into his neck.

THE MOMENT he joined Reynolds in his truck and locked eyes with her, Cade wondered if they would make it out of the station's parking lot. His pulse raced as he held her close. Pushing aside her hair, he ran his lips down her neck, feeling her shiver. Her scent was intoxicating. Reynolds moaned softly as his lips parted, his tongue on her tender neck. She pushed him back as her lips found his.

"Why don't you put it in?" she asked in a voice just south of a whisper.

"Pardon?" His brain foggy, not entirely sure he'd heard her correctly. "What was that?"

"Why don't you put it in gear and bring me home? It may not be the best career move to have the station's top anchor caught making out with the top cop in our parking lot."

"Time to leave," he announced and started the truck, heading the FJ Cruiser out onto University Avenue as fast as he dared. He hoped there wasn't a cop around.

THE KILLER LOOKED for signs of police presence as he drove down her street. A car with occupants, maybe a flash of light or reflection from a window, possibly someone walking a dog or out for a late-night run. However, the street was quiet.

He drove up several blocks and turned into an alley. Behind the last house, a fence with an overgrown hedge blocked the home's view of Sweetwater's car. He left it there because he could return to it from several directions and within moments be out of the neighborhood and onto the interstate. It wasn't actually his car; he'd borrowed it from an old woman he'd come across. No way she'd miss it after 10 p.m. And if everything went according to plan, he'd have it back at her house, and she'd never know.

Out of the car, a baseball cap pulled down and his collar turned up, Sweetwater moved down the alley. He crossed the street and continued down the pavement. He started his reconnaissance behind her house, looking for movement. Seeing none, he moved to the front which was equally quiet. He knew where she was and didn't expect her to be home anytime soon.

Back in the alley, he walked as casually as he dared. He hopped the low chain-link fence separating her small yard from the alley. A dog barked nearby and Sweetwater crouched low as he listened. After several minutes of nothing, he cautiously rose and moved across her back yard. Before approaching her door, he paused again to listen. Caution was hard-wired into Sweetwater, and he mentally counted to one hundred as he waited.

Sweetwater once read that serial killers were among the most alert and cautious of all human beings. He had to agree. In his case, such caution could be explained by Sweetwater's foremost concern, his personal security. As long as he wasn't caught, he would be able to continue enjoying his specialized pursuits.

Time to continue. He pulled a chisel from his jacket pocket and crept up her back steps.

Listening at her door for several long moments, he deemed it safe to enter. Pulling on the knob to created space between the door and the latch plate, he pushed the chisel into the gap. Using his shoulder, Sweetwater shoved the door open. He paused once again as he listened intently for signs his forced entry had been detected. All was quiet. With a glance over his shoulder, the killer stepped into her home.

CHAPTER
24

The drive over had been a tense affair as he sped through the dark streets, need pushing caution out of the equation. Little was said as they drove, and Cade didn't trust himself beyond an occasional glance in Reynolds' direction. The smoldering glance he received in return promised more than words ever could.

Inside Reynold's home, Cade pushed the door shut and pulled Reynolds close.

"You are so sexy," he said, his voice thick with emotion. He kissed her passionately, tangling his fingers in her hair. It wasn't the safe, trim cut many professional women had. It was long, blonde and flowing, barely contained, offering a hint of her untamed inner self. It was the look of a woman supremely confident in her appearance, secure in her sexuality. Reynolds uttered a soft moan as he tenderly kissed her neck, making a monumental effort to slow down, wanting to savor the moment. Her scent was intoxicating, as he opened his mouth and tasted her smooth skin. He couldn't help himself as his right hand slid down the back of her silky blouse, enjoying the firmness of her body.

This moment had played through Cade's imagination from the day he'd first met her. The way she'd used her physical presence to calm him, to draw him in. To seduce him.

"What are you thinking?" she asked in a low voice that had him wanting her even more, if that was possible. The ability to form words and a cohesive sentence were beyond him as his blood pounded. He ran his tongue slowly, ever so slowly, along the delicate skin of her neck, blowing a light breath over the moist spot. She shivered and said, "I'm getting a clearer idea of what's on your mind."

They stood inside the entrance, the glow of the overhead light the sole source of illumination in the otherwise dark house. Cade pushed her gently back to the stairs leading to the second level, the shadows merging into darkness as he glanced up the stairwell. "We are alone here, aren't we?" Reynolds nodded, as she sat back on a step looking expectantly at Cade.

"We are. Don't be worried about making a little noise." She leaned back and placed one of her heels on Cade's thigh. "This is an older neighborhood and my neighbors all go to bed right after the ten o'clock news. Most right after the weather. We could make a lot of noise if we wanted." She slid her purple stiletto up a little higher.

"Are you telling me your neighbors miss out on the clever ad-libs you guys make at the end of the news? A shame." Reynolds narrowed her eyes and pushed a bit harder. Cade smiled and lifted her foot. He was about to say something and paused, listening. A creak came from upstairs. They both looked up the dark stairwell.

"Are you sure we're alone?" he asked, his hand sliding down to his hip.

"Just Toby," she replied and called up the stairs, "Toby."

Cade heard the creak again and a medium-sized brown and white dog moved into the light. Toby was an older cocker spaniel who appeared to have some difficulty with the stairs. He came down and sat beside Reynolds, nuzzling her. She gently stroked his head, "This is Toby. He's my rescue shelter dog. We go back a lot of years."

Cade reached his hand out, allowing Toby to sniff him. Cade must have passed Toby's muster, as the cocker pushed his ear against Cade's hand. "You like to have your ears rubbed, do you?" he asked the dog. Apparently, the answer was yes, as the dog turned his head, pushing against Cade's hand again.

Reynolds laughed. "All cockers love to have their ears rubbed. It's just their nature." She stood up, excusing herself to let Toby out and feed him his dinner. Clearly, the dog was not a master of timing. Cade took a seat on the stairs and waited.

After Kim fell out of his life, he'd thrown himself into his work and tried to forget her, looking to move on. His track record with relationships, which was far from inspiring, made him much more tentative while looking for a new one. In fact, Cade wasn't looking when Reynolds DeVries came into his life. He was taken by surprise as much as she was. And now, here they were, mostly alone in her home. Cade took a deep breath.

Reynolds came around the corner, leaning against the wall. She folded her arms and appeared to be sizing him up. Her playful smile looked to be a good sign. "Sorry about the interruption. I believe we were talking about making some noise." The corner of her mouth turned up, her eyes twinkling.

Cade held out his hands, and when Reynolds reached out, he pulled her into him. He was well aware of how high her skirt rode as she straddled him on the stairs. She put a warm hand on his cheek and he pulled her in, his lips finding hers. Her lips warm and soft as he not-so-gently kissed her, their passion building.

Reynolds broke the kiss, leaning back, her breathing heavy.

"Would you like to see the upstairs?" she asked.

"I thought you'd never ask," Cade answered.

CANDAN SPRING PUSHED OPEN the seventy-something year old door and stepped into her quiet house. She dropped her keys into the basket and slipped off her coat. Her feet were sore from the heels, but the pain was worth it. The governor's fitness gala was a huge success and she'd had the opportunity to meet several potential clients. Two were high profile, one an elected official and the other a newspaper columnist for the Minneapolis paper. Both could benefit from her training regimen. As her business was built on referrals, having such visible clients would attract even more business. The bottom line was

Candan knew she could have a profound impact on the quality of their lives, and that was important to her.

Candan paused. One of the picture frames on her "table of history," as her friends called it, had fallen over. She picked it up and studied it. The picture showed a much younger Candan in her basketball jersey standing next to her father. Both had the same we-won-the-championship grin. She set it back in place next to the one with her and her mother wearing their Twin Cities Marathon race numbers.

Growing up, her father was her basketball coach and her mother was a runner, entering a dozen races each year. Candan played school sports and summer leagues, which transitioned into cycling and running her own races after college. Her degree was in sports medicine and she found a position soon after at the Minneapolis Athletic Club. The life of a certified personal trainer was exactly what she needed. Being such an extrovert, it gave her the opportunity to meet a variety of people and make a difference in their lives.

She slipped out of her heels, rubbed her feet and padded into the kitchen. Candan grabbed a bottle of water from the fridge and headed upstairs. Knowing it would be a late night, she'd rearranged the schedule so her first client, Greg Anderson, wouldn't be until the afternoon. Often, her first appointment of the day was at 5:30 in the morning. It was a rare luxury to be able to sleep in, and she looked forward to it.

Slipping out of her blouse and skirt, Candan tossed them onto the hamper with plans to hang them up in the morning. She stood in her small upstairs bathroom as she brushed her teeth. Tightening her abs, Candan appreciated the definition she saw. She worked diligently at her fitness and kept to a strict dietary regimen, avoiding most sugars and carbs. It worked, she thought, as she turned and looked at her rear. So firm you could crack an egg on it—if you were into that sort of thing. She smiled at her humor.

Her eye caught movement in the mirror and she looked up. A man stood behind her.

CHAPTER
25

Marlin Sweetwater lived for this moment. That delicious moment when his chosen one realized her life was going to change—and not in a good way. Each of them reacted uniquely. Some cried and pleaded, others fought back, while some panicked and screamed, and others quietly accepted their fate. Most were a combination of these behaviors and emotions. Sweetwater loved them all. After all, these women were his.

Screaming, the woman spun around and went to slam the bathroom door shut. Sweetwater slipped his hand into the door before she could get it shut. The woman slammed into it, desperate in her attempt to get the door closed and locked. However, Sweetwater had muscles for days, and the door didn't move at all. Her struggles didn't dampen Sweetwater's mood, in fact, he welcomed her efforts at survival. This was a rare moment for him these days. Unlike his recent kills on the state highways, he actually had the time to play with her. Just the thought of being able to take his time and enjoy his thoroughness made him excited. Spring would be so...tasty.

He gave the door a little push, wanting to toy with her. He felt her pushing back, as he enjoyed the moment until a sharp pain sliced across his fingers. Caught by surprise, Sweetwater yanked his hand from the door. The door slammed shut and he heard the lock being set. The bitch must have used a razor on him. He looked at his fingers to see how bad they were sliced, but the heavy blood flow obscured the wounds. He needed to stop the bleeding before he left a blood trail. It could be the end of his fun if crime scene techs got his DNA.

Sweetwater stepped across the hall into Spring's bedroom and spotted her laundry hamper. Wrapping a pair of her panties around his fingers, he cursed himself for being so incredibly careless. He would make the woman pay. Squeezing his hand into a fist, Sweetwater was relieved the cuts hadn't sliced into his muscle or caused nerve damage. He'd finish what he started. Time to get her out of the bathroom.

CANDAN SPRING FELL BACK against the door and stared at the bloody razor. She knew the cut would only slow the man down. He was much too large to let a small thing like a bathroom door keep him out for long. Her mind raced, desperate to find an escape. The window on her second-floor bathroom was too small for her to get out, and besides, she didn't have much time. Her eyes scanned the room for anything to use. Unbelievably, she'd carried in her cell phone and there it was, sitting on the back of the toilet. She lunged for it.

SWEETWATER STEPPED up to the door. A smear of blood on the frame marked his struggle as well as his presence. He'd have to do a cleanup after he finished with the woman to make sure the crime scene techs wouldn't find blood traces. He didn't want his DNA to become a threat to his survival. However, the sound of her voice made clear a real threat was imminent.

SPRING FRANTICALLY UNLOCKED her phone and pushed the three numbers that could save her life. A voice answered, "911. What is your emergency?"

"There's a man in my house. I'm locked in the bathroom and he's right outside."

SWEETWATER HEARD her words and knew his window was fast closing. He backed up and launched himself at her door.

REYNOLDS LAY across Cade's chest as he brushed her hair back, wanting to see her eyes. Even sweaty and spent, Reynolds was gorgeous. She studied him for a moment. "What's it like being a cop?"

He laughed. "That's a tough question. Sometimes it's challenging, sometimes rewarding, sometimes terrifying, sometimes boring, and usually unpredictable. Cops are out on the front lines, bringing gray to a black-and-white world."

"Not sure what you mean."

"Black and white means following the letter of the law. Gray means following the spirit. By following the letter of the law, I am treating everyone by the same standard without a lot of room for pity or common sense. Sometimes you need to focus on the greater good and ignore the little things—which can be especially difficult for anyone new to law enforcement. It's a crisis of faith every new cop goes through as they adjust to their new environment."

Reynolds ran her hand across Cade's chest. "Tell me more."

Cade smiled, enjoying being the center of her attention. "High-speed chases look like fun because they are. Take away alcohol and stupid, and the world would require about 90% fewer cops. Most would say if we could make one change to improve society, better parenting would be toward the top of the list."

"I absolutely agree," Reynolds said. "If every parent taught their child to be responsible for their actions and own the consequences—good or bad—our community would be significantly better."

"You've been chasing windmills for a long time?" Cade grinned.

Reynolds laughed. "A girl can dream, can't she? I've always wondered about something. Why do so many cops show up for some minor incident like a fender bender or a traffic stop?"

"The official answer is wanting to support and protect our fellow officer. The real reason is probably boredom. Simple boredom. You drive around for hours on end and when something happens, you want to be part of it. Cops are people too. The laws of human nature apply to us too."

"Are you a gun nut?" Reynolds asked as she glanced at his pistol on the nightstand. "Just wondering."

"I have a healthy respect for them. Typically, cops run the gamut from those who only shoot to qualify with their duty weapon, all the way up to passionate gun enthusiasts with safes full of guns, who go to firing ranges as a hobby, and buy and sell among one another. Cops generally support the right of people to own, use and carry guns, so long as people act reasonably and responsibly. Cops who carry concealed firearms in plain clothes or while off duty are careful to keep the weapons concealed. And speaking of concealed, the gun on his hip, that's the one he wants you to see. It is not alone. There's always a backup weapon hidden somewhere."

"Cops get a bad reputation," Reynolds said. "I heard a joke recently. How many cops does it take to push a suspect down the stairs? The answer: None, he fell."

Cade laughed, shaking his head. "Unfair, so unfair. I heard one too. An officer stopped a guy for speeding and put him in the back of the squad car. The officer says it's his birthday and he's feeling benevolent. He tells the guy if you give me a good, original excuse for your excessive speed I won't write the ticket. The guy replied that some years ago his wife left him and ran off with a police officer. Confused, the officer asked why is that an excuse for your speeding? The guy smiled and said, 'I thought you were bringing her back!'"

Reynolds laughed, a musical sound Cade could get used to. "I bet the troopers hear it all," she said. "I'm sure your favorites are the ones beginning with 'Do you know who I am?' or 'I pay your salary.'"

"Surprisingly, I've never heard either. But I'm not concerned about those people. It's more the regular repeat offenders that are the issue."

Cade rolled Reynolds onto her back as he kissed her. When they broke for air, she asked, "I've heard it's the 80/20 rule: 80 percent of the crimes are committed by the same 20 percent. Is that true?"

Cade looked into her eyes. "Let me put it this way. If you get a group of four or five cops together and ask them to name the last time they arrested someone who'd never been arrested before, be prepared for a thoughtful silence." He stroked her cheek, "Enough about work. Let's get back to pleasure."

She giggled and Cade felt her hand slide south. "It would be my pleasure," she said softly.

Mine too, he thought. Mine too.

AFTERWARD, Reynolds set a plate of cookies and several bottles of water on the bedside table. "Figured you might be hungry."

Cade nodded and picked one up, looking at it carefully. "Is it chocolate chip or raisin?" he asked. "Raisin cookies that look like chocolate chip cookies are the reason I have trust issues." Reynolds' giggle was exactly the response he hoped for.

Life was good.

CHAPTER
26

The door split down the middle under the force of Sweetwater's attack. Shards of wood sprayed across the small bathroom. The woman stood frozen, her mouth open, cell in hand. Spring's eyes were wide with terror.

Sweetwater reached and plucked the phone from her trembling fingers. The 911 operator's voice could be heard asking questions, questions Spring would never answer. Sweetwater locked eyes with the trembling woman, lifting the cell to his ear. He listened to the 911 operator ask for Spring's location. The killer growled, "She's mine now," and dropped the phone and ground it into the tile floor with his boot.

Sweetwater looked up, letting his eyes take a walk over Spring's body. The killer took his time examining the nearly naked woman in front of him. She wasn't going anywhere. And he knew the police couldn't stop him. The closest the authorities could get to his location from Spring's 911 call was the nearest cell tower. If the call was quickly lost, the 911 center typically only knew the location within a mile radius of where the call originated from. Not much help. The FCC's plan to enhance cellular technology would eventually provide more precise location information; specifically, the latitude and longitude of the caller. This information would be accurate to within 50 to 300 meters. However, their plan was years away from being realized.

His prize looked exceedingly vulnerable standing there in her matching bra and panties, her last lifeline smashed into pieces at her feet, framed by the jagged remains of her bathroom door. Sweetwater enjoyed the firmness of her well-toned body. This would be a night to live up to his every fantasy. Reaching into his jacket pocket, Sweetwater pulled out the lengths of cord he'd pre-cut to restrain the woman. Time to get started.

CADE'S CELL VIBRATED, the sound penetrating his slumber. He slid out of bed, disoriented as he searched for the offending device. A glance at Reynolds' bedside table clock showed him the time: 1:24 a.m. Shit. His pants were discarded on the floor, his cell in the front pocket. He fished it out, noting the source of the call was dispatch. There could only be one reason.

"Dawkins," he said as the adrenaline kicked in, pushing away the fog from his brain. Getting woken up in the middle of the night had to be near the bottom of his list of favorite life events. Right down there with car trouble and girlfriends telling him, "We need to talk." On the phone was the 911 call center's watch supervisor, Russ Horstead. They'd met on several occasions and Cade like him.

Horstead got right to the point. "At 1:21 a.m., our Roseville communications center received a call from a cellular phone. We pinged it to a tower located in east St. Paul, near 35E. Let me play the call for you." The Minnesota State Patrol 911 Communications Center in Roseville handled the emergency calls from much of the state with a secondary facility located in Rochester.

Cade heard several clicks and then, "911. What is your emergency?"

A woman's voice. "There's a man in my house. I'm locked in the bathroom and he's right outside." Cade could hear the panic in her voice.

The 911 operator: "What is the address there?"

A loud crashing sound, reminiscent of splintering wood. A sharp inhalation of breath followed by rustling, the phone being jostled.

Cade could hear the sound of breathing. Then a man's voice. "She's mine now."

The voice came out as a low growl, but Cade recognized it just the same.

A loud sound, the phone clearly dropped. And then the call ended with a crushing noise.

"The call came in roughly three minutes ago?" Cade asked. He moved fast now, gathering his clothes, getting dressed. Reynolds looked at him with a concerned look. Cade held up a finger.

"That's right," Horstead answered. "But we don't have an address, just a mile radius in St. Paul. There could be thousands of homes in our target area."

Cade slipped his boots on and leaned back, touching Reynolds' cheek. "We need to flood the area with every squad you can round up. Get Ramsey County, State Patrol, and divert as many St. Paul officers as you can spare from the other precincts. See if Maplewood and Roseville can offer help as well. We may not be able to stop him, but maybe we can catch him."

Taking the stairs two at a time, Cade was downstairs and out the front door in a heartbeat. "There shouldn't be many cars on the side streets at this time of the morning. Instruct the responding squads to look for solo male drivers, maybe with a military-style haircut. Everyone needs to be stopped. Any other vehicles moving in the area should have the license plates recorded."

"You're talking a massive operation here." An implied question was in Horstead's hesitation.

"This is the blonde-killer we're talking about here. Our response has to be immediate and it can't be massive enough. We have to get this guy, so get everyone rolling." Cade looked back at Reynolds' house. A dark thought colored his urgency to move. Could this be a diversion? The killer, clearly strategic in his planning, the call could be a feint to open up Reynolds' defense for a direct attack. "One more thing Russ, can you get a unit to my location?" He gave Reynolds' address as he gunned the truck, taking the corner hard.

The FJ Cruiser fishtailed as Cade pushed the Toyota to its limits. Best to cover his bases. The killer would definitely have his covered.

THE KILLER WAS ALMOST GIDDY with the excitement of the moment. After breaking down the bathroom door, the woman had resisted vigorously—which Sweetwater both admired and enjoyed. It was always better when they fought back. He let her hit him, knowing she couldn't possibly hurt him. Yet, she'd been able to stun him with a poke to the eye. Angry, Sweetwater caught her with an open-handed smack to her head. The blow took the fight out of her, allowing him to carry the woman to her bedroom.

Her chest rose and fell as Sweetwater waited for her to come to. He didn't have to wait for long.

Candan Spring's eyes fluttered open and after a moment, panic took her as she realized her predicament. She struggled, thrashing against her restraints as she held Sweetwater's eyes. She knew her life was in his hands and it wouldn't be for long. Sweetwater leaned closer. "Recognize me?"

Spring's eyes narrowed. Sweetwater could see the moment of realization as her eyes widened. "But, you're a cop."

Sweetwater smiled, not a warm smile in the least. "Yes, but I have a little hobby on the side. One that can be a little indulgent." He produced a knife and held it up for Spring to see. "Let's get started, shall we?"

CHAPTER
27

Cade's truck roared up the ramp from 35E, turning left onto Wheelock Parkway. He swung into the elementary school parking lot, a convention of flashing emergency lights. A dozen squads were circled wagon train style around the St. Paul watch commander. Cade recognized him as Matt Gralinski and headed in his direction. Gralinski held up a clipboard and shouted out patrol sector assignments. As quick as a squad arrived, the veteran commander sent them back out. He nodded at Cade and continued until the last squad headed out. "I've got Fire and Paramedics coming to block the interstate ramps. I don't want anyone getting by us." The watch commander ran a hand through his reddish hair. "I hope we get this guy."

"Me too. It kills me to know he's nearby with some woman. Do we know who she is?"

Gralinski nodded. "Caller registration records showed this as belonging to Candan Spring, with the Minneapolis Athletic Club as the address. Looks like it's a company-issued cell phone. We've got people working on getting ahold of someone there, but we haven't been able to find a local address for her yet.

"Seriously?" Cade spat out the word.

Gralinski shook his head. "Afraid not. It's not like the old days when everyone had a landline and we'd have an address. Cell phones and digital internet phones play havoc with 911 calls."

"That has to be our number one priority." Cade wanted to punch something. Anything.

"It is. Maybe tonight will be our night," Gralinski said. "You better get moving. I'll have you cruise the east side of the freeway and direct you in whenever a squad pulls someone over. That way you get eyes on each suspect. We're not letting this asshole get away."

Rob pulled up and got out of his truck. His hair stuck up, and his plaid shirt was misbuttoned and hung over his paint-splattered Packers sweatpants. Rob looked more homeless than most of the street people he'd come across. "I see your mom finally stopped laying out your clothes for you," he told Rob who held up a finger.

Rob was assigned the west side of 35E and they both rocketed out of the lot as more cruisers pulled in. Cade headed across the interstate on Wheelock Parkway, slowing after the four-way stop. *The killer is here. Now we have to find him.* He swiveled his head, intent on finding any sign of movement. The strobe on his dash didn't do his night vision any favors, but it was necessary so he wouldn't be stopped by the saturation patrol himself.

Within a minute, the first call came through. St. Paul had a single male in a pickup truck pulled over on Larpenteur Avenue. Cade cut over at the next intersection and was behind the officer within a minute. He pulled his Glock, holding it at his side. The officer exited his vehicle and approached the driver's side. Cade crossed behind the pickup, noting the construction debris in the bed. At the passenger door, he peered in at the driver who was obscured by the hoodie he wore. The officer glanced across the top of the cab and Cade hooked a thumb at him. Get the suspect out of the truck.

The moment he was out and the hoodie came down Cade knew it wasn't the guy. This one had shoulder length stringy blond hair and a mustache. He also knew right away the guy should not be behind the wheel as the guy lost his balance and almost fell before catching himself on the front of his Chevy. "Good luck," he called and headed back to his own vehicle.

Another vehicle was stopped on Nebraska, a half-dozen blocks to the north. Cade flew past the tree-lined streets on Payne Avenue. He made a left on Nebraska and saw the flashing emergency lights up a block. He decided to cruise by and get a look first this time. He went past the Maplewood squad and pulled even with the Toyota. The man looked to be in his forties and wore glasses. Not our man. He reversed and shook his head to the Maplewood officer.

Cade continued down Nebraska and turned left on Arcade Street. Another vehicle headed his way. He was about to pull a U-turn when a state trooper squad shot out of a side street and slid in behind the sedan. The trooper activated his emergency equipment, lighting up the smaller green sedan. The car pulled over right away. Cade slowed, pulling alongside. The driver was heavy-set with a baseball cap and there was a woman in the passenger seat. Continuing along, he waved off the trooper. Our guy travels alone.

Another call came in, another stop. This one at Edgerton and Maryland. Cade pulled a U-turn and gunned it. He was worried their time was getting away from them. At the same time he received two more calls of stops. It looked like it was going to be a busy night.

SWEETWATER TOOK A SHOWER, wanting to remove any trace evidence. The key now was to slow down and be methodical. Take the time to eliminate any DNA, any evidence that could implicate him. Sweetwater lingered in Spring's shower as he washed up, smelling her shampoo. Women always had so many bottles in their showers, choice clearly important to them. He had exactly one bottle of shampoo and one bar of soap in his shower. Really, it was all he needed. Why have choices in the shower when you're there simply to clean up? He'll never understand women, but he sure liked to use them. Sex, killing, whatever.

After getting dressed, he moved to the front window and peered out into the night. The problem with breaking in was you always looked guilty on your way back out. It must be the chief occupational hazard for burglars. There's no explaining away the 50-inch flat screen you're lugging down the front steps. One glance and everyone knows the story. So, Sweetwater, ever cautious, surveyed the neighborhood looking for signs of life. Fortunately, it was a quiet neighborhood. No one should be out cruising—especially in the middle of the night.

As these thoughts ran through his head, Sweetwater saw the headlights of an approaching vehicle. Time slowed to almost a complete standstill as the vehicle moved into his field of view. It was a squad car. Sweetwater held his breath. The St. Paul squad rolled down the tree-lined street and continued on out of sight. After a long moment, Sweetwater let loose his breath.

What was the squad doing here? If they knew where he was, the squad would have stopped. And there would have been more. Lots more. Maybe all of them.

Another squad rolled past. This time it was a state patrol squad. Shit.

Sweetwater turned and sprinted. Now was not the time to be patient. He grabbed his jacket, frantically searching for his radio. He slid the radio's power switch and waited. It took a minute to get the gist of the situation. They didn't know exactly where he was, so they called in as many cars as possible. A saturation patrol. Dozens of squads in a small area stopping every single driver they encountered. Saturating the area would make it nearly impossible to get the block and a half to his car, let alone get to the interstate. And he was inside the cop's perimeter.

He pounded down the stairs, spun around the corner and headed for the kitchen. Sweetwater needed to know if the alleys were covered. It took just over a minute before the sweep of headlights move down the alley. *Damn that Dawkins.* Had to be him behind this. Sweetwater shook his head. He'd wanted a worthy opponent. It looked like he had one.

Options ran through his mind. Wait it out here. Move to a neighboring house. Leave the vehicle and stay on foot until he could get clear of the perimeter. Get to the vehicle and stay on side streets until he made it back to his Frogtown neighborhood. As fast as the options came to him, he ruled them out. He couldn't stay here. After

Spring's 911 call, he knew Dawkins would find her house soon enough. Moving to another house would require a home invasion and bring its own set of problems. And once Dawkins determined where the killing took place, a house-to-house search would be the first tactic employed. Fleeing the area on foot would be too risky. The same could be said for staying on side streets. The police were targeting single occupant vehicles.

He paced for a moment and moved back to the woman's second floor. Sweetwater looked down at her body, lifeless now, but earlier so full of life as she'd struggled with the inevitable. The experience was remarkable, but he couldn't let it end here. He had so much more to accomplish, including finishing his game with Dawkins. Dawkins' voice was on the radio just then, asking for the officers' continued vigilance on stopping each single occupant vehicle. Apparently, Dawkins wanted eyes on each stopped driver.

A question occurred to him. *Why?* As careful as he'd been, there shouldn't be a physical description circulating. Dawkins had heard his voice, but that wouldn't be enough.

An idea came to his mind as he looked down at the Spring woman. The Twin Cities had several HOV lanes. These high occupant vehicle lanes were designed to encourage carpooling. Carpool cheaters tend to get more brazen—and imaginative—when the traffic got worse and the weather heated up. Drivers used creative schemes to bypass rush-hour gridlock and break the HOV lane rules. A stuffed sweatshirt topped with a low-tipping ballpark cap was not an uncommon tactic for drivers seeking an instant passenger. Some were meticulous about strapping the clothes into a seatbelt, just in case. Empty car-seats covered in blankets are standard ruses, although the particularly crafty sometimes place a plastic baby doll inside. One woman employed a life-sized mannequin—topped with a wig and even wearing makeup.

Sweetwater smiled as the idea formed. If Dawkins had his saturation patrol targeting single occupant vehicles, he could use his own mannequin—Spring—and slip right through the net. He darted to the bathroom and grabbed a towel. Surprisingly, it made him uncomfortable to touch her lifeless body. But necessity drove him to clean her up and dress her.

Like a fireman, he hefted her body over his shoulder and carried her down to the main floor. He'd use her vehicle, knowing he'd never get back to his stashed vehicle. Parked out front on the street was her green Honda. He found the keys in a basket, moved to the window and waited. It was almost five minutes before a squad made its way down the street. This one was from Maplewood. After it passed out of sight, he counted to 30 and opened the front door. Baseball cap pulled low, Sweetwater stepped outside and looked around. He walked as matter-of-factly as he could and opened the passenger side door. So far, so good.

Sweetwater went back and picked up the lifeless body of Candan Spring, carrying her across the threshold, out into the cool night. Down the three steps and the length of the walk, keeping his eyes on the Honda. If a squad came now, there would be no way out. He gently placed the dead woman in the vehicle and buckled her seatbelt. Safety first. Almost as an afterthought, he tucked the woman's hair under a knit cap.

He drove the Honda down the still-quiet avenue. Home was roughly five miles due west. However, he decided to continue heading east, away from the interstate—since most of the police presence would be concentrated there. Once he got far enough east, he'd go south before turning west. Glancing at the dead woman beside him, he turned onto a busier thoroughfare and thought things might work out after all.

That was until out of nowhere, a trooper shot out from a side street, the squad's emergency equipment activated. The bright strobes lit up the car's interior. He glanced at the dead woman. Her head lolling lifelessly to the side. She would not fool anyone who gave her more than a cursory glance.

Another vehicle pulled alongside. Sweetwater slouched down in his seat as he glanced sideways. It was Dawkins.

Surprisingly, Dawkins continued, pausing briefly alongside the trooper before he pulled a U-turn and accelerated down Arcade. The trooper turned off his emergency lights and waved Sweetwater to go, making it clear he was free to leave. He let out the breath he'd held and headed for freedom. Of course, there was still the matter of his passenger's body.

CHAPTER
28

Tensions ran high. Daylight fast approached and nothing had happened except for seven DUI arrests and a vehicle full of stolen goods and burglary tools. Cade knew their time was slipping away. Officers needed to be relieved, departments needed their squads back. Something had to give. He didn't believe the killer had gone to ground. It wasn't in his nature.

Capt. Rejene called. "We have an address for Candan Spring. Finally. It's near your location. I'm getting everyone headed there. Be careful." He jotted down her address but didn't need the GPS to find the house. He'd driven up and down the area all night long. Cade's frustration level was nearly redlined knowing he had been so close. Cade accelerated up Edgerton, anxious to help the woman.

A St. Paul squad blocked Spring's street at the nearest intersection. Squads converged from multiple directions. Gralinski, the watch commander, pulled up by Cade. "SWAT is en route, maybe ten minutes out."

Cade shook his head. "The killer could do a lot of damage in ten minutes."

Gralinski nodded gravely. "I know. Let's get the neighboring homes cleared now, so SWAT can focus on the entry." Rob joined the group, as the veteran watch commander directed the officers.

"I want a look at the house," Cade said. "Rob and I will approach it from the back. We'll use the street behind, Nevada, and come up through the yards to the alley. I see the look you're giving me Gralinski. We won't get closer than the alley. Scout's honor."

"Aren't you supposed to hold up a finger or two to make the scout thing official?" Rob asked as they walked away.

Cade held up a finger. "Happy?"

"No, not really," Rob said with a shake of his head. "But I'll come with you anyway."

Weapons in hand, the two investigators jogged to the corner and turned left on the sidewalk. A brick church sat on the corner. Nevada Avenue, like much of the east side neighborhood, was a quiet bedroom community of pre-World War II homes. Built in close proximity, the yards were small. At the fifth house, Rob gestured them to cut between two homes. Not wanting to be seen by the homeowners, they both instinctively hunched down. Both officers knew the pitfalls of chasing suspects through a homeowner's property. Whether it was enforced by a Doberman or a shotgun, some homeowners could go to the extreme to protect their property. Neither officer wanted to be a grisly anecdote to be shared with rookie officers.

They crossed the alley and used Spring's one-car garage for cover. He glanced inside, but didn't see a vehicle. The back yard was fenced in with overgrown foliage obscuring much of the house. Confident he could not be seen, Cade edged around the garage corner. The house had a large picture window on the main floor and a smaller set of windows on the second story. A window overlooked the patio on the main floor in the corner of the house. No lights were on.

Cade studied the windows, looking for movement, a shadow, any sign of life. He leaned close to Rob. "It feels empty. Know what I mean?"

Rob nodded. "I'd be surprised if the killer was still here," he whispered in reply. "Which wouldn't be a good thing for the Spring woman." He self-consciously checked his pistol.

Cade's anger rose and he fought the urge to enter the home. He needed to do something. His cell phone picked that moment to vibrate in his pocket. The display told him it was dispatch. He held it up for Rob to see and ducked back behind the garage. "Dawkins."

"Cade, it's Russ Horstead. A woman's body was discovered under the bridge on 94 near the Lafayette Bridge. Someone took their time with a knife."

"Shit. Does the woman have blonde hair?" Cade asked—though he already knew the answer.

"She does. Sorry." Horstead told him the crime scene techs were on the way to the scene. Cade said he'd be there in ten minutes.

He reached around the corner and pulled on Rob's jacket. "We have to go. She's not here. A woman's body was found under a bridge on 94 near downtown St. Paul. She's blonde and had multiple knife wounds."

They sprinted down the alley and found Gralinski. Cade briefed him on the discovered woman's body. "I know SWAT still needs to clear the house, but he's gone." A dark thought came to him. "And I bet he was driving a green sedan."

Gralinski raised an eyebrow but didn't ask.

"If her body is laying under a bridge on 94, it means our killer had to drive her there. Ask yourself what would be the best way to get out of a saturation patrol targeting single male drivers."

Rob shook his head.

"I saw a green sedan being stopped, but because he had a woman passenger, I waived the trooper off. Our killer was supposed to be traveling solo."

"This guy is smart. Don't beat yourself up over this." Rob put a hand on Cade's shoulder.

Cade shrugged it off. "The passenger was a blonde and I didn't put it together. I should have seen his play coming. We'd taken away all his options, what else could he have done? I'm going to kill him when I find him."

Rob gestured toward their vehicles. "Let's get rolling. You can drive."

His eyes narrow, jaw tight and nostrils flared, Cade said, "Have dispatch clear the way. We're coming in hot." He took the corner hard at Wheelock Parkway just as the SWAT vehicle was making the turn onto Payne. "Too little, too late." The speedometer surged to over 80 miles per hour as he flew down the hill. He ran the first stop sign they encountered.

♪

WITH INTERSTATE 94 CLOSED, it was gridlock for miles around. Cade shot down the shoulder, passing the line of vehicles on the jammed 35E freeway. He slowed and went around the trooper blocking the ramp to eastbound 94. The cluster of emergency vehicles gave him a clear beacon to where Spring's body was discovered. He added his truck to the group and together they jogged to the bridge.

A State Patrol trooper stepped forward. Cade recognized her as Kelly Kirkland, a tough trooper surviving and thriving in a male dominated world. Stone-cold and single-minded when action needed to be taken, she took it without hesitation. Cade was witness to her dogged determination at the 35W bridge collapse several years back. Even with the immense scope of the disaster she never gave in to tiredness or depression. She simply did what needed doing—for 17 hours straight. "Kelly," he said and offered his hand.

"Dawkins," she replied giving him a firm handshake, nodding to Rob. "Gentlemen, I have bad news, some good news, and maybe more bad news."

Cade glanced at Rob. "Okay, let's have it then."

Kirkland led them up the incline under the bridge. A group of law enforcement officers stepped aside. Representatives from the State patrol, St. Paul police and sheriff's department were in the group, a particularly haunted look to their faces. Cade had never seen such a morose group gathered in one place. One look at the body on the cold concrete surface explained why.

The woman—blonde of course—looked to be in her late 20s. Her eyes looked horrific with broken blood vessels, the red replacing the normal white in her eyes. She wore a black coat, opened to reveal multiple cuts. Cade had to look away.

Kirkland spoke after a moment. "Her subconjunctival hemorrhaging—burst blood vessels—were caused by intense struggling. She looked to be alive for most of her ordeal." Her voice trailed off.

"I'm not sure there could possibly be good news involved in something so sickening." He looked at Rob, who wore the same haunted look as the other officers.

Kirkland led them back down the concrete embankment. "There is a witness." Her voice had a tentative quality to it.

"Really?"

"Really. Says he saw the killer carry her body and display it. However, that brings in the other bad news." She brushed back her sandy-blonde hair.

"Go on," Cade prompted.

"Our witness is a borderline homeless character. And he claims to be psychic." Kirkland folded her arms. A take-it-or-leave-it expression on her face. She pointed to the back of a Patrol squad. A man in his 30s pressed his face against the glass as he smiled and waved like they were old friends. "His name is Gordy Stensrude. And he's all yours."

"Let's see what we got." Cade opened the door.

Gordy Stensrude rolled out of the squad, falling to the ground. Lying on his back he looked up at Cade and then over to Rob. "Hey," he said. Stensrude was dressed in camo pants, fur boots, and a vivid Hawaiian shirt over a long sleeve flannel shirt. He was stocky in build, had spiked blond hair and a weathered face which showed many hard miles. Cade thought the expression, "Rode hard and put away wet," to be particularly apt in this situation.

Cade held out a hand. "Let me help you up."

Stensrude shook his head. "I'm good. I've been on my feet way too much lately."

180 | ALLAN EVANS

"Have it your way. I'm told you witnessed something involving our victim." Cade chose his words carefully, not wanting to lead Stensrude. It was always better to get the witness's own words and impressions. You never knew where it might lead.

"I guess I had the vibration something was going to happen and I thought I'd spend some time under this bridge."

"I can see why. It's a nice bridge," Rob said as he looked around wearing a surprisingly deadpan expression.

"I've seen better, I've seen worse. Anyway, I was coming here this morning..."

"You didn't sleep here?" Cade asked.

Stensrude looked irritated. He sat up and crossed his legs as he stared at Cade. "I'm not homeless. I may move around a lot, but I'm not homeless. You're being racist, dude."

"That's not being racist," Cade stood up for himself.

"Whatever. I have my own trailer home. Someday I may get a double-wide when I have a family, but for now, I'm nice and cozy the way I am. But, like last night, I often stay in motels just for the room service. You see, I have rather sophisticated tastes." He looked Cade up and down. "Not that you'd know anything about it."

Rob shook his head and covered his mouth.

"I do see a lot of homeless guys around here though. Just saw a homeless guy on Franklin Avenue yelling at his shadow yesterday. Looks like six more weeks of recession..."

Cade folded his arms. "Say, Gordy, can you tell us what you saw here? Under the bridge."

Stensrude scratched his head and kept at it for an uncomfortably long time. "It wasn't a homeless guy. He had a car."

"Did you see what color the vehicle was?" Rob asked.

Stensrude nodded. "It was a green Honda. Four doors, it had one of those parking lot security stickers on the driver's side windshield and the rear tire pressure was a bit low on the passenger side. It was a woman's car though, so he must have borrowed it."

It was Cade's turn to scratch his head. "What makes you say that?"

Stensrude smiled a smug little smile and pointed to his forehead. Cade looked over at Rob, who shrugged.

"Okay Gordy," Cade said, "tell us what you saw."

"This green Honda pulls up under the bridge and right away this guy is out. He books around the back of the car and opens the passenger door. He reaches in, unbuckles the blonde woman and pulls her out. At this point, it's obvious something's not right."

Rob asked, "How's that?"

"He pulls her from the car and drops her. Like she's something he's throwing away."

"That's probably an accurate statement," Cade said quietly.

"This guy is strong. He just bends over and picks her up, putting her over his shoulder. Like you or I would pick up a bag of wood chips. He carries her to the spot over there," gesturing toward the body. "He drops the woman like he doesn't give a shit. And then does something odd." Stensrude looks between the two investigators, clearly playing up the drama of the moment. It worked.

"What did he do?" Cade asked, even though he wasn't sure he wanted to hear the answer.

Stensrude gets to his feet with a groan, stretched and twisted his back. Both investigators could hear the cracks echo under the bridge. "You," he said to Rob, "lay down."

Rob looked at Cade.

Stensrude laughed. "I'm not going to do anything to hurt you, big guy. Just showing what the man did with her body."

Rob didn't look convinced. "Okay, but if you touch my junk, I'm going to shoot you. You've been warned." He pointed a finger at Stensrude and sat down on the concrete.

"When he dropped her, she was on her left side. Almost fetal. Do that." Stensrude gestured to Rob to lie down. With a glance up at Cade, Rob leaned back and rolled onto his side. "So, our guy gets down on his knees..."

Stensrude got on his knees and rolled Rob onto his back. He unzipped Rob's coat and opened it as much as possible. "At this point, the guy stands up and looks like he's going to leave. But then, he looks down at her for a long moment or three and brushes back her hair. The guy moves her arms and legs like he's posing a Barbie doll. What you see up there didn't happen randomly, he posed her that way." Stensrude moved Rob's limbs, lifting his arms up by his head and spreading his legs apart. Rob didn't look at all comfortable.

"When he was done," Stensrude continued, "the dude stuck his finger in her mouth. No lie. Sort of sexual if she'd been alive, but super creepy 'cause she wasn't."

"Then..." Cade prompted.

"He left. Ran down to the Honda, slammed her door shut and sped off." Stensrude shivered.

"Can you describe the man?" Rob asked as he got to his feet and zipped his coat.

"Like I said he was strong. Stocky build, like he lifts weights. He had a baseball cap, but you could tell he had short hair. Buzzed like he's in the army. Not super tall."

Cade stepped up to Stensrude. "Taller or shorter than me?"

Stensrude sized him up. "Shorter, but more muscular. He looked army like, you know: military."

"So, he didn't see you?" Cade asked.

"No man. I wouldn't be here if he had. That guy was badass."

"Where were you?" Cade gestured around the bridge. "The guy had to have looked to make sure he was alone."

"I was stealthy, dude. See those shadows over there?" Stensrude pointed to where the sloping concrete met the bridge deck. "I was hanging there."

Cade shook his head. "I have to say it strains credibility you just happened to be hanging out under a bridge in the dark on such a cold Saturday morning." He didn't say anything further, letting his words hang there. Waiting for Stensrude's response.

Stensrude looked back and forth between the two investigators.

He shrugged. "It is what it is," he offered. "Bad situation. I don't care what anyone says, it's time to put the rocks back on the moon. It's out of balance down here."

⚘

CADE'S PHONE VIBRATED. It was Capt. Rejene. "What do you have?"

"Definitely our killer. It was brutal."

"Any evidence we can use to find this guy?"

"A witness, actually."

"That's great. So, he saw the killer dump the body?"

"He did, but there's something seriously off about this witness. Not convinced he'd play well before a jury. But it's better than nothing."

"How bad could he be?"

"Let me put it this way. You know how there are people who secretly deal drugs out of ice-cream trucks? He's dressed like a drug dealer who secretly sells ice cream."

Rejene let out a snort. "Really, that bad?"

"Yeah, he's the type you see riding the bus at night wearing sunglasses. And get this: he said he could tell the killer's car had been borrowed from a woman."

A pause. "How?"

"He's psychic, I guess." Cade let out a long sigh. "I'm surprised he didn't know the license plate number."

Stensrude spoke up. "It's 3AV-071."

Cade spun toward Stensrude, who held up his hands. "You never asked."

Rejene repeated the plate number and said she would have the number run. "We may have something then. Good work."

As Cade talked strategy with Rejene, he was drawn into Stensrude's discussion with Rob. Rejene paused and Cade held up his phone so she could listen. Stensrude was talking about his motel stay. "So, there's only one channel in this motel, and in the morning while I was getting ready, I was watching Sesame Street. They were doing this bit where some clown was trying to wash his hands but kept washing his feet or his elbows and Elmo would go, 'No Mister Noodle, your HANDS!' and all the TV kids would laugh. Around the fourth or fifth time when he couldn't find his hands, I heard a grown man yell from somewhere else in the motel, 'DAMMIT, MR. NOODLE.'"

"I'm starting to understand what you mean about your witness," Rejene observed. "But if he helps, great. He can link the killer to the body. We can put Stensrude on the witness stand and he'll identify the killer—once we catch him—as the one dumping her body."

Cade, completely perplexed, watched Stensrude as he hopped on one foot and pointed up to the sky. He shook his head. "Which would perhaps sound more convincing from a person whose home featured a foundation, but sure."

"Hey, you're not going to believe this," Rejene said. "But your witness was correct. The plate came back registered to Candan Anne Spring. I'm putting the plate out metro-wide now. With all eyes searching for it, maybe we'll get lucky."

"We need some luck," Cade said looking back toward Spring's body. "And we need it soon."

THE MINUTE SWEETWATER was back in Spring's Honda, he knew time still wasn't on his side. He needed to drop this vehicle faster than a wasp after a sip of Cuban coffee. He wanted to abandon it far away from his neighborhood. Options ran through his mind, the Mall of America, maybe the airport. However, he couldn't risk the twenty-minute drive out to Bloomington. He knew it wouldn't be long before an all-points broadcast went out for Spring's Honda.

A thought came to him and Sweetwater tingled with its boldness. The Ramsey County Law enforcement center was on Grove Street, just a few blocks over. The last place anyone would look for a killer's getaway vehicle would be in the law enforcement center's parking lot. And conveniently, there would be a variety of unattended vehicles for him to choose from. Decision made, he headed north on 35E and took the first exit on Pennsylvania.

CHAPTER
29

Saturday was a complete mess. The media was all over them once the story broke. The blonde-killer, as he was now almost universally referred to, had struck again. Word of Spring's panic-stricken 911 call got out and everyone was pointing fingers. Governor Ritter showed himself to be particularly adept at deflecting unwanted attention. Over the course of the day, Ritter pointed at nearly everyone: the State Patrol, BCA, St. Paul police, media, and of course, Cade Dawkins. To quote the Governor, "I still believe Dawkins is the right man to lead this investigation. Face it, everyone screws up. It's what you do with the situation and how you handle it that's important. I'll be there, watching to make sure the investigation gets back on track." Ritter looked directly into the television camera, adjusted his $180 Salvatore Ferragamo tie, and proclaimed, "And that's why you elected me. To be accountable."

Cade was livid. "That slippery bastard is anything but accountable. I love how in the same sentence he says that I'm the right man for the job and I screwed up."

Rob shook his head. "Like Ritter is going to come anywhere near our investigation. Not a chance."

Cade paced around the shared office. "What are we going to do about it?" He punched the wall, ignoring the worried looks of the State Patrol staff. "What the hell do we do next?" His voice grew louder.

Rob stood up. He gently tugged on Cade's sleeve, leading them out of the office. "Waffles. We're going to get waffles."

"I like waffles."

Rob nodded. "I know. Everyone likes waffles."

"My mom used to make us waffles every Sunday."

Rob steered them around the maze of desks and out the door. "Mine too. Waffles make everything better. There's something about the combination of butter and syrup that makes all the bad just melt away."

THEY ENDED up at an IHOP restaurant off White Bear Avenue. Apparently well-liked by the law enforcement community, several troopers sat in an adjoining booth. They were greeted warmly, handshakes and fist bumps all around. One of the things Cade most appreciated about being in law enforcement, especially in times of stress and persecution, was how cops had each other's backs. "Sorry to hear Ritter throwing you under the bus," Mike Swanson offered. "I thought you did the best with a near impossible situation. I'd like to see Ritter do any better, the sanctimonious prick."

Cade sat back in their booth, taking a sip of decidedly average coffee. Rob leaned forward, rubbing his eyes. "I am absolutely beat. Lack of sleep is killing my brain. I'm having serious issues with stringing together coherent thoughts."

"Where do we start?" Rob stared off in the distance. "What's our next step?"

"It's time to get back to the basics. Good old-fashioned police work. Start with running down all the stops and registration checks in a two-hour window around each of the killings. Maybe we'll get something. In New York, police finally caught the Son of Sam serial killer due to a witness who'd been walking her dog when she saw a parked car being ticketed near a fire hydrant. Moments after the traffic police had left, she heard shots fired nearby. The witness stayed silent about this experience for four days until she decided to contact police, who then closely checked every car ticketed in the area that night." Cade took a sip of coffee.

"There's a rhythm to these cases," Cade continued. "Even when it looks bad—like it does today—I feel the momentum shifting. If we check back over everything, we'll find something and we'll have this guy soon. Things are coming to a head."

Rob nodded. "I hope you're right. We can't keep going like this."

The waitress dropped off matching plates of waffles. Conversation gave way to attacking their breakfasts. Both men were lost in thought, dwelling on the case.

Rob was the first to speak, with a mostly empty plate in front of him and a half-chewed bite still in his mouth. "I still don't get how the blonde-killer found these women in the first place. These aren't random killings, crimes of opportunity if you will, where he randomly came upon his victims. Whatever he does for his work must give him occasion to come into contact with these women."

Cade finished his breakfast and pushed the plate away. "And then he stalks them. He followed his earlier victims, marking their vehicles with a reflective dot, and attacked them on quiet stretches of state highways."

Rob picked his teeth with a toothpick. "And because the crimes happened on state highways, the case comes to us. Some guys get all the luck."

"Not sure I believe in luck anymore," Cade said, standing up. He grabbed Rob's check. "I've got your breakfast. Go get some sleep. I'm going to do the same. I need to get my brain functioning properly."

On the way out, they stopped by the trooper's booth. Three uniformed officers lounged over coffee as one of the troopers, Julio Roque, finished an anecdote about a traffic stop that had gone as wrong as one could. When the story was done, they all shook hands and Roque said, "This was a big day for science. He ordered chicken nuggets," nodding to the veteran trooper, "and Swanson ordered eggs. Couldn't help but wonder which would come first." He burst out laughing and the others joined in. The thing about cops is, you learn to deal with the job's pressure through humor. If you didn't, you'll be walking a mall or selling insurance within five years.

As they headed to the cashier, Cade was stopped by the older trooper who was at the next table. Cade knew the veteran trooper as Harvey but had never spoken to him.

"Dawkins, a word if you have a moment." Cade noted the man's serious expression and waved Rob to keep going.

Harvey looked to be approaching the Patrol's mandatory retirement age. His hair had mostly gone gray, but he still looked fit. Older men tended to go into one of two directions: they went soft and pudgy, the years of inactivity catching up to them, or they became lean and wiry, their body composition shifting to bone and gristle. Harvey fell into the latter camp. "What can I do for you?" Cade asked.

Harvey ran his fingers through his thinning hair. "Couldn't help but hearing you guys talk about the killer stalking those women." He paused.

"And?" Cade prompted him. He was bone tired and his patience was draining away.

"I know you haven't been with the Patrol long. There's an old highway trooper trick you may not know about. Back in the day, we'd mark a few of the regular cars at the bar and then follow them at a distance. It's how we'd get some of those hard drinkers off the road."

"How'd you mark them?" Cade was intrigued.

Harvey glanced around. "I'm not admitting anything here. But I've known some to crack a taillight. Most would put something reflective on the car so they could spot it easily. I suppose it's similar to the whiskey plates they put on repeat DWI offenders today. It made them easy to spot, and certainly helped make our arrest numbers look good."

Cade thought for a moment as he edged towards the door. His brain had that fuzzy feeling that only lack of sleep could bring. He knew it wasn't firing on all cylinders. "So, you think the blonde-killer used one of the trooper's old tricks?"

Harvey nodded.

"So?" He could hear frustration creeping into his voice.

"So, ask yourself how he knew about it. That's all."

They shook hands and Cade headed out into late morning sunshine, eager to find his bed.

ELEVEN HOURS LATER, Cade woke with a start. He glanced at the clock, seeing it was after 10 p.m. already. He shook his head and dragged himself out of bed. He padded over to his small office located off the bedroom and picked up his cell. After a moment, Capt. Rejene answered.

Without preamble, Cade said, "The killer is a cop."

Rejene's voice was slightly above a whisper. "Hold that thought. I need to move somewhere more private." The phone jostled and she came back on after several long moments. "Why do you believe the blonde-killer is a cop?"

"I've been so sleep deprived, I couldn't see it. But my brain made the connection and woke me up. I was talking with one of the veteran troopers last night, Harvey something..."

"Harvey Reed. Yeah, he's been with the Patrol since the stone age. Solid guy."

"We were discussing how the killer stalked his victims using the reflective dot so he could easily follow their vehicles from a safe distance."

"Yeah," Rejene said.

"He told me it was an old trooper technique to mark vehicles at the bar by breaking a taillight or putting something reflective on the car. Then the trooper follows from a distance and pulls them over."

"I've heard tell of troopers using that trick. Most troopers know about it, but I don't believe it's used much these days. Not on my watch anyway," Rejene growled.

"The point Reed tried to get across wasn't that cops did it, but how would this guy know about it? So, that's why I believe this guy is a cop. Or worse, a trooper."

"That would explain finding Spring's Honda at the Law Enforcement Center." She told him about how the car was found and another was taken. Not surprisingly, it was found in Spring's neighborhood.

Neither spoke for a long moment.

"I had a thought," Cade said. "Several times now, witnesses have said the killer looked military. Stensrude said our killer looked like he was in the army."

"So, we check out recent military discharges or National Guard. Not troopers." Rejene sounded frustrated.

"Let me ask a question: Have you looked at our troopers? Most have short hair, and most look like they spend their off-time pumping iron."

Rejene sighed. "In other words, they look military."

"But I don't get why Stensrude described the killer as military when the description also fits cops. He never said the killer looked like us and Rob and I both spent considerable time with him."

"The trouble is, neither of you looks like a cop, Rejene said with a chuckle. "You look more like the barista at my coffee shop. No offense. And Rob looks even less like a cop. He looks like he should be working as a pastry chef on Grand Avenue. And don't tell him I said that."

"Your secrets are safe with me, boss."

Rejene laughed. "Go talk to Stensrude again. Bring along someone who does look like a cop. Swanson, maybe. He's got the right haircut and build. See if that sparks anything in our witness."

"I have my doubts if there's much sparking in Stensrude's head. Better living through chemistry has eroded his brain beyond the point of no return."

"What else have you got going? Go see if you can jostle something loose in that crusty head."

Cade laughed and headed for the shower, hoping this would be the day they caught a break.

He reached Swanson at home. "Hey, Mike," Cade said as he climbed into his truck.

Swanson sounded wary. "Hey, Dawkins. What's going on?"

"What are you up to? I need a favor." Cade knew he was pushing his luck. If he couldn't convince Swanson on his own, he'd resort to using Rejene's name. He hoped he wouldn't need to go that far.

A pause. "It's 11:00 on a Saturday night. My girlfriend and I just finished watching our romantic comedy."

"Good, so you're free." Cade smiled to himself as he accelerated down the freeway entrance ramp. "I need you to meet me in downtown St. Paul."

"Are you nuts?" Swanson asked. "You're a single guy. What do you assume is going to happen after I gave up two hours of my life to watch a chick flick with my ultra-hot girlfriend?"

"Dessert? Maybe swing by Dairy Queen?" Cade heard Swanson snort as he signaled and moved into the other lane, wanting to get around a minivan that drifted into the center lane. He could see the woman was talking on her cell. The woman gestured animatedly as she moved into the middle of the two lanes. Cade hit his brakes and pulled in behind the minivan. "Dang, the woman in front of me is bouncing around the lane like a bowling ball hitting the bumpers at a kid's birthday party. Good chance the stick figures on her back window are her kill scores."

"Listen, Dawkins, I'd love to help, but those two hours are ones I'm never going to get back again." Cade could hear a second voice now, one that didn't sound exactly happy. "No, that's not what I meant. I really did enjoy the movie. I—"

Cade shook his head. He slowed down, wanting to put some distance between himself and the minivan.

Swanson was back on the line. "Okay, it looks like I'm available now. Where do you want to meet?" Swanson didn't sound at all happy.

They made arrangements to meet by the Union Gospel Mission in downtown Saint Paul. Cade took the Pennsylvania exit, thankful to be away from the minivan. With distracted drivers, the highways were more dangerous every day. Never a cop around when you needed one.

THE UNION GOSPEL MISSION operated a hotel of sorts for the area's homeless population. On average, the shelter's 88 emergency shelter beds were used every night, and the 140 plus transitional rooms were almost always spoken for. A hub of activity with the itinerant crowd, it was a safe bet Cade would find Gordy Stensrude at the Union Gospel Mission. He parked and walked through the lot, looking for Stensrude. From the wary looks he received, Cade knew he stuck out. He continued toward the entrance where a group of men in army coats gathered around a beefy security guard. They looked up when Cade approached.

"Looking for Gordy. You seen him tonight?" he asked.

A large black man with salt and pepper hair stepped forward. "He in trouble?"

Cade shook his head. "He witnessed a crime early this morning, so I had some follow-up questions. No big deal." Cade held his palms up and waited.

The man searched Cade's eyes and shrugged. "It's early for Gordy. He'll be here. Can I tell him who's looking for him?"

Cade smiled. "No, I'll wait. Appreciate your help though." He walked back to the lot, finding a vantage point where he could watch the entrance without being too obvious. Swanson pulled into a nearby spot and joined him.

"Thanks for coming. Your girlfriend didn't sound any too happy with you."

Swanson laughed. "Just another day. She'll get over it. That movie, though..."

Cade grinned. "You know how you can tell if it's a chick flick you're watching?"

Swanson shook his head.

"When you wake up, your girlfriend is crying."

Swanson laughed. "Too true, too true."

Cade caught a glimpse of color. He grabbed Swanson's arm. "C'mon. He's here." Stensrude's Hawaiian shirt was an orgy of color: pink, fuchsia, red, white, green and orange. The blue flannel shirt he wore underneath didn't exactly match, but Cade wasn't sure if anything would have. It must be tough to be such a slave to fashion.

Stensrude spotted him right away and stepped away from the group. "I knew I'd see you again," he said.

Cade glanced at Swanson. "Gordy here is psychic."

"No," he said. "I just figured you hadn't been exactly thorough this morning."

Cade raised his eyebrows. "Really?"

"Really. Most cops ask the same questions at least three times. You and the other guy only asked once. So, I knew you'd be back. It didn't take psychic abilities to see that." Gordy took out a well-used handkerchief and blew his nose, loudly.

Cade couldn't help but smile. "I wanted to ask you about the man you saw. You described him as muscular, and military like."

Stensrude coughed up something and spat. "Sorry dude, I have sinus issues."

Cade waved Swanson to step closer. "Hey Gordy, this is my friend, Mike."

Stensrude looked him up and down, before reaching out a hand. "Hiya, Mike."

"I like your shirt," Swanson told him with a slight grin.

Stensrude laughed, a high-decibel braying sound. "People probably think I'm doing the walk of shame every morning. It's worse, they're actually my clothes."

Swanson laughed and hooked a thumb toward Stensrude. "I like this guy," he said to Dawkins. "He's different. In a good way."

Cade stepped closer to Stensrude. "How does Mike here compare to the man you witnessed this morning? Hold on." Cade pulled out a baseball cap from his jacket and handed it to Swanson. "Put this on."

Shrugging, Swanson pulled the cap over his head.

Cade pointed to the parking lot. "Could you walk over to that Jetta and walk back? I want Gordy to see you in motion."

Both men pivoted toward the lot and watched as Swanson walked away. At the Jetta, Swanson gave a self-conscious wave and started back. Cade studied Stensrude on Swanson's journey back.

An educated observer didn't need the uniform to distinguish a cop from a regular citizen. It's the build, the haircut, the alert eyes, the swagger. Cops look like cops. However, they also look like military personnel at a superficial glance. Cade hoped to make the distinction clear for Stensrude.

"What do you think?"

"He's close, you know. The guy was darker. The hair color, the skin too. But they both have the same aura." He looked between the two men. "They have the same movement, the same kinda attitude."

"Would it surprise you if I told you Mike here is a cop?" Cade said. He looked at Stensrude for a reaction.

Stensrude folded his arms. "No. And it wouldn't surprise me if the guy I saw was either. Damn, I knew he was badass." He shook his head.

Cade put a hand on Stensrude's shoulder. "I'd appreciate you keeping this quiet. We're desperate to catch this guy and if word gets out that he's a cop, he'll disappear." Cade handed him some bills. "Why don't you go hit some of the skyway shops on me. Go enjoy yourself."

Stensrude tucked the bills into his front pants pocket. "Awesome, I love the skyway. Can't wait to spread joy and creepiness all day by smiling and staring at strangers for uncomfortably long periods of time. Life is good, my friends." He gave a little bow and ambled off toward the group of men by the mission's entrance.

"And that was Gordy Stensrude." Cade laughed as they turned and headed for their vehicles.

Cade's face turned serious as the implication of Stensrude's confirmation hit him. He knew this killer was exceptionally dangerous, but finding out he was also a cop brought it to an entirely new level. He'd have to proceed with extreme caution going forward. Clearly, his life depended on it.

CHAPTER
30

The killer plotted.

    With the stakes so insanely high, the killer's game brought together everything that mattered. Pitting his mind against a worthy adversary while satisfying his carnal desires made this a game he couldn't walk away from. Ever.

When he bested Dawkins, as Sweetwater knew he would, it would be time to leave. Sweetwater already had things in motion. An Albuquerque police detective recently had solved a series of cartel-style killings through the use of their Real Time Crime Center. Modeled after systems adopted in Chicago, New York and Boston, this state-of-the-art center allowed Albuquerque officers to look up fingerprints from the field and use FBI facial recognition software. It also allowed analysts to send intelligence from dozens of public and private databases directly to the officers in the field. A detective using this high-tech crime center would make an interesting and unusual opponent. Knowing his time in Minnesota was coming to an end, he'd already initiated his transfer request.

Sweetwater always imagined himself to be the consummate chess player. Able to easily strategize a dozen moves ahead, combined with his ability to unerringly react to his opponent's fumbling, should make him a master chess player. However, the act of sitting two feet across from someone for an hour at a time was far too intimate. It made his skin crawl to picture being so exposed to someone. He simply couldn't do it.

Watching Reynolds DeVries relate the story of yesterday's events got him thinking. Sweetwater rewatched the broadcast a dozen times, carefully studying DeVries to make sure. He was sure he saw something in her eyes when she spoke of the investigator Dawkins. Combined with the fact she wasn't speaking ill of him—despite the fact that most others were—sparked a thought in Sweetwater: there was something between the cop and the reporter. Something he could use to his advantage.

Sitting in the dark with the house completely still, the killer's mind raced with possibilities. He'd have to orchestrate the situation, but he could use DeVries to lure Dawkins into his trap. In the final moments of Dawkins' life, with the last of his warm blood flowing, the detective would see the light and know he'd been outplayed. Delicious.

And so, the killer schemed.

MORNING COFFEE IN HAND, Cade walked through the deserted Patrol headquarters and found Rob at his desk. "May have something here," Rob said as he ran his fingers through his hair. "Remember the night Stephanie Harding was murdered?" Rob's voice was breathless and Cade could sense his excitement.

"Yeah." Cade handed over Rob's coffee. "That was a bad day."

"The Patrol caught a lot of heat because Harding was allowed to leave—despite considerable evidence of intoxication—after the trooper stopped her for a DUI."

"Sully appeared to be a bit distracted by Harding's appearance." Cade laughed. "Not our finest hour."

"I can sympathize," Rob said. "God gave us men both a penis and a brain, but unfortunately not enough blood supply to run both at the same time."

"I'm guessing with you being married and all, you don't have much opportunity to run either." Cade grinned.

"I shouldn't dignify that with a response, but I will." Rob cleared his throat, pausing dramatically. "You have no idea what you're talking about. You're missing out on the carnal playground that is the marriage bedroom. Let alone the deep, soul-stirring conversations that happen between two starry-eyed lovers."

"I'm no medical professional, but it sounds like your testosterone patch might need a booster." Cade switched gears. "You were saying that Sully had our victim stopped just before her murder."

"Yeah, her body was found less than two miles up the road." Rob paused, pointing at Cade. "The thing is, Sully is a good cop. He's thorough and usually has good instincts. So, I ran his log before he stopped Harding."

"And?" Cade prompted.

"And get this: Sully ran a plate check several minutes before stopping Harding. The vehicle in question was registered to a Marlin James Sweetwater."

Cade ran the name through his head. It didn't sound familiar. "Should I know the name?"

"Sweetwater is a trooper."

"Really? Shit."

"Hang on, it gets better. He's on the Governor's protection detail. Sweetwater does advance security reconnaissance for Ritter's appearances. And guess where Governor Ritter's last appearance was?" Rob didn't wait for an answer. "The Minneapolis Athletic Club."

"Candan Spring was a personal trainer at the Minneapolis Athletic Club. Chances are, Sweetwater would have seen her during his reconnaissance." Cade shook his head. "We need to see if the other victims had crossed paths with Sweetwater and the Governor."

"If this gets out..."

"It can't." Cade paced in front of his desk. "But we both know how cops are. If you're investigating one of your own, cops will talk. If word gets back to Sweetwater, he's gone. We're too close now, we can't let it happen. We need to keep this between ourselves."

Rob leaned back in his chair. "I have an idea you're not going to like. Protocol says we should hand off the investigation if it concerns our own department. In cases such as this, the BCA is brought in to negate any possibility of impropriety or favoritism. That way, the reputation of the Minnesota State Patrol won't be tainted."

"Tainted?" Cade spat the word out as he stepped close to Rob. "Tainted? One of our own is out there killing women on our highways. And he's on the Governor's staff. We are so past tainted you can't even see it from here. This isn't damage control. This is cut off the leg to save the life."

Rob crossed his arms. "I knew you wouldn't like it."

Cade took a deep breath and willed himself to settle down. "No, it has to be just us. We need to be sure before we point fingers. We'll look for links between Sweetwater and the victims. I bet we find both the event planner and the attorney had dealings with the Governor. When the evidence is there, we grab the killer. End of story."

Rob cleared his throat. "What about Captain Rejene?"

Cade shook his head. "Uh, uh. It's just us."

CADE REACHED TOM SODERHOLM, Holly Janek's boyfriend, and arranged to meet in the West Seventh area of St. Paul. He found Soderholm on the third floor of a construction site where a large apartment complex was going up. "We're putting in all the kitchens here. Something like 450 kitchens. That's a lot of granite."

"Nice job," Cade commented as Soderholm and another man laid the center island piece. "I wanted to talk to you in person. The questions I need to ask are sensitive and it's critical you don't share the information with anyone else. Are you good with that?"

"If it helps catch Holly's killer, sure." He hooked a thumb toward the balcony. "Let's go out there and talk."

They leaned on the balcony, watching the activity of a construction crew three floors below. Cade counted seven different trucks parked outside the entrance. A panel van from a plumbing supply company turned into the lot and joined the others. He turned toward Soderholm. "As I said, this needs to remain confidential. Did Holly ever work for the Governor? I didn't find anything on the copy of Holly's schedule you gave me."

Soderholm looked at Cade, studying his face. "The Governor," he repeated. "Not exactly what I expected. But no. Holly hadn't worked for Ritter. We're not Republicans." He grinned.

The two men from the plumbing van rolled a cart of materials up the sidewalk. "Had she been to the capital or the Governor's residence for an event?"

Soderholm shook his head. "She was supposed to have Ritter at a corporate event for Ecolab though. The Ecolab Foundation hosted its annual fundraising gala several weeks before Holly's death. Holly put the event together and I guess Ritter was to stop by to rub shoulders with St. Paul's elite. However, something came up at the last minute and he never showed. So, I guess the answer is no, she never met the guy."

Cade pushed off the railing. "Thought there'd be a connection there. Damn."

Hand on the door, Soderholm paused. "You're not really suggesting Ritter killed those women, are you? It doesn't sound right —even for a Republican."

"I wasn't suggesting anything, just looking into a possible connection involving the Governor's staff. Even if it doesn't pan out, I'd appreciate you keeping this quiet."

"No problem." The men shook hands and Cade stepped out into the hallway. He paused for a moment and stuck his head back into the kitchen.

"Hey Tom, one more question: how did Holly know Ritter was supposed to make an appearance?"

Soderholm pulled off his cap and wiped his forehead. "You know, you should ask Sarey, her assistant. She would know. She runs the floral shop on Grand and Victoria. Not sure of the business name, though..." Soderholm's voice trailed off, as did his interest.

"Hey Kevin, the corner doesn't look right there." Soderholm

turned away and Cade ducked out. He maneuvered around the carpenters hanging the front door and headed for his truck. Next stop: Grand Avenue.

Sun, Stems and Vines, as it turned out, was a block off the busy Grand and Victoria shopping area. Located in a bright green Craftsman-style house, the florist shop was empty as Cade made his way through the displays. One nice thing about flower shops, they always smelled like spring. A dark-haired woman had her back to him as Cade approached. She turned around, and let out a sound, clearly startled by Cade's appearance. "Oh, sorry, I hadn't heard you come in."

Cade smiled. "No worries, I scare a lot of people. It's just a curse I have to live with."

The clerk, a pretty Asian woman in her twenties, smiled back at him. She gave him an appraising look. "Somehow I don't think you've scared off too many women. How can I help you?"

"Are you Sarey?" Cade asked.

"My day keeps getting better," she replied. "Yes, I am. And color me intrigued," she grinned.

Cade pulled out his badge case. "Tom Soderholm sent me over. I'm working on Holly Janek's murder case." The smile left Sarey's face, as her expression turned grim.

"Oh. How can I help?"

"You worked with Holly on her events, specifically the Ecolab Foundation event?"

"I did. That was a massive undertaking, with over 500 guests. Our largest event so far..." Sarey paused, as tears welled in her eyes. "I guess it will always be our largest event. Poor Holly." Her chin trembled.

Cade stepped forward, unsure how to react. Law enforcement training suggested a professional detachment in these types of situations. His brain told him to do one thing while his heart told him to do another. Maybe it was that this woman reminded him of his previous investigative partner, Daisy. Daisy was a striking woman of Asian descent who had made a bad choice and was now living in a women's correctional facility. Maybe it was the fact it was Holly's deceased body that first pulled him into this case. But either way, his heart won out. He put his arm around the petite Asian woman and pulled her close. She melted in his arms as he felt the shake of her sobs. Cade gave her time to let it out. After a few long moments, they awkwardly disengaged, the woman wiping the tears from her cheeks. She looked up a Cade, "Sorry. I thought I was past all this."

"No apologies needed," he said, putting a hand briefly on her shoulder. "When you lose someone, sometimes it can be the smallest thing bringing a rush of memories and emotion. It was that way after I lost my dad. I'd see a favorite book of his, or smell his cologne and I'd lose it. It eventually stopped, though I can't say if that's a good thing or not."

Sarey looked into his eyes. "You're an unusually sensitive guy for a cop. No offense." She gave him a little smile. "I mean it's a good thing. I appreciate your kindness."

Nodding, Cade changed the subject. "Tom said Holly had mentioned the Governor was supposed to attend the Ecolab gala. Do you know how she knew the Governor planned on attending?"

"He didn't actually make it. I remember Holly saying it was just like a Republican to stir things up with special accommodations and then not show up." Sarey shook her head with a wistful smile. "Holly and Tom were so into politics."

"What do you mean when you say stir things up with special accommodations?"

"Ritter sent over a state police officer to arrange for security precautions in the event he was mobbed by his adoring fans. Like that was ever going to happen," she added. "For over an hour, this guy had Holly lead him all through the facility, checking the kitchen, back hallways as well as each and every possible exit."

Cade struggled to maintain his composure. "I don't suppose you saw what this officer looked like?" Cade asked.

"No, I never saw him. But I can do better than a description. Hold on," she requested and stepped into the back room. She returned carrying an expandable folder and pulled out a business card, handing it to Cade. "He left this in case we needed to contact him."

Cade looked at the card. The name read, "Marlin Sweetwater, Minnesota State Patrol, Executive Protection Detail."

Got you.

CHAPTER
31

Riding up to the Lineker & Marsh law offices, Cade silently cursed the inventor of elevator music. What piece of pond scum had decided that watering down the Stones classic, "Start Me Up," would make the twenty second elevator ride more enjoyable? He jabbed the lighted 17 button again in the vain hope it would speed up his trip. Mercifully, the doors opened.

Richard Schusterman greeted him warmly. "Good to see you again, Mr. Dawkins. How can I help?"

"Could you get me into Jennifer Allard's old office? I want another look at her power wall. There's a photograph I'd like to see again."

Schusterman's face went from a smile to a frown. "I had to clear it out last week. We have a new partner starting today." He motioned Cade toward the hallway. "But I have all her photos boxed in our storage room. We don't throw away anything here. You never know when something will be needed."

Cade smiled. "That's how hoarding begins. Before long, you have twenty-year-old newspapers stacked to the ceiling in your bathroom."

"We actually have a seven-year retention policy on all documents."

"You know I was kidding, right?" Cade asked.

Schusterman laughed. "You'll have to forgive me. The legal profession has never been known for its sense of humor." He led them into a room with row upon row of shelved boxes. They turned down the fourth row and stopped halfway. "Here are the boxes from Jennifer's office."

They took out each of the boxes, pulling the covers to look over the contents. Three of the boxes contained the framed photos Cade was looking for. Sitting on the floor, he pulled each out, examined it, and stacking it next to the box. Jennifer Allard sure liked to have her picture taken. Toward the bottom of the first box, he found the picture he had come for. Allard, wearing a conservative business suit, was posed next to a smiling Governor Ritter. A number of people were scattered around the background, but Cade couldn't recognize the setting. He handed the photo to Schusterman. "Do you know anything about this picture? Specifically, where and when it was taken?"

Schusterman nodded. "This was taken this year, maybe a little less than a month before Jennifer's death. She was part of a roundtable discussion on women's issues. The governor was there, as well as several prominent senators and congresswoman Betty McCollum. It was held at the Woman's Club of Minneapolis near Loring Park." He handed the photograph back, a frown clouding his face. "And you believe this event is connected to Jennifer's death?"

"There's a remote possibility, however I need to request your discretion on this." He stacked the frames back in the boxes and stood up. "Can I hang onto this photo?"

Schusterman opened the storage room door. "No problem. Since she didn't have any family, it won't be missed. I just hope it helps."

Cade shook his hand. "Me too." Cade looked around. "Where are the stairs?"

Schusterman looked confused. "The stairs? We're on the 17th floor."

Cade shrugged. "I have a thing about elevator music."

Laughing, Schusterman pointed across the hall.

◆

"I HAVE SOMETHING." Rob's excitement was evident in his voice when he picked up Cade's call. "Stephanie Harding worked as a sales rep for Medtronic, selling an implantable medical device for chronic back pain. Well, it turns out Ritter has had back issues for years and had one of these devices implanted in January. It worked so well, he visited the Neuro division a month ago to meet all the people responsible. Apparently, they made a big deal of it. Brought in food, had all the senior executives there for speeches and gave out special bonuses for each and every Neuro employee." Cade heard the sound of shuffling paper. "Since she started with Medtronic in January, Stephanie Harding would have been there."

"That sounds like a promising connection."

"If Ritter planned to make an appearance, he would have had his protection detail do an advance sweep. We can't say for certain it was Sweetwater, however. I'm sure we can pull the duty logs and confirm it was him."

Cade swung his truck around a slow-moving sedan and turned onto Robert Street. "We may not have to. I was able to put Jennifer Allard at the governor's appearance at the Woman's Club of Minneapolis in January."

"Nice work," Rob commented.

"It gets better," Cade said as he hit the entrance ramp to 35E. The FJ Cruiser made a satisfying roar as it sped down the ramp. "Holly Janek planned an event where the governor was supposed to attend. The fact that Ritter never actually made it there only helps us. The advance security reconnaissance trooper left his business card. It was Marlin Sweetwater."

"Now we're talking," Rob's enthusiasm came through loud and clear. "That links him with four of our victims. Allard, Janek, Harding and Spring."

Cade passed the Roselawn exit as he headed up 35E. "Hang on, I know we said Ellie Winters was so high profile, most everyone knew what she looked like. But have you found a link there? Had she crossed paths with the governor?"

"While she worked events, they were never the same ones as Ritter. She was at promotional events, while he would be at fundraisers and causes. No, they lived in different worlds. Winters was all about the nightlife, working a lot of promotions at the clubs in downtown Minneapolis and some of the larger suburban ones."

Cade laughed. "No, I doubt Ritter frequented the dance clubs."

Rob cleared his throat. "What about your girlfriend? The killer reached out to her as well."

As he took the looping expanse of ramp onto eastbound 694, Cade pondered the question. "She's even more high-profile than Winters being on camera every night. It's obvious she fits his profile. But yes, she would have many opportunities to cross paths with Ritter and his security detail."

"We have enough to bring to Capt. Rejene. We should read her in." Rob said.

"I'm five minutes out. Let's discuss it when I get there." Feeling the urgency, Cade darted past a cluster of vehicles merging onto 694. His speedometer climbed above 80 mph. Each second ticking on the clock brought them closer to the case's conclusion.

REYNOLDS DEVRIES WAS RUNNING LATE for her afternoon yoga class. Again. The one nice part about working later hours was the flexibility to hit the gym early and avoid the crowds. Keeping in shape was an important component of her daily regimen. Unless you were at the absolute top of the news business, women were always held to ridiculous standards of appearance. It wasn't a level playing field for men and women. Men seemed to be given a pass as they aged, while women were often pushed out of the top spots when they begin to show signs of aging. Of course, the wave of high definition television screens had changed everything—but not in a good way. Reynolds read about television actresses in their forties who often had in their contracts that they were to be shot slightly out of focus. So, wanting to be proactive, yoga class was on Reynolds' schedule.

Grabbing her keys, she stepped out into the warm spring air. Reynolds pulled her door shut, locked it and turned around.

The Taser hit her hard. Intense pain joined an alarming mix of muscle spasms, confusion and involuntary movement as she lost all control of muscle function. When the five seconds of electrical charge was over, the killer lifted Reynolds to her feet. "If you fight me or scream," he hissed into her ear, "I'll shock you again."

Reynolds was beyond panic. Each of the five seconds felt like ten minutes as the electricity coursed through her. It was like hundreds of plastic baseball bats were hitting her in the back thirty times a second. She would do almost anything to avoid a repeat episode. "No, please no," she pleaded.

The killer propelled her forward, a dark green minivan with an open side door in front of her. "The barbs are still in, so cooperate or be shocked. Your choice." It was no choice really, and Reynolds climbed into the rear seat, feeling the soreness of each and every one of her muscles. She was used to thinking on her feet—being a broadcast journalist taught some important life skills after all—however being zapped and trapped by a serial killer was beyond her current coping skills.

CHAPTER
32

C ade ushered Rob into Capt. Rejene's office and pushed the door shut. Her eyes darted between them. "You have him. Tell me you have him."

Cade nodded.

"Thank God," Rejene announced as she slammed a fist on her desk. "Our nuts have been in a vice."

Rob leaned close to Cade. "Our boss has nuts," he whispered. Cade shook his head.

Rejene looked at Cade. "Who is it?"

Clearing his throat, Cade glanced at Rob. "There's good news. And bad news."

"Give me the bad first." Her brown eyes looked at him impatiently.

Cade sat in the chair across from Rejene. "He's State Patrol. Name is Marlin James Sweetwater."

"We are so screwed," she said shaking her head. "Yet, you say there's good news?"

"Sweetwater's on Governor Ritter's staff. Executive Protection Detail."

A hint of a smirk colored Rejene's face. "This is good. I can work with that." She leaned back and folded her hands behind her head. "This is the kind of leverage that will save our butts."

Cade ran Rejene through the connections tying Sweetwater to each of the victims. For her part, Rejene listened and jotted notes as he spoke. Her phone rang several times while they talked, but she ignored it and focused on the evidence trail Cade laid out for her.

"What should our next step be?" she asked. "We can grab him now or get in front of a judge first to get a search warrant to look for evidence of his crimes."

Cade nodded. "He'll have souvenirs. Research shows this type of pattern killer often takes something from each victim. Something of use to embellish their mental reliving of their kills. I'd put the odds pretty damn high Sweetwater has a stash of mementos hidden away. It may not be at his residence, but he has it somewhere nearby. Maybe a storage locker or a bolt-hole."

"Bolt-hole?" Rejene asked.

"A place where the killer can get to quickly to hide out if his plans go south on him. Serial killers are extremely cautious and their instincts for self-preservation are unparalleled. He'll have someplace set up to hide and buy time should he need it."

Rob spoke up. "Either way, we need to get Sweetwater under surveillance right now. We can't have him skipping on us."

Rejene spun around and got on her computer. "I'm going to pull his state employment file. We'll get his personal history, work records and posting schedule."

Rob looked surprised. "You can get that?"

"You bet your sweet ass I can. You don't work your way up through the ranks without making some well-placed friends and learning a few of their best tricks," she boasted. Cade caught her smug smile and decided his opinion of her ticked up several notches.

Cade learned early in his law enforcement career that his new world wasn't nearly as black and white as he'd expected it to be. Cops survived and thrived by living within the copious shades of gray. It was a matter of looking at the greater good, the result you were reaching for, and then deciding just how far you were willing to go for the result.

The critical point was the line, however. There is a line—albeit a moving one—that you don't cross. Honoring your badge meant staying on the right side of the line. Over the years, Cade knew the line well because he'd treaded close enough to smell the actual line.

Rob moved behind the desk, joining Rejene at the computer. "He lives in the Frogtown area," Rob pointed out. Frogtown was the name given the St. Paul neighborhood surrounding University Avenue to the west of the capital. "Geographically, that fits with the murders."

"You mentioned work history," Cade asked. Rejene looked up from the screen and nodded. "How long has he been with the patrol?"

The light from the screen lit up Rejene's dark eyes as she studied the display. "It looks like he's been with the state for about five months. Transferred in mid-November."

"Transferred?" Rob quizzed. "From where?"

Cade leaned back in his chair and stretched. "Chicago. Chicago PD."

Rejene ran her finger down the display. "Yeah. Chicago police. Sweetwater was with them for six years. He worked as a patrol officer and promoted to field training officer after four years on the job." She looked up at Cade.

"The Chicago detective, Martinson, was the final victim of a series of murders in Chicago last year. A tip from an anonymous patrol officer had set him up."

Rejene nodded grimly. "So, this is our guy."

Rob cleared his throat. "Boss, look at this."

Rejene leaned over. "Crap. He's put in for another transfer. To Albuquerque."

"He's started his exit strategy," Rob said. "We need to get a team on him ASAP."

"His duty roster shows him off both today and tomorrow. We'll have to catch him at home." Rejene tucked some loose strands of hair behind her ear. She glanced up; her face wore the sort of expression the Titanic captain would've had after realizing the ship could actually sink. "We can't lose this guy."

"There's something you both are forgetting," Cade offered as he leaned forward. "Maybe Sweetwater isn't ready to skip town quite yet. He hasn't made his big play."

Rejene moved around to the front of her desk. She folded her arms. "What big play?"

"You have to think like him. This is a game for Sweetwater. The entire run of kills and tips to Reynolds DeVries was designed to pull the Patrol in. To pull me in."

"Why you?" Rejene prompted. "No offense."

Cade grinned. "None taken. "These killers are all about patterns. The first kill may not be perfectly choreographed. But, inspired by the intense satisfaction the killing produces, he starts to plan each one out in earnest. Killings become a pattern the killer can't depart from. As he perfects his trade, his future victims may increasingly undergo a more torturous, orchestrated, even ritualistic death."

"Patterns. Got it." Rejene shrugged.

"It's all about the patterns. Look at Martinson. He was widely recognized as a genius for his breaking the Syrian terrorist case. Lots of media attention for solving the biggest case Chicago had seen since Capone. Martinson was a star. And he was absolutely brutalized in a public display by the killer. After that, the killer killed no more."

"In Chicago, anyway," Rob added.

"Exactly. He moves north, establishes a pattern even a blind detective couldn't miss, and makes damn sure I'm involved. No bragging, but I received a lot of media attention for bringing down Bishop. They promoted me as the poster boy for smart law enforcement. No way Sweetwater would have missed the story in nearby Chicago. So, now he's up here killing again—and the bastard actually called to taunt me. Without a doubt, I will be his final target."

"Okay," Rejene paused. "We're going to be cautious with this. This has to be a tight group; no word can leak out. If either the media or Sweetwater gets wind of our surveillance, he's gone and we're screwed. We'll all be riding Segways at the mall chasing shoplifters."

Rob shook his head. "I don't like this. Cops like to talk."

"The Patrol doesn't," Rejene replied. "Really. When the feds want to close a bank, why do you think they use the Patrol? They need absolute confidentiality or there's a run on the bank. We can put troopers in place without a single word leaking. Ever." She looked between the two investigators. "Okay, you two head for Sweetwater's neighborhood and establish his location. I'll put together a team and get them rolling in your direction."

Rob stepped out from behind Rejene's desk. "Got it. Let's roll," he said to Cade.

They walked out the front entrance, headed for their vehicles. "I'm going to catch up with you," Cade said. "Now that we know more about our killer, I want to reconnect with my BCA forensics contact. Grace can help me get into his head, maybe figure out his endgame.

CADE FOUND her in the BCA crime lab where she spent most of her days. When she wasn't on scene, Grace was a lab rat of the highest order. Before Cade left the BCA, he'd often physically drag her out of the building, telling her he was medically concerned about her lack of vitamin D. Together, they'd taken daily walks to nearby Lake Phalen and discussed life.

"Hey, Grace," he announced as he pushed through the door. "Time to get outside and play." She looked up from a stack of papers and grinned.

"Everyone needs a little sunshine in their lives. Especially someone who looks at crime scene evidence all day," he said offering his arm. "Now, let's go chat about serial killers."

Grace batted her eyes. "How can a girl refuse such a fine offer?"

They'd just rounded the corner of the building when the rumble of thunder broke the late afternoon calm. Cade stuck out his hand, palm up, in the near universal gesture of checking for rain. "This might be a short walk."

"You are such a wuss," she teased. "A little rain won't hurt."

Of course, it wasn't a little rain. A flash of lightning and a roll of thunder were followed by a torrent of rain. Grace let out a squeal and grabbed Cade's hand, pulling him toward the loading dock area at the back of the building. They jumped up on the platform and leaned against the brick wall, protected by the overhang. The rain came down in sheets, the visibility reduced to a dozen feet.

Cade glanced at Grace, as they stood shoulder to shoulder, a drop of water hung precariously from her nose. "I have to work on my timing."

"My sentiment exactly," she offered. She laughed and Cade joined in.

"So, let's talk about our killer," he suggested after a moment.

"Go ahead, it's your party."

Cade ran his fingers through his wet hair. "We know who the killer is." Grace's eyes widened, but she remained silent. "He's in law enforcement, which means he knows our protocols and procedures. As if he wasn't already dangerous."

Grace nodded. "Extremely dangerous."

"What I need to know is what this guy is capable of doing. What lengths he'll go to achieve his objective."

"By objective, you mean killing blonde women," she said.

"There's more to it with him. This entire thing is a game to him and I'm the ultimate prize. That's what happened down in Chicago. He built a pattern of murdered waitresses and lured the prominent lead investigator into a trap. Eviscerated him on the hood of his car. Now, he's moved here and began again. I need to get into his head to stop him."

"You shouldn't discount his targeting blonde women though. I'd bet there's more to it than simply providing an easily discovered pattern."

"You mean somewhere in his past, there's a blonde who done him wrong?" Cade asked.

"Don't make the mistake of ignoring his triggers. You might be able to use this," Grace replied.

"That's good, Cade nodded. "I know these killers are not wired like the rest of us. Help me to understand this guy."

Grace shivered, as she paused. "The truth about the people who commit serial murder is both scary and eye opening. Evil is alive and well in these killers. They are likely to have come from broken homes and have been abused or neglected. Most are shy and introverted. Yet, others are gregarious and outgoing. But they feel almost universally isolated from the world. Often, serial killers exhibit three behaviors in childhood known as the MacDonald triad: bed wetting, arson and cruelty to animals."

"I've heard that, especially the cruelty to animals part." Cade glanced up at the dark clouds swirling overhead. A flash of lightning danced across the sky. "Torturing and killing small animals is how it begins."

Grace nodded. "We're dealing with a mature killer here. His needs escalate as the intervals between kills shrink. He can achieve satisfaction through the reliving of previous killings, however, the mounting hunger he has for real-life violence against a real-life captive can be contained for only so long. His need is driving him. Whether it's a game or not, he will need to kill again soon. At the conclusion, I'd expect him to make a big play to draw you in. His meticulously prepared killing scheme will have a variety of contingency plans designed to snare his victim: you."

"Great," Cade growled.

"The price of popularity. You didn't have to be so good at your job."

Cade grinned. "Somebody has to."

Cade's cell buzzed. The display read Reynolds DeVries.

CHAPTER
33

The stench of decay assaulted her senses, making her eyes water, making it hard to breathe. Reynolds was dragged and chained to a roughly hewn post in the corner of the bleak building, far from the door. The iron manacle around her ankle bit into her skin, but she was otherwise unhurt.

Her captor had driven them out of town, headed east on Highway 36 until houses gave way to farmland. Not a word was exchanged for the entire trip. At a stoplight, with cars nearby, Reynolds gauged her chances of escape. The man simply held up the Taser and any hope she had disappeared. They eventually turned off the highway and soon traversed a rutted dirt road. When they pulled up alongside a large outbuilding, he got out long enough to swing open the doors before driving inside. Nothing about the road or the dilapidated structure suggested anyone had been there in decades.

Time meant little as the afternoon sun waned and the rumble of thunder heralded a change of weather. Soon, the rain attacked the metal roof, and Reynolds was forced further into the corner by the persistent leaks that followed her as she shifted position. After he first chained her to the post, the man moved around the building for nearly an hour tucking away various sharp objects around the structure. To Reynolds, it looked like the entire building was to be a trap, and the killer wanted to have as many weapons at hand as possible.

She knew who the intended victim would be.

Glancing up, she was startled to find her captor mere feet away. He was unnaturally quiet in his approach and she hadn't heard him, not having any idea how long he'd stood there. She held the man's gaze as she fought the urge to look away. He seemed normal enough: muscular, clean cut, professional in his neatly pressed patrol uniform. There weren't any scars, piercings, or neck tattoos. Nothing that marked him as a monster. That was, until she looked at his eyes.

As a reporter, she'd learned to study a person's eyes because they told you a lot about what they're thinking. Not this one. His eyes gave away nothing, but took away everything—all her plans, all her dreams, and all her hope. It was at that exact moment she knew she'd die today.

He knelt down, undoing the clasp on her manacle. She tried to pull her leg away, but his hand shot out and his fingers locked onto her ankle. Each finger dug into her leg, pressing muscle, tendons and nerves until she gasped from the pain. He didn't say a word, as he dragged her across the dirt floor, his rigid fingers never loosening their grip. Abruptly, he squatted and effortlessly hefted her up and tossed her onto a weathered wooden table. Landing hard on her back, she panicked as she tried to get a breath.

The man worked quickly as he secured her to the table with bungee cords. Reynolds, now in full desperation mode, flung her head from side to side as she scanned her surroundings. Knives of varying sizes were spread around the sides of the table, as well as rope and more bungee cords, and an assortment of farming tools. Something about the sickle with its sharp, curved blade terrified her far more than the other tools.

Looming over her, the man paused to glance at his watch and spoke his first words since the minivan. "Looks like we have a few minutes to play," he murmured as he began to unbutton his shirt.

⚔

THE VOICE on the phone was not Reynolds'. Cade's stomach dropped and his face burned. His fight-or-flight instinct was engaged as he grabbed Grace's sleeve and put the call on speaker. "What did you say?"

A pause. "I have her."

Cade's eyes locked onto Grace's. "You have her?" he questioned.

"We've had some playtime." The smirk in Sweetwater's voice was maddening. "I've enjoyed getting to know her, every inch of her tight body."

Cade's blood pounded, his anger rising. "If you—."

"Don't presume to threaten me," the killer hissed. "I'm smarter than you'll ever be," Sweetwater bragged. "You don't realize it yet. You will, though." He laughed a horrible joyless sound. "But don't you worry, Miss DeVries and I have much more to accomplish. She is very much alive." The phone jostled, and a soul-wrenching cry overwhelmed the phone's tiny speaker.

Agitated and afraid for Reynolds' life, Cade looked to Grace for help. She shook her head as tears ran down her cheeks. Cade summoned as much strength as he could and asked the one question he could think of. "What do you want from me?"

"You have a chance to save your fine little blonde girlfriend. But first, you have to pass a modest test I have set up for you. Do that and you both survive."

"And if I don't pass the test?" Cade knew the answer before he finished the question.

"Her blood will be on your hands."

Cade searched Grace's gaze, looking for a way out. She moved her hand in a keep-him-talking gesture. "Where do we go from here?"

"Get your ass moving on Highway 36 toward Lake Elmo. You need to be here within twenty minutes. I'll text you the turns. And Dawkins, I'm more connected than you could possibly guess. Contact any branch of law enforcement and I'll know. We need to keep this simple. Just you and me, so I want you to come in exposed. No shirt or shoes. If I spot a weapon, she's done. You disobey me and your blonde is sliced and diced. And I'm in the wind."

The line went dead.

Grace had her cell out, a focused look on her face. "I can get everyone moving in that direction. That way backup is close."

Cade closed his hand around hers, sliding the phone from her fingers. She glanced at him, clearly puzzled. "He's not going to know."

"What if he does? What if he sees our squads? If I were him, I'd be in position to see if I brought help. He'll keep me waiting while he ensures there's no backup. He has our radio, and he will be listening." Cade headed for his truck.

"Wait," Grace called.

He turned on her. "Grace, I can't take the chance. I really can't."

Stepping close, she held his gaze. "I agree with you. But let's not give him all the cards. I need a minute to grab something." Not waiting for his answer, she turned and raced for the BCA entrance.

CHAPTER
34

C ade was in a flat-out sprint, flying down Highway 36, the other vehicles slow-moving masses as he maneuvered around them. At the Hadley stoplight he moved onto the shoulder to get around a particularly slow pickup truck. The moon-faced driver held up his middle finger as Cade went past. The rules of the road could wait until everyone was safe. Speed was Cade's priority.

As he flew past the exit north of the interstate, Cade's cell chirped with an incoming text. *Left on Lake Elmo Avenue.* He didn't know much about the stretch of road west of 36, other than it was dotted with farms. He remembered seeing not only endless rows of corn, but cows and sheep along the two-lane country road. After cresting a hill, he could see his turn up ahead. A car waited ahead of him in the left turn lane. He slid in behind it as the light changed to green.

As he made the turn, Cade scanned the area around the intersection looking for an observer. "Where the hell are you?" he asked loudly, slapping the dash in frustration. *This is where I'd be.* If he could corner Sweetwater here, away from Reynolds, the risk would be much less. But if he was here, Sweetwater was well-hidden.

After making the left turn onto Lake Elmo Avenue, his cell chirped to announce another text had arrived. *Pull over and wait.*

Cade swung the Toyota to the shoulder and checked his rearview mirror. No one behind. The pickup he'd followed from the intersection continued on, oblivious to the unfolding drama around him. Such was the nature of life. Events of great magnitude could be happening right next to you, and you may never know. The neighbor you wave to each morning could be quietly suffering. It may not be something as dramatic as having your girlfriend kidnapped by a deranged serial killer, but a loved one with cancer could be just as devastating.

Cade ruminated on this for several long minutes as he tried to contain his mounting agitation. He picked up his cell, desperate to at least text Rob and clue him in. He jumped when the cell chirped in his hand. *Proceed,* was the brief message. It was followed by, *Right turn at the yellow flag.*

He put the truck in gear and slung gravel behind him as he sped for the top of the hill. After cresting, he saw the yellow flag next to a neglected dirt road. He pulled over briefly by the wooded area and glanced at his watch. It was 7:52 p.m. and the sun was going down. He hoped it wasn't a metaphor for his and Reynolds' lives.

Cade turned at the flag. The ride was rough as he steered around the deep holes and the exposed rocks that comprised the desolate road. Large boulders blocked the road after Cade rounded a curve. Cutting the engine, Cade stepped out into the damp evening air. On his left were the remains of a farmhouse, long ago burned to the ground. It looked as if the farm hadn't seen life since Reagan was in the White House.

As directed, Cade stripped off his shirt, kicked off his shoes and slipped off his socks. Leaving the relative safety of the truck, Cade moved past the boulders toward the single metallic outbuilding ahead. Seeing a flicker of light from the interior, he knew this was his destination. Without a doubt, this was a trap. But Sweetwater wouldn't try to take him with a rifle, instead he'd want the killing to be close and personal. Sweetwater would choose something sharp for his coup de grace, something to make him bleed and suffer. This was personal—for both of them.

Instinctively, Cade reached for the comfort of his pistol and remembered he'd left it in the truck as instructed. No second gun in an ankle holster, either. He stepped up to the large door and paused, feeling naked and exposed. He pushed the door open. Let's get this over with.

⚊⚊

OPENING WITH A CREAK, the door swung on its hinges and slapped up against the wall. So much for a quiet entrance. Cade took a step inside and waited for his eyes to adjust to the dim light. A dozen candles flickered around the structure leaving pockets of light in the otherwise dark space. The brightest spot was lit by a gas lantern across the way. A large wooden table held both the lamp and Cade's attention. It took a moment for his brain to register what his eyes were seeing. Reynolds was on the table, lying motionless.

Cade knew this was when the trap would be sprung. The moment he went to Reynolds, Sweetwater would be there. He knew this, yet he couldn't not go. A large part of why he became a cop was because the protector instinct was hard-wired into his DNA. He would always watch over the weak. He ran to her.

Reynolds was covered in blood. Cade couldn't tell where the source was, there was so much. Her clothes were in tatters and she was strapped to the table. Even though she was gagged, her eyes were trying to tell something.

He reached over and swept the blood-streaked hair from her face. Reynolds eyes kept flicking to the side.

Her warning and his flinch saved him when he heard the sound of the blade cutting through the air. If he hadn't moved, Cade would have lost his arm. Sweetwater stood in front of him, shirtless and marked with what looked like war paint, a matching pair of sickles in his hands. The man was ripped with muscle, outweighing Cade by a good thirty pounds. His dark eyes were fixed on Cade, streaks of red around the killer's eye sockets. It was a terrifying visage, especially when he realized it was Reynolds' blood Sweetwater had adorned himself with.

The killer took a step forward and Cade sidestepped, wanting to offer the smallest possible target. Sweetwater's breathing sounded like animalistic grunts, and his eyes never wavered from his prey. He took another step toward Cade.

The attack was vicious and sudden. Recognizing when your opponent tensed up before he struck was one thing, getting out of the way was another thing altogether. Cade saw Sweetwater shift his weight as he lashed out with the right sickle, followed by the left. Cade spun to his left, twisting away from the first blade, the second nicking the back of his neck. Cade reached a hand back, touching the cut. A smear of warm blood appeared on his fingers, but the wound not life-threatening.

Sweetwater stared at him as a malevolent smile played across his face. "Just getting warmed up," he hissed. "I'm going to bleed you." The cord of muscles in Sweetwater's jaw twitched. Cade sized up the killer. To say there was more animal in him than human would be unfair to animals. However damaged, a human psyche had to be buried in there somewhere. That would be where his weakness lay.

Cade spotted a six-inch blade with a wooden handle on the edge of the table. He grabbed it and held it in front of him. He knew there were two outcomes in most knife fights, one fighter goes to the hospital while the other goes to the morgue.

The look on Sweetwater's face conveyed little concern about Cade's chances with the knife. No matter, the weapon was simply a delaying tactic.

The trouble was, Sweetwater wasn't going to be delayed.

He lunged at Cade, the twin blades cutting through the air. The man was a whirlwind, his quick movements forcing Cade to step back to avoid the blades. Cade's defensive training taught him to anticipate the attacker's strike and when to counter. When the moment arrived, Cade brought the knife up, going for the soft tissue area above Sweetwater's elbow. However, his counter attack appeared to be expected and the blade clanged against the steel of a sickle.

Sweetwater paused, wearing a grin which looked like it would be more at home on a hyena. It was at that precise moment that Cade realized he was in way over his head. Physically, he was no match for the killer.

And then things changed.

"Marlin."

Sweetwater's head whipped around. His grin disappeared as he took in the blonde woman standing at the shadowy entrance. She wore a form fitting skirt and blouse, much the same as his victims. He lowered the blades.

"Marlin," the woman repeated as she took several steps toward him. "What do you think you're doing?"

Sweetwater said nothing, but he pulled his hands behind him, looking as if he wanted to hide the sickles. Cade took the opportunity to move away from him.

"Marlin!" the woman shrieked, moving forward. "You are such a disappointment. Your constant bed wetting disgusts me. How can you live with yourself?" Sweetwater hesitated and took several steps backward.

Cade moved to his left, putting more space between him and the killer. He knew time was running out. Fast.

"How could you hurt those poor animals?" she demanded. "Doesn't it ever disturb you to torture, maim and murder those small, defenseless creatures?" She made a show of wiping her eyes.

Cade glanced over at Sweetwater. The man stood still, absolutely rigid. His mouth hung open a little.

"And the fires. Always burning things." The blonde woman jabbed her finger at Sweetwater as she took another step forward, pushing her perceived advantage. "You've always been a disappointment, Marlin. Do you know that?"

Cade flicked his eyes between the two. It intrigued him that Sweetwater retreated every time Grace stepped forward. There had to be some remnant of human psyche inside Sweetwater's twisted mind. Grace was correct after all. When they discussed Sweetwater, she'd pointed out that even though the pattern was designed to draw him in, it still had to mean something. A blonde woman had to have had a major impact on his life. "If I had to speculate," she'd said, "it would be his mother. No one can mess with your head like a mother," she insisted.

After Cade received the call from Sweetwater, Grace had wanted to grab something from her office. She returned with a gym bag and insisted on climbing into the rear seat of the truck. "I can help," she'd argued. "No one can get into his head like I can." On the way over, she proposed a plan. "This might be our only way to save Reynolds. Otherwise, it's getting ugly. You go in first, and I will make an entrance that should mess him up bad. I'm going to become his worst nightmare: his mother. I have a change of clothes to fit the bill. No peeking," she declared as she pulled up her shirt.

As Cade rocketed down Highway 36, he'd catch an occasional glimpse in his rearview mirror as Grace transformed herself. First, it was a form fitting silk blouse, followed by a diminutive black skirt. Caught in a line of traffic at a stoplight, Cade glanced over his shoulder. She turned sideways in the seat as she slipped on a pair of black heels. Gone was the slightly shy lab nerd he'd known for the last few years.

"Grace," he began.

"I had plans after work. You didn't think I'd wear my work clothes, did you?" She reached into her bag and pulled out a blonde wig. She leaned forward and studied her reflection as she pulled on the wig and tucked her hair underneath. She glanced at Cade. "I can be whoever I want to be when I go out. Don't judge."

That was the last words they'd spoken before he left with a quick, "Good luck."

Now, Grace stood in front of the serial killer, using nothing but her wits to take him down. And she was playing him perfectly.

Like most of life, every moment can be ephemeral. Life can be a series of ups and downs, with change being the only constant. Disasters can be short lived. However, success can be just as fleeting. Sweetwater took a step toward Grace and said, "I never started fires."

The sickles were no longer hidden behind his back and menace radiated from his eyes.

Sweetwater took another step toward Grace.

"This is over, Marlin," Cade announced as he closed the distance to Grace. He tossed the knife toward Sweetwater, wanting to distract him. The lob wasn't meant to be an attack and Sweetwater stepped back, easily avoiding the knife. Cade put a reassuring hand on Grace's back as he stared down the killer. "We are going to put you in a cage. Where you belong."

Things happened fast after that. Sweetwater let out an animalistic howl and lunged at them, blades swinging. Cade slipped his hand down, grabbing the Glock tucked into Grace's waistband. They both dove, desperate to avoid the sickles. Cade rolled on the floor and leveled the pistol as he looked Sweetwater right in the eye. "Didn't anyone ever tell you not to bring a knife to a gunfight?"

Shock registered on Sweetwater's face as Cade squeezed the trigger until the clip emptied and would fire no more.

Ears ringing, he let the pistol slip from his fingers and rolled to face Grace. She thrashed and let out a scream between clenched teeth. Cade was at her side in an instant, yet his mind told him he was too late. Blood covered her fingers as it coursed out of a long gash from her knee to the hem of her short skirt, her artery pumping out copious amounts of fluid. "Give me your belt," she directed.

Cade had never felt so torn, but he whipped his belt off and offered it, eyes flicking towards Reynolds. Grace pulled the belt from his hands and worked to get it around her leg. "You need to help Reynolds. Go."

He went to Reynolds, fearing the worst. There was so much blood.

CHAPTER
35

I t was difficult to leave Grace, but Cade knew Reynolds needed immediate medical attention as well. After a quick check on Reynolds to see she wasn't bleeding out, he sprinted out to his truck for his cell, calling 911 to get the paramedics rolling. Cade suspected he was in shock as he talked to the emergency operator. He heard his voice, sounding far removed, as he pleaded for them to hurry. It felt like an out-of-body experience.

Rob was patched into the call right after that. Hearing his partner on the phone brought him back a little. Rob's voice was a blend of anger and frustration. "We can't find the bastard. He hasn't shown up at his house or his work. It's like he's gone off the grid."

Cade found his voice. "I killed him."

A momentary pause, and then Rob barked, "What? You did what?"

"I put him down. He's dead."

No pause this time. "Cade, give me something here. What happened?"

Leaning against the FJ Cruiser's front bumper, Cade ran a shaky hand through his hair. A siren could be heard off in the distance. "He took Reynolds and sliced her bad. He cut Grace too. I'm wearing half of her blood."

"Holy shit. Where are you?"

"Lake Elmo, not far from Stillwater." He gave Rob the address. There were numerous sirens now and they were getting louder.

"I can hear the paramedics coming." Cade felt tired, so incredibly tired as he struggled to stay on his feet.

"It's not just the paramedics, brother."

"Who else is coming?" Cade asked, his voice sounding oddly thick in his own ears. The sirens were getting close, approaching from multiple directions.

"Everyone," Rob reassured him. "Just hang on."

The sirens were upon him when his legs gave out.

*

AFTER THAT, a blur of images: a light shining in his eyes, an oxygen mask, Rob's overtly concerned face, a doctor—or possibly a nurse—leaning over him, Rejene's hand on his as a tear made its way down her cheek, and finally a white ceiling with mounted lights.

*

CADE BECAME AWARE.

His eyes were open and his brain caught onto the fact it was receiving stimuli again. His eyes focused and Rob stared back at him. Rob wore an expression of a man who wasn't sure if someone can see him through an interrogation room two-way mirror. He waved a hand in front of Cade's face.

"I'm here, partner. I'm here," Cade croaked. His throat felt impossibly dry and he reached for a cup of water from the side table. Rob handed it to him and Cade gulped it down. "How long have I been here?" he asked.

"Just a day. But to be honest I was worried. You wouldn't wake up." Concern shone in his friend's eyes. "Even though your wounds weren't that bad, the doctors said you'd been through so much..." He paused, letting the words sit there.

A flood of memories hit him hard and he sat up. "The girls. It was bad." Cade held Rob's gaze. "I tried to stop the bleeding. But he sliced Grace's artery."

Rob moved closer, putting a comforting hand on Cade's. "I am so sorry. That had to be incredibly rough, but your belt saved her life."

"She was so brave. Grace insisted on coming along when I got the call from Sweetwater. We both knew it was a trap, but she said we had no choice. She said she could get into his head, give us some options. So, she grabbed clothes and a blonde wig to look like our blonde victims. Grace argued that the pattern meant something, that it was more than a ruse. She said Sweetwater had serious mommy issues and she could use that to mess with him, buy us time and get a pistol to me."

Rob shook his head. "That took a lot of courage."

Cade nodded. "She never backed down from anyone. Ever. You don't find her kind of combination of bravery and audacity any too often."

"Agreed."

"It was such an impossible situation. I wanted to get Reynolds out of there, but she was strapped to a table and sliced up bad. She was still alive, but I knew she'd be gone in minutes. Nothing I could do." Cade wiped his eyes.

"Reynolds was..." Rob began, but Cade held up a hand, silencing him.

Cade's gaze slid to the floor. "I don't know where to go from here."

"Hang on buddy," Rob replied, as he went to the door. "I was supposed to notify the nurse when you woke up. Be right back."

Cade ran his fingers through his hair, sighing. He remembered the words of his mother, as she comforted him through the struggles of his teenage years. She'd sit him down and tell him how every day was a new beginning, and when life was at its darkest, that's when things would get better. Her strength and conviction had gotten him through many dark times and was the prime cause of his normally optimistic viewpoint. However, nothing was normal about today. He wrapped his arms around himself and shivered.

Rob pushed open the door and held it. Seeing something in Rob's expression made him glance toward the open door.

It took a moment for Cade to register what he saw when the doctor entered, pushing another patient in a wheelchair. It was Reynolds.

Emotions coursed through him, and Cade was out of his bed in a heartbeat, pulling his IV stand behind him. "Reynolds!" He went to her and got on his knees. Looking tenderly into her eyes, he reached up and touched her cheek. "I can't believe you're here." His eyes teared up as he looked at her. "How can you be alive?"

Reynolds held his gaze and smiled. She pulled back her hospital gown, showing off her heavily wrapped upper arm. "It was all for show. He cut the soft tissue of my arm and bled me. He took his time and used his knife to spread my blood around, basically painting me with my own blood. I was terrified, but he used a rubber hose to curtail the bleeding. He said he wanted to save me for later when he could take his time." She gestured to her arm. "This is my only wound. I'm going to be fine."

Cade leaned into her and pulled her close. Relief washed over him, as he gave in and broke down, his tears welcome as he held her.

CADE LEFT the hospital the next day with Reynolds. After what they'd been through, no way he'd be leaving her side anytime soon. They tried to get out without anyone noticing, but the media was all over the hospital. It wasn't long before they were cornered by the pack of reporters. Cade let Reynolds speak, deferring to her media experience. He stood back as she lit up the room when the cameras were turned on. She was brave, passionate and articulate as she related her experience. No longer a star in the making, Reynolds had truly arrived.

The media had insisted on speaking with Cade and eventually, he relented. But just one question, he told the assembled group. This caused a moment of hesitation as everyone looked around. The Twin Cities' most-senior anchor from WCCO stepped forward. "How was it that Marlin Sweetwater ended up dead, with 13 of your bullets in his chest, instead of being arrested?"

Cade stepped forward, looked directly at the camera and gave his answer. "I could give you the safe, politically correct answer that law enforcement officers are trained to keep shooting until the threat was over, but it's not that complicated. The killer was playing cat and mouse with me and I was tired of being the mouse."

Cade's statement had led the news that night, as well as splashing across the front page of every paper in the state the following morning. Requests for interviews came in from all the national news programs. The story spread around the world, as the video went viral, of the outspoken cop who gunned down a serial killer. That Cade had gone off grid after that had only fueled the controversy.

After leaving the hospital—and the media circus—Cade steered the truck onto 35, headed north. Reynolds asked about their destination and Cade smiled and said they needed some alone time. The five days spent at a lakeside resort in Duluth was exactly what they needed.

They returned for Grace's hospital homecoming. When it was one of your own that stood up and fought against a killer—and was severely wounded—the law enforcement community banded together. The "just a small get together" was actually a packed house at a local Saint Paul restaurant, Cossetta's. Officers filled the second level and cheered wildly when she emerged from the elevator. The head of the BCA guided her wheelchair through the throng, as Grace received handshakes, fistbumps and hugs from hundreds of cops.

Cade had been asked to speak and was torn on what to say and ultimately hadn't prepared anything. As Cade watched the officers greet her with passion and tears, he came to the conclusion that Grace lived her life without fear. She did what she believed was right without concern for failure. Whether it was her career or her life, Grace approached life head on, consequences be damned. Hers was truly a life to be celebrated. Cade stood up in front of the packed gathering, looking out at the hundreds of law enforcement officers lining the hall, and spoke about his friend Grace. There wasn't a dry eye in the house, especially Grace's.

"You didn't have to make up all that nice stuff," Grace said when they found a moment together. Her hug felt better than he could have imagined. "But it was nice to hear."

"You are an amazing person, maybe a little too cautious in life, but amazing nevertheless."

"That's me, little Miss Cautious." She batted her eyes at him.

"I can't argue with your results, you got into his head alright. But I'm guessing his mother must have gotten there first. Sweetwater was a piece of work."

Grace held his hand as she studied him. "Tell me you're doing okay. That couldn't have been easy for you either."

Cade took a moment to answer, memories of that night flashing by. "I'm going to be okay. I'm taking a little time away from work, and I'm in no hurry to get back. In the meantime, people will continue to do bad things or stupid things, so I'll have plenty to keep me busy when I return."

"Ain't that the truth," Grace said with a chuckle.

"And I'm sure I'll be reaching out again for your help. It'll give you another reason to wear that blonde wig." Cade tried to keep a straight face.

Grace gave him a look. "That went so well last time. Maybe we just meet for a beer instead."

Cade laughed and Grace joined in. "That sounds like a better plan. You take care."

The parting hug was long and heartfelt.

A WEEK LATER, Cade went back to work for the first time.

Rob stopped him in the hallway, asking how he was doing. When someone stares you down as they ask if you're okay, it goes beyond concern—they were having serious doubts about your stability. Cade smiled and reassured his partner everything was just fine. He could read Rob's expression well enough to know he didn't believe it, either.

They sat in Rejene's office discussing the case's fallout. "There's been some heat on the Patrol," Rejene said. "But the majority has been on Governor Ritter. When the media discovered the killer was on Ritter's own security detail, they had a field-day. It was amazing. I've never seen a political animal have his nuts removed in prime time before. The slippery bastard finally got what was coming to him." She smiled, clearly enjoying herself.

Rob spoke up. "He's in full damage-control mode now, trying anything and everything to repair his reputation. I even heard he signed up for the Big Brothers program," he said with a grin. "Now a guy comes and takes him to the circus every other week." That broke up the room.

"There's been a shift of power in the state's law enforcement management," Rejene continued. "The Commissioner for the Department of Public Safety—who oversees the State Patrol, as well as the Bureau of Criminal Apprehension and Homeland Security and Emergency Management—is putting together a major crimes task force. They wanted the task force to be immune from jurisdictional issues and political maneuvering. This task force will be called in for any high-profile cases." She leaned back in her leather chair, putting her heels up on her desk. "This is where you come in."

She had his attention now. "Really? I'm going to be part of this task force?"

She nodded. "Really. But it gets better. I've heard through back-channels that you *are* the task force. When something major comes along, the Commissioner will be handing it off to you. It will be up to you to pull together whoever you need, from wherever you want."

Rob waved a hand at Cade. "You can bring me in anytime you'd like. I need the overtime."

Cade leaned back, taking it in. "This sounds interesting, but not at all what I expected. I thought my answer to the media was a little too honest and I'd be reassigned to regulating commercial vehicles down in Worthington."

"Your statement sparked a big commotion. Of course, the politicians were holding up a finger to see which way the wind of public opinion was blowing. Fortunately, the public saw you as someone who got things done and as someone not afraid to speak their mind. And just between us, both have been missing in our state leadership for a long time. So, you, my prized investigator, are safe. You have the state's full backing on this."

"All of our state?" Cade said, thinking of Ritter.

Rejene smiled. "Yes. The governor, in a rare moment of common sense, decided to stay out of it and gave his blessing."

Cade stood up and moved toward the door. "Thanks, boss. This should make things interesting."

"Dawkins." Rejene held his gaze, studying him. "Just don't make it too interesting."

Cade simply smiled and kept walking.

ACKNOWLEDGMENTS

Like parenting, writing takes a village. To bring this novel from the germ of an idea to a published book, took the help of so many.

- First and foremost, my lovely wife. Her belief in me moved mountains. Thank you, Jen!
- My family in no particular order (other than alphabetical), Abbey, Andrew, Ben, Cade, Dan, Suzanna, as well as my brother, Mark and mom, Eleanor.
- Tony Policano, who was responsible for Governor Jesse Ventura's and Governor Tim Pawlenty's security, for providing the background on the governor's security detail function the Minnesota State Patrol provides.
- Troopers Mike Swanson and David Kalinoff, for exciting ride-alongs. There's nothing like a 100-mph ride with lights and siren to get one's heart racing. Thanks for all you do.
- Officer Robert Zink with the Saint Paul Police Department for his inspiration for the oddly similarly named character.
- Staci Olsen, from Immortal Works for discovering this book during the Twitter #pitchmad event.
- My editor, John M. Olsen, for his great insights.
- Everyone at Immortal Works who touched this book— and my heart—with your passion and creativity, including Jason King, Holli Anderson, Ashley Literski, Rachel Huffmire, Megan Nerdin and Ruth Mitchell.
- John Sandford for writing such amazing books (The Prey series and Virgil Flowers) that I was inspired to write my own.

ABOUT THE AUTHOR

 Allan Evans has been an undercover investigator, fitness trainer, bodyguard, magazine producer, retail manager, advertising copywriter, employment recruiter and marketing manager. Beyond filling out his bio, these experiences have added color to his writing—which brings us to today. Evans is obviously the writer of this book, but he's also the author of *Abnormally Abbey* and the "Silent Night" short story published in the *Haunted Yuletide* anthology.

A soccer coach, he can usually be found on a soccer field somewhere, teaching kids about soccer and life.

Allan lives in the Twin Cities of Minnesota with probably the cutest puppy ever. Pictures (and some writing stuff) are posted on his website evanswriter.com or on his social media accounts.

This has been an
Immortal Production